Praise for SUSANNA JONES

The Missing Person's Guide to Love

is a mistress of unexplained menace and keeps you guessing
to the end' *Mail on Sunday*

one familiar with Jones's two previous books will know that, in
liciously disorientating fictional worlds, nothing is ever quite
eems . . . Jones is a mistress of disguise, not just in her charac-
tion and plotting, but in her blurring of the divisions between
and wrong. Hers isn't quite the deliberate amorality of Patricia
smith, but she similarly denies us any easy options when it
s to taking sides for or against her protagonists. With Isabel,
s has fashioned her most complex, involving heroine yet and
ar her most audacious sleight of hand in terms of a storyteller.
ll it a twist would be to devalue what is really a hidden under-
ent of the whole narrative; nevertheless the revelation, when it
es, is breathtaking' Martyn Bedford, *Literary Review*

written and the mystery is more mysterious than most'
Times

intriguing tale about the deaths of two friends . . . An engross-
g read, and one that's quite mysterious at times, this is a book that
ou won't be able to put down' *Easy Living*

The Earthquake Bird

'Compelling and haunting, this delicately crafted debut novel's tremors are felt long after the final page is turned' *Observer*

'Jones' candid portrayal of Lucy's insecurities makes her solitary heroine incredibly affecting. It's remarkable the way Jones shows how when we think we're being unflinchingly honest, we're really moving blindly from the truth. You'll find this story still lurking in the dark corners of your mind long after you've put the book down' *Face*

'In its spare way, this novel, which I have now read three times, is one of the best accounts – and this is not all that it is – of female sexuality, that subject of and mystery for any male reader . . . Try it – *The Earthquake Bird*' A. N. Wilson

'An astonishingly accomplished debut . . . it's hard to believe that this skilfully constructed and beautifully written work is a first novel' Susanna Yager, *Daily Telegraph*

'Jones renders Lucy's painful realisation of love lost and missed opportunity with seductive delicacy' *Guardian*

THE MISSING PERSON'S
GUIDE TO LOVE

Susanna Jones grew up in Yorkshire and lived in Japan for many years. She currently resides near Brighton.

Also by Susanna Jones

THE EARTHQUAKE BIRD

WATER LILY

THE MISSING PERSON'S GUIDE TO LOVE

Susanna Jones

PICADOR

First published 2007 by Picador

First published in paperback 2008 by Picador
an imprint of Pan Macmillan Ltd
Pan Macmillan, 20 New Wharf Road, London N1 9RR
Basingstoke and Oxford
Associated companies throughout the world
www.panmacmillan.com

ISBN 978-0-330-45083-6

1 3 5 7 9 8 6 4 2

A CIP catalogue record for this book is available from
the British Library.

Typeset by SetSystems Ltd, Saffron Walden, Essex
Printed and bound in the UK by
CPI Mackays, Chatham ME5 8TD

Visit www.picador.com to read more about all our books
and to buy them. You will also find features, author interviews and
news of any author events, and you can sign up for e-newsletters
so that you're always first to hear about our new releases.

In Memory of Mike Jones

Thanks to Maria Rejt and all at Picador,
to my agent Bill Hamilton, to Judy Jones and all the other
Joneses, to Colin McGranachan and Tolga Önce.

MAGGIE

– i –

She wanted something to delay the start.

After a few minutes of waiting, the telephone rang. There it was. She edged her way around the study walls and descended the stairs. A stripe of sunshine from the kitchen window cut the staircase in two and she stepped into the light. She sat in the sunny half of the bottom step, in the place where the carpet was worn. She sniffed the air; the hall smelled of old orange peel. Occasionally she was able to recognize this house as being her own and her husband's but more often it seemed to belong to the people who had come, stayed, and gone over the years. They left traces and they left odours. The carpet on the bottom step had always been thin, but she had not been eating oranges.

She lifted the receiver. 'This is Maggie speaking. Hello?'

No one answered but someone was there. There was effort in the silence, the tightly held breath. She sensed quivering tips of hair, an unsteady hand. Somehow she knew that the person crouching in the void was female.

'Leila, is that you? Is that Leila? Hello? Will you speak?' Her fingers twitched. 'No? Who is it, please?'

I

The silence rippled for a few more seconds, and the line went dead.

She returned to her study. She shut the door and saw that two of the screws on the handle were loose. She should find a screwdriver and fix it but she'd had her postponement for the day and there was nothing for it now but to get on with her work. As her hand rested on the back of her chair, she remembered something from her childhood and stopped. She held the wooden chairback for balance — as they used to do in the church hall — and took up first position, then second.

Plié. Grand battement. *Rest, and* bras bas. Rond de jambe. *It was still inside her.* Plié. Bras bas. *First position, second position, third and fourth. Her limbs seemed to remember them all. In fifth position, her legs shook. That never used to happen. She gripped the floor with the soles of her feet and checked her posture in the window. Perfect, almost. Bend from the waist and sweep the arm to the floor.*

It might have been her sister, not Leila, on the phone. Bess hadn't called for more than ten years. She might have dialled the number, then been too shy to speak. Bess had always been afraid of everything. She hid her fear behind pious disapproval but fear it was. If Bess hadn't been such a prig and a coward, Maggie thought, and lived as though all that mattered was keeping safe from sin, Satan and danger, then I wouldn't have had to be quite so much the opposite and I might have had an easier life, when all is said and done. I would not have had to be fearless just so as not to be Bess. Maggie twisted to the wall and raised her arms above her head. Not that she blamed Bess, not at all. Arms down. Rest. Bess had lost almost everything.

She felt better. Never mind the phone call. It made no difference. She didn't want to talk to Bess or Leila now. Leaves were falling outside the window, almost as graceful as she was. She stretched her

2

arms behind her back, said, 'Mmmaaa,' as they released. She moved to her table, sat at the computer, ready to begin righting. That was what she called it. Her day of righting the wrong that once happened. But her body was still dancing around the room. She saw it flit from wall to wall. She was wearing a tutu now. White and slender, she was a lily.

She tried to concentrate on the girl who had died. She drummed her fingers on the table edge. But what to think about her? The sweet girl appeared all around the room, photographed, framed and lightly coated with dust. Could the dead girl, somehow, have been the silent person on the phone? Was it possible? 'Don't be an idiot,' she said. 'Stop getting ahead of yourself and calm down. There is work still to be done and there will be time to listen to ghosts, but we are not there yet. You know you have hardly thought of anyone but the girl for years. You may as well be honest. You can't put it off another day because tomorrow you are going back to the place where it happened.'

The ceiling made a crackling sound. She looked up. The mice were chasing each other under the attic floorboards, playing tag or Hunt the Crumb. One day soon she would go up there and lay a few traps, but not yet. The window-pane wobbled in the breeze. A curled sycamore leaf brushed the glass and came to rest on the sill. Now she was ready. She pressed the button on the CD player. 'Sunday Girl' by Blondie began to play.

ISABEL

— I —

Almost the end. It's past midnight, and in the morning I return to Istanbul. The room is cold. A wind sometimes catches the curtains and they billow over the dressing-table mirror till the empty window-frame sucks them back and holds them for a moment. Each time it happens I think someone is trying to creep in from outside and my breath stops in my chest, but I want the window open. I pull the covers up to my neck and tuck them under my chin. The bed is cosier and cleaner than the guesthouse bed I should have slept in tonight and I am glad. I have a friend on the other side of the wall, an old friend I found again this evening, so that is something good. In this sense, at least, my journey has not been wasted but I wonder if I have made any other progress today. My investigations have not led me to the answer I wanted, or indeed any useful answers, and I cannot see that I shall have another chance to find out the truth. If I leave tomorrow – I *must* leave tomorrow – I shall take the bus away from the village, down from the moors to London and the airport, and journey back from the past to the present. Mete and Elif will be waiting for me and we'll be a kind of family again.

In the lamplight, I can see the books on the shelves. It is a comfort, in this unfamiliar room, to see books whose covers I know so well. There are several by Eva Carter, the pen-name of my aunt Maggie. *Goose Island*, *The Missing Girls' Club*, *The Hotel on the Moor*. I don't think I've read any of these, not all the way through, but if I wake in the night, I may pick one up. They are romantic thrillers, all set around here, on the moors and in villages like this one, though Maggie moved to London years ago. When I was a teenager, she would press one of her books on me each birthday, with a gift of lacy underwear or a bottle of perfume. 'Always a happy ending, in my books, Isabel,' she'd say. 'It always turns out well for the girl.' And then I'd get a thickly mascaraed wink, so I guessed she was referring to sex, though I was never sure. I was embarrassed that my aunt wrote such racy stuff. Later, when I was working in Maggie's second-hand-book shop in London, I used to hide in the basement thumbing through old copies of Anaïs Nin and Erica Jong, and I was no longer interested in Maggie's romances of the moors. I avoided them for I had left the area, had no friends here and never wanted to think about the place again.

Now I'm back. One day has chewed up fifteen years and left them ragged. It's almost as if I never went away, almost as if every year I have lived since then has been pretended, as if Mete and Elif were some preposterous and beautiful dream I once had before I was an adult, the perfect man, perfect daughter who would be posted into my life one day, gift-wrapped with a bow. Early this morning I was touching them with these hands and lips. Then we were separated, and for the next few hours I was lost. My fingertips, every moment, were itching to reach through the air and find the soft top of Elif's dark head, and my voice ached to whisper her name. But time has passed. It is night, and I can hardly believe that she is even real any more. She is not with me and not away from me. Her essence is in the air outside the window, a membrane stretched across the black sky. It's as if she is waiting some distance in the future, not ready yet to enter my life and so hers. This should feel wrong but it does not. When I think of things this way, it is a huge relief to me.

I should be sleeping at the Lake View guesthouse – my bag is there, next to the bed where I dropped it, and I'll have to collect it in the morning – but, thank God, I'm here and not there. For one thing, there was no view of the reservoir. I had booked a room at the Lake View especially because I wanted to see the water. Since there is no other lake in the area, I took the hotel's name to be a genteel reference to its situation. The reservoir was to be the starting-point of my search and I had imagined that it might be helpful to keep a distant eye on it, to look down from time to time, allow it to seep into my thoughts and bring fresh ideas. Everything that happened here, I believe, happened near the reservoir and I would find the answers nearby. I saw rooftops, telegraph poles, the ugly backs of dressing-table mirrors blocking bedroom windows, but not the water.

But what have I achieved even now that I have escaped the

Lake View? I went to Owen's funeral, said goodbye to my old schoolfriend. I breathed within centimetres of his coffin. I spoke to his mother and managed, more or less, to be polite, knowing that she would still like to kill me. What good it would do her, I don't know. I cried through the hymns and smiled through the eulogy. I have spoken to many people during the day and asked the questions I could think of, for what use they were. I took a spade and dug a big hole in the ground, certain I had found the answer. But the mystery is still there, a black fingerprint smudge over every thought I have of Owen. I don't know whether I am nursing a ludicrous suspicion, or holding the answer to a secret that everyone would like to know yet no one but I have understood.

Owen's death was an accident. He was in his car on the way home from a sales meeting and was hit by a drunken teenage driver who tried to do a U-turn on the M62 near Pontefract. There is no possibility that it was suicide or anything more sinister. I'm not sure why I need to reassure myself on that point but I found it odd, at the funeral, that the mourners appeared to accept Owen's death with a kind of ease. There were tears, of course, but other than his mother no one seemed shocked and no one was angry. I am sure they should have been angry. Owen's family and the vicar spoke as if an elderly person had died, not a young man in his thirties. They could not have expected him to die. Or am I wrong? Perhaps you don't need to be sickly for people to assign you a short life. Perhaps they looked at Owen's life, saw how difficult he had found it, and simply thought that he could not last a full seventy or eighty years. He had screwed up so many times, he was bound to die young.

However, this was just a feeling I picked up in the church and I may be wrong so there is no point in dwelling on it now. I came here to find out what happened not last week but almost twenty years ago. There are two deaths to consider tonight and Owen's is only one of them. The other, the one that interests me more, is the death of Julia Smith. Julia was another school-friend – my friend and Owen's girlfriend – and she vanished at the age of fifteen.

I have always been able to picture the scene of Julia's disappearance with clarity. She was doing her paper round, visiting the cottages near the reservoir. A bright light shines over the landscape of that afternoon like the round beam of a torch in darkness, and I feel as if I must have been holding the switch when she opened and shut the brightly painted gates, slipped the evening newspapers through the letterboxes, reached bitten fingernails deep into her bag for the next copy. Of course, I saw nothing and this vision is based only on what we learned later. I finished my own round, returned to Grimshaw's, the newsagent, to collect my weekly pay and wait for Julia. We usually bought sweets and ate them on the way home. After twenty minutes Julia hadn't shown up so I left. I wasn't worried. We didn't hang around for each other every week. Mrs Grim-shaw put the money aside for her at the back of the shop. Later the newsagent's big canvas bag, almost empty, was found by the reservoir. Julia's post-office savings never went down. She had had no belongings with her. At school, people – police, teachers, Julia's relatives — started taking us out of our classrooms, one by one, to ask if Julia had told us anything, dropped any hints about being unhappy. It made us feel guilty, though we did not know why. A few weeks later, Mrs Grimshaw slipped the two pound notes into a brown envelope and dropped it through Julia's letterbox for her parents.

We liked to make up stories among ourselves that gave Julia a happy ending. We invented relatives, penfriends, secret pregnancies. We exaggerated the postal romance she'd had with a soldier fighting in the Falklands. We reported sightings of her, saw her in city centres when we went on holiday, in photographs in magazines. She became outrageous and exciting to us: a junkie, a spy, a prostitute, a model in a photo-story. We were optimistic. The adults in the village understood what the rest of us wouldn't accept, of course, that Julia had not run away and that she would never come back.

But her body was not found and, as far as I have always known, no one was ever charged with her murder. And so, eighteen years later, I left my flat in Turkey, while it was still dark, to come to Owen's funeral. I must have imagined, stupidly, that I would climb off the bus from London, breathe the old air of the moors that had once belonged to me and, by magic, watch the answers flash up in my head like numbers on a screen. I thought I would know exactly what to do. I have talked to people in a fairly random way, filled up my head with a lot of conversations that I cannot now disentangle and that do not tell me what happened. I should have used the long journey to plan. I could have done it better. I am a journalist. I do know how to ask questions. I know how to tease answers from the unwilling or unknowing and weave them into a fabric that is more or less as helpful as truth. But today I might as well have been seventeen years old again as, it seems, I was too stupid to do anything properly.

I roll over on my side and look at the sky through the gap at the top of the curtains. It is thick and cloudy and its blackness has a dark green tinge. Was Owen strange? How strange? Why did he return to the village when he came out of prison? Did he like to visit certain places in the area, perhaps a favourite spot on the hills or near the reservoir? How did he react when people spoke of Julia? Did he want to talk of Julia when no one else did? Was he questioned at the time? Was he jealous in his relationships with women? Did anyone think that a boy of sixteen could have hurt a girl of almost the same age? Perhaps that never occurred to them. These are the questions I forgot to ask, or when I remembered to, I discovered that I didn't have the skill to lead the conversation where I needed it to go. I found out about some bloodstains but am not sure what they meant or that the blood was real.

Owen spent most of his life in the village. After his short time in prison he could have left and started a life in a new place but he didn't want to. I managed it after my own release, or thought I did. I see now that if I leave tomorrow, still not knowing, I will never have escaped. I rub my forehead, then the base of my neck. It's stiff. There are tight knots of muscle under my skin. Perhaps I have found the answer but I don't yet recognize it. I have collected spoken words all day and maybe

I need to sift through them, again and again, until I identify it. But what? The only solution is to finish the job while I'm here and I'm going to need more time. I don't know how much but I'll start with tomorrow. So, then, I cannot return to Istanbul in the morning. I fumble on the floor for my phone and switch it on. I send a message to Mete. He won't like it.

Can you manage if I stay one more night?

The little envelope in the screen tells me that the message has been sent. I stare at it. Any second now my words will pop up, still in their envelope, in a telephone at the edge of the Sea of Marmara and at three thirty a.m. I wonder if it will wake him.

So, let me try to salvage something from today. One feature of some of the conversations has been particularly upsetting. I knew that people here would remember and recognize me, and I knew that they would be surprised to see me and, in some cases, not especially pleased about it. However, several people have told me that they had believed me to be dead. I cannot make any sense of this since I don't know where the rumour began. I know that it passed through Owen at one point, and on to his mother, but I don't know that Owen started it. It's possible. He might have been angry that I never replied to his letters after I left the village. The letters were messy and too disturbing to make much sense so I ignored them. What else could I do? It wouldn't surprise me if he had decided to kill me off as a sort of revenge for this snub. If this is the case, it only confirms that he was, at best, confused, which may support my theory that he was responsible for Julia's death.

I also heard that the rumour came from my own aunt Maggie, who knows perfectly well that I am alive. She might have started it to keep Owen away from me, though it seems unnecessarily heavy-handed, and that never appeared to be her intent. I am sure that, if it was Maggie's idea, she only meant it for the best. None the less, to be told that I was dead – or 'passed away', as Owen's mother kept saying – leaves me somewhat queasy. I keep looking at my limbs, touching my skin and pressing it to feel the bones underneath. I keep holding the back of my hand against my cheek to find warmth and measure it. I keep checking that I'm alive.

My phone vibrates on the bedclothes. A message from Mete.

OK. But what shall I tell Leila?

I smile. He means Bernadette. I send one back.

I don't know. Why does she want to see me?

This bed is soft and white, comfortable. I wriggle around, pulling part of the duvet between my thighs and stretching it out, warm inside from this tiny piece of contact with Mete, beginning to feel aroused. I rest my head on one pillow and cuddle the other, meaning to think of Mete but my mind fumbles instead for a picture of Owen, a photograph I saw today in his parents' house. It was a recent picture so it was of an Owen I never knew. He was in the pub with a couple of friends. There was a pint of dark beer in his hand and his face was red. He was smiling. His hair had receded a centimetre or two since I knew him. The picture was nothing special but the smile has lodged itself behind my eyes and spreads and bulges, like the leering mouth of a clown. I try, but I can't get Mete back.

This is not what I want at all. I climb out of bed, put my notebooks on the dressing-table, push aside the pots of cream, coloured jars of makeup and a hairbrush tangled with fine brown hairs. I peer behind the mirror to catch a glimpse of the narrow street. It is empty. The other houses are in darkness. The neighbours are sleeping. I can't see the reservoir from here. I can't even make out the shapes of the moors, but I know that they are there, just a mile or two away. I pull the window down until it is almost closed. I am still a little cold, wearing a borrowed T-shirt that hardly covers my thighs. I sit on the purple-cushioned stool and roll my shoulders back. I'm stiff, an ex-dancer whose movements have become lazy and rough. If I flex my feet, the bones crackle. A quick gust of wind chills my face. My legs stretch out, blue-white gooseflesh. This is good. I don't sleep when I'm cold. I shall stay awake.

This afternoon I arrived at the Lake View guesthouse, hoping for a view.

The Lake View guesthouse stands at the end of the street, near the beginning of the sycamores. The shadows of the trees darken the garden and the far side of the house. The paint on the window-frames is chipped in places, but the small front lawn is neat and the gate is shiny green. Beyond the houses, the moors slope and curve away to the edges of the sky. There are two or three other small hotels nearby, smart bed-and-breakfasts with signs in the windows advertising vacancies – one even boasts a swimming-pool – but I chose the Lake View for its name.

I arrived two, nearly three hours before the funeral was due to begin. The sky was a mucky white and the damp moors were blurred out of focus. From the pavement outside the guesthouse there was no sign of the reservoir. I could see terraces of houses, telegraph poles, hedges of privet and leylandii, but no water. I knew that the reservoir was there, at the bottom of the hill behind thick rows of trees, but a stranger would not have guessed. I stood at the gate and wondered what I should do. A red tricycle sat in next door's garden, its front wheel cocked, looking like a dog awaiting a homecoming. That might be the best welcome I could hope for, and I considered finding another place to stay. But I decided that it would be unwise to change my plans so soon before the funeral. Perhaps, I thought, if I have a room in the attic, the water will be visible after all.

I stepped up to the door and read the labels on the three bells. There was *Lake View Main Bell*, *Lake View Reception* and *Lake View Private*. There was also a large brass knocker in the middle of the door. I dithered between the top two bells, lifted the knocker, then put it back again. Paint fell away in dandruff flakes. Finally I pressed *Lake View Reception* and waited. The house was similar in shape and proportion to the one I had grown up in, a few streets away. It made me nervous and I found myself twitching and turning from the door to the street and back again. I had been travelling since early morning and was beginning to feel light-headed. Was I right to have come? I had no idea, but at that moment I wanted only to pull off my shoes and rest. I wanted to lie down for a little while, perhaps take a shower, before dressing for Owen's funeral. After a few moments' silence, I heard feet stumbling from high up in the house down the stairs to the bottom. A large honey-coloured hairdo appeared at the other side of the glass. I stepped back as the door opened to about thirty degrees of its full swing. A pink, puffy face peered out. Soft bags of skin lapped gently around the woman's dark green eyes. She wore a loose cardigan and long denim skirt that had slipped too far around her waist, as though she had come down the stairs spinning.

'I have a reservation.' I cleared my throat. I had hardly spoken all day and a thin film of ice covered my voice. I made a note to do some vocal exercises in my room before my next encounter to prepare myself for the conversations ahead. If I were speaking Turkish, it would be all right. I have developed a personality that operates well in Turkey. My Turkish self is used to haggling over prices and payments, striking up conversations with strangers in lifts and in queues to pay bills. She gets what she wants every time but I don't think she's here when I speak English. I wasn't sure, before I set off, how this would work but now I knew. 'It's Isabel Clegg,' I rasped.

'Oh, right.' She looked at me, then over my head at the path. 'Come in, then. Did you drive here? Do you need parking?'

'No. I walked from the bus station. I'm early. Is it all right? It's just that I'm going to a funeral and I'd like to leave my bag, please.'

'Yes, that's fine, love. Your room's ready.'

Her accent was local. She opened the door wide and stood back, as if there were several of me to let in. I didn't even have a suitcase, just a small rucksack, and I slipped it off my shoulders, let it trail at my ankles as I walked.

The hall was square and dark. There was a shelf of ballroom-dance trophies, a payphone, a range of yellowing signs about keeping noise down and check-out time, and a bell for attention at night. The woman asked me to sign the visitors' book and pay in advance, no credit cards. She leaned against the wall, folded her arms under her heavy breasts and watched with narrowed eyes as I wrote a cheque and signed it. It seemed old-fashioned – *Who do I make it out to? Doreen Fatebene, please* – but somehow in keeping with the era I was travelling back to, the 1980s, my teenage years. She pushed a large key into my hand and told me to head for the top floor, to room nine.

'The bathroom's opposite. If the light doesn't work there's a bulb in the cupboard on the landing. There's an extra blanket under your bed if you need it.' She nodded towards the door. 'It'll be parky tonight.'

It was November but feeling wintry rather than autumnal. At least I would be indoors most of the time, except for one or two visits to specific locations. When I was half-way up the stairs Doreen shouted after me to ask what I wanted for breakfast.

What could I have? I was flummoxed. I don't live in this country any more. I'm almost a foreigner now and need a little more help. I was afraid of saying the wrong thing, of saying cake when the answer should be bread.

'It's just easier if I know in plenty of time.' The woman tried to sound relaxed but it was clear that not knowing in advance would trouble her. 'You can change your mind when tomorrow comes, within reason.'

'Of course.'

A sign on the wall opposite me boasted English breakfasts so I asked for this.

'Full?'

'Yes, please.'

'And would you like a map of the village or have you been here before?'

'Oh, I used to live in this village.' It sounded like an apology. Perhaps it was. 'I was born here.'

And then I didn't know what to say so I pushed my hair from my face and continued up the stairs to the top floor.

I lifted the key and unlocked the door. I stepped into a long thin room with a single bed and coffee-coloured walls. It smelled of detergent. A television was mounted high on the wall, like a closed-circuit surveillance screen. The window was open and a little sunlight spilled across the carpet. I hadn't noticed any sun at all when I was outside and I peered out to see where it had come from. There was a small crack in the clouds, just a graze, and a pale lemon light seeped through. Lake View. Even from up here I couldn't see the reservoir. I saw grey rooftops, chimney pots, the paths leading out to the moors, brown and cold behind the village. And there was the tower of St Peter's, dark grey and shiny. I put my head out of the window to breathe fresh air.

I had known, without having to read all of Maggie's message, that the funeral would be held at St Peter's. It is the main Anglican church in the community. Owen and I sang in the choir there when we were children, along with our friend Kath. We wore purple cassocks, white ruffs and surplices, and in our treble voices we sang through practices twice a week, communion and evensong on Sundays. We did puzzles and read joke books together in the choir stalls and I have no recollection of ever having heard a sermon so we must have been busy daydreaming when we were not singing. We were perfectly at home in that church. If God was present too, we expected Him to fit around us. We had a sense of ownership, popping in and out of the vestry, putting the hymn numbers up on the boards, lighting and snuffing out the candles. The smell comes back to me sometimes, when I am near old wooden furniture, dusty books, the place where a flame has just been extinguished. It reaches me with a poke in the face, as if it's a memory that must belong to someone else. It doesn't seem like me and it doesn't seem like Owen. We weren't angels. Kath is the only one who fits that memory still.

I hadn't been inside the church since my childhood. Soon Owen's body would be lying just a couple of metres away from where he had stood, and knelt, more than two decades ago. I swallowed hard, took big breaths of cold air and let them out slowly. I could not afford to be squeamish now. I had to keep a clear head so that I could observe and understand. When I felt steady, I forced myself to picture both the coffin and the choir stalls again. I needed to measure and understand the space in between.

Then I closed the window and pulled back the bedcovers to check for spiders, mice or monsters, a tic from childhood that I have never shaken off. There was just a sheet, blue and bobbled. Its roughness under my fingertips made me wince. A key went into the lock of the room next door and the wall shook. Voices came through, both male. *If we'd come up the M1 we wouldn't have got stuck and had to take the M6. It probably added half an hour to the journey, if not a whole hour, and we wouldn't have had to eat at that place. I'll choose the bloody route tomorrow.* The walls were just flimsy partitions. Strangers would be opening and closing doors to the other rooms and I would miss Mete all night. Doreen Fatebene was moving around downstairs, clattering crockery in the kitchen. I listened to her, feeling both irritated and ashamed that I was staying in a strange hotel in my own hometown. Surely, I thought, there should be a friend's house, some old haunt where I am one of the family and there is a bed or sofa that is as good as mine. There should be a place where I slip through the back gate and tap on the kitchen window to be welcomed in, where someone knows me and we share a meal together, at least. There should be something better than this.

If this were the house I'd grown up in, I would be in a corner of the spare bedroom now. The wall between this room and the next was more or less where their bed started. I wondered who would be living in my parents' old house now. They may both have had their own funerals, for all I know. They left the area some years ago and gave no forwarding address. I suppose that if they had died, someone would have had to tell me, but I can imagine Aunt Maggie not quite getting round to the job, not wanting me to know if she thought it would upset me, or interfere with some plan she had of how I ought to be feeling. Maggie would say, *Goodness, Isabel. Surely I told you that. You must be in denial.* But I am sure they are alive, somewhere, and one day we may even see each other again.

I put the kettle on and dropped a teabag into a mug on the floor. I kicked my shoes into a corner and spread out my clothes on the bed. I had brought a couple of black tops, black trousers and a black skirt, but I didn't know which to choose. I hadn't been to a funeral since I was a child. Did people still wear black to funerals, these days, or were you supposed to wear what you felt comfortable in, or what the deceased would have liked? I had no idea what Owen would have thought about this. My only aim was to be inconspicuous.

The kettle boiled and clicked. I made the tea and sat on the floor by the bed. When I let Owen's face into my mind, his deep, narrow eyes and shy, freckly frown, I didn't have any sense that he was dead. I believed he was still somewhere in the world, living his life with people I didn't know and couldn't see. 'Sorry, Owen,' I said aloud. 'I'm thinking of you. I'm trying to think of you.' I had a letter in my rucksack, one that Owen had sent to me fourteen or fifteen years ago. Most of the letters made no sense. They were strange expressions of rage directed at no one except, possibly, himself and sometimes me. I threw them away, half knowing, even then, that I would want to see them again. But there was a letter that referred, briefly, to Julia and I had kept that one. I had brought it with me in case it helped. I did not need to unfold the soft, yellowing scrap to remind myself of what Owen had written.

You accused Mr McCreadie of hurting Julia but that was wrong. He never did it. Julia did it to herself and made her body disappear, maybe with somebody's help. Maybe with God's help. It was what she wanted. I've thought about it and I understand. She didn't want to be alive any more. No one could have murdered her because she wanted to die.

I fell onto the bed, lay on my back and thought, in spite of the swirling blue butterflies on the bedspread and the breeze through the window, how it resembled a cell. The walls and ceiling were just a little too close to me. The thought was followed by dark clouds gathering, a sick sense of travelling backwards and downwards, a weight on my chest. I had to stop myself falling so far that I would never come up again. I shut my eyes tight and let the clouds move around above a picture of the reservoir. I rose up, as if to the water's surface, and there, around me, were the boats, bobbing in the sun. I dreamed myself into the nearest one, lay in the warmth and let the water's ripples rock me.

I thought I might clear my head by working for twenty minutes or so on an article I was writing for an English magazine in Istanbul. I took out my laptop and began to type. It is part of a series called 'Millennium People'. Every month I've been writing a profile of a foreigner who lives in Istanbul and will be there in December for the millennial celebrations. The editor of the magazine is Turkish and his original idea was that I should write pieces in which foreigners told of their great happiness since giving up their lives in other countries for the sun, the friendliness and the good food of Turkey. To the editor, it was obvious. In practice I have found that it is never quite so simple: though these elements may be relevant, there are often secrets and darker stories underneath.

Accordingly, I have moved away from the brief somewhat, and he has not complained. This month I interviewed a cosmetic surgeon from New York who came to Istanbul to take up painting. She had made a fortune from her work so had an income to finance her new studio. She talked for a while of downsizing, of taking a break in life, but soon I asked her about the deep scars across her face. They were the result of a car crash, she told me, and would be so easy to fix with cosmetic surgery that she couldn't be bothered to get it done. She had come to like them. 'I lost my appetite for chopping up human faces. I want to see them as they are. I wish I could have my old skin back, the sagging one, but since I can't, I'm fortunate to have these scars.' She lived in a large apartment looking out over the Bosphorus and painted nothing but the faces of strangers, mostly women. I tapped this into my computer. I had taken photos of some of her paintings but had left them in Istanbul. I forgot where I was and, for a second, thought I could stand up, go into the next room and find them.

Just on the other side of the partition, a man began to cough. I switched on the television to disguise the noise. There was some interference and then an attractive young woman's head appeared on the screen, talking with great enthusiasm about a broken-down bus near Wakefield. I liked the sound of her voice and left it on in the background, but found I couldn't concentrate on the article. I saved what I had written and switched off the computer.

But what was I supposed to do? How should I go about solving the mystery of Julia's disappearance? How does one investigate secrets when one is neither invisible nor anonymous? Talking, I guessed, as always. I had not brought my tape-recorder or my camera. I didn't know whom I should approach. I had to make a list. There must be people who could help me and some of them would still live here.

The first was Kath. I knew from Maggie that Kath lived in her parents' old house, passed on to her when her father died and her mother moved into a nursing-home. She was my best friend but I never saw her after I was taken away from the village. I had no idea whether she would want to talk to me now. If she was not at the funeral I would knock on her door

later, see if she would let me in. What could she help me with?
We would talk together of the days around Julia's disappearance.
We'd put it together one more time. We both saw her at
school. We knew about her love letters to the soldier in the
Falklands, and we had watched as she dropped her dull boyfriend, Owen Carr. I had never had time to tell Kath of my
suspicions about Mr McCreadie, my boss, I went away too soon
afterwards, but I could tell her now and perhaps it would jog
something in her memory.

The next was Mr McCreadie himself, manager of the
supermarket. He must have retired by now. I had no idea if
he still lived in the area but he had been a public figure so someone would know. He might have died, of course. If he was still
alive, he would be old. Apart from Owen, he was my only
suspect.

There was Aunt Maggie – if she showed up – for, though
she hardly knew Julia, she knew Owen's mother well and may
have picked up pieces of information about Owen.

Who else? Owen's immediate family would be able to tell
me things, though they might not want to. I would have to
tease very carefully to find out what kind of life he had lived
since I last saw him. I knew that he had an older sister. He must
also have had other relatives and friends.

There was Julia's family, but her parents had moved away
a few years after Julia disappeared. Maggie told me that after
staying at home every day, not having a holiday in case Julia
turned up looking for them, they had decided to set themselves
free and start afresh in another town, I forget where.

It was not much of a list but this did not bother me. At the funeral I would see a lot of people from the old days, friends from school, people who lived locally, worked in the shops, taught at one of the schools. It is a small community and someone would be able to help. Julia would not have been forgotten. If the older generation had never wanted to talk about it, mine would be different.

I sat up on the bedspread, drew my knees to my chest, sipped hot tea and pulled apart a soft custard cream from a complimentary packet of two. I scraped the filling from the biscuit with my teeth and savoured the synthetic sweetness. I rocked slightly, side to side, as I often find myself doing when I'm in the foetal position. I hadn't eaten all day. I had almost missed my flight from Istanbul and then the bus from Victoria coach station, so there was no time to change money. There would be food after the funeral, of course, if only I had the courage to attend. What would Owen's mother say if she saw me? The last time we had met was in a crowded market-place. She was screaming at me. Her son's funeral was hardly the occasion for reconciliation, not that I wanted to be her friend. If I could just sneak into the back of the church and not be recognized, it would be all right.

A knock on my door. I opened it to find Doreen Fatebene with an armful of dark brown towels. 'Not sure I remembered to put towels on your bed before.' She gave them to me.

'Thanks very much.'

'Funeral at St Peter's, is it?'

The woman on television was still talking. I picked up the

remote control and turned it off. 'Yes, it's later this afternoon.'
Then I realized she wanted more. 'His name was Owen Carr.
I was at school with him.'

'Didn't know him. He'll have been young, then.'

'Yeah. It was a road accident.'

'Would you like me to make you a cup of tea?'

'I've just had one, thanks.' Did I look upset?

'You just say if you want one.'

For a moment she reminded me of my mother.

'That's very kind of you.'

'Is there a wake as well?'

'I think everyone's invited back to his parents' house. After
that I might go to the pub with old friends, depending on who
I bump into.'

'Well, if you're going to be late, get a taxi. Don't walk
home on your own.'

My mother again. I picked up my sponge-bag and one of
the towels to show that I was about to have a shower and
perhaps encourage Ms Fatebene to go back downstairs. She
took the towel from my hand and gave me the other. 'This is
the bathsheet, if you're having a shower. That one's just a hand
towel.'

'Oh, thanks.'

'And if you wash your hair, come to me for a hair-dryer
you can borrow. Don't go out with damp hair. You'll catch a
chill.'

'I won't.'

'Right, then.' And off she went downstairs.

The shower was an attachment in the bath that did not stretch quite high enough to reach my head unless I knelt or crouched. The bath was stained and the water pressure low. I had to rub the water over my skin with my hands to get completely wet. There was no soap and I hadn't brought any. I dried myself on the bathsheet feeling dirtier than before and a bit cold. I wrapped the towel around me and carried my things back across the landing to my room.

My clothes were crumpled lumps of black on the bed. I tried on each combination, watched myself change from a student to a woman dressed up for a party to something androgynous in trousers and a black polo-neck. I decided to wear the skirt and the less fussy top. I would go to the church and see. I could always turn back if it looked as though it was going to be bad. I hummed a few scales, up and down, then arpeggios. My voice was stuck somewhere under my ribs but gradually I teased it out and progressed from humming to singing. The song that came to mind was 'Sunday Girl'. On the flight I'd been thinking about Kath and Julia and me singing along with Debbie Harry in Kath's bedroom. As I sang, I slipped into the black clothes again, tried to conceal my green bra straps under the sleeves, and brushed my hair back into a demure knot. I checked myself in the mirror, smeared a touch of blusher on my cheeks. I looked all right. Black suits me, though I am pale. I put on the pointy-toed shoes I'd bought in a hurry from a fancy shop near Taksim Square. They pinched my feet and I wasn't used to wearing heels but I looked better than all right. I looked quite good. I added lipstick, then changed my mind and rubbed it off again. I checked my profile from each side. Yes, yes, but it didn't matter what I looked like.

My handbag was empty. I filled it with pens and notebooks from my rucksack, a handkerchief. I put my black raincoat over my funeral outfit and left Lake View. I still had a couple of hours to spare and I would begin with a visit to the police station. I had painful memories of that old-fashioned little building, with its lamp on the outside wall, but there were likely to be new people now and they would help me. Was the case of Julia Smith ever solved? I would ask them, certain that it was not and tell them that, perhaps, I had the answer. A voice in my head began to pray. *Lord, please help me know what to do and give me the strength to find out—* No, no. It was not my voice that I could hear and this work was all down to me.

I sat in a comfortable black chair and watched a couple of sparrows hopping on and off the low wall outside. The police station had changed since the 1980s. There was now a pleasant area with low chairs, a small table and a water-cooler. Signs on the walls gave phone numbers and helpful information on everything from drug addiction and domestic violence to bicycle theft. In the old days this area had been smaller, darker. I remembered a high, severe counter, dingy cream walls, and one or two upright chairs. I remembered a lower ceiling. It was a more relaxing place now, there was no doubt. I didn't have to feel small here but could lean back in the soft chair and stretch out my legs. I smoothed a wrinkle in my tights. It was not so terrible to be in this room once again, after all. Indeed, I felt quite at ease, looking through the window – it seemed larger than the old one – at the birds now pecking at a small twig on the bonnet of a police car.

The plump young female officer returned from the corridor and smiled. 'I've just checked for you. The case is still open. She was never found. It was a suspected abduction but there were no key suspects and no reported witnesses to her disappearance.'

'Was anyone arrested?'

'A few local men were questioned and all released without charge. It doesn't appear to have been our finest moment – the police force's, I mean.' She laughed.

A panda car drew up outside. The doors opened and two male police officers unfolded themselves into the daylight. I looked to see whether I recognized either from the past. I could not see their faces but their bodies were thin and they moved with the quick fluidity of young men. I turned back to the woman behind the desk. She had a pretty round face with soft rosy skin and I liked her. She made me feel as if it would be all right to confide in her. I wished I could take her to a pub and tell her the whole story over a pint or two.

'So if nothing has changed, after all these years, does that mean we'll probably never find out what happened? I mean, as time passes people forget things, people who knew things will die off—'

'Not necessarily. I'd say there's every chance we'll find out. The case will be reviewed at some point and, anyway, it's very likely that new information will come to light. For one thing there's the possibility of DNA evidence now. For another, you have to trust that people do remember things after years, even decades. Or they might keep the information secret to protect someone but then something happens to change their mind, a falling-out or bereavement, say. It seems to you and me now as though she disappeared into thin air, but the truth is, someone out there will know something, and not just the person who abducted her, if that is what happened. I don't think your friend will be lost for ever. I really don't.'

'Can I show you something?'

I stood and handed Owen's letter to her.

She ran her eyes over it a couple of times. 'I don't understand.'

'Owen Carr wrote it to me. He sent me a lot of letters but this is the only one I kept.'

'The young man who died last week on the motorway? The same one?'

'Yes. He was Julia's boyfriend when we were at school. Do you think it means anything?'

She read it again and shrugged. 'Should it?'

'I don't know.'

In Istanbul I keep the letter in a painted wooden box with other treasures. The box was a birthday present from Mete a couple of years ago and it stays in a drawer next to our bed. It is decorated with pictures of Ottoman warriors and sultans, in red, blue and green. Most of the letters inside were sent by old friends before we started using email; one or two are from Maggie. Whenever I find myself wondering about Owen and Julia, I take his letter from the box and read it again. It makes my head ache but I can't let go of it.

Now the police officer held the letter tightly between her finger and thumb. I wanted to warn her not to tear it but I kept quiet and waited for her to speak.

'If he knows – sorry, knew – anything, he's not being very clear about it, is he? When did he write this?'

'Years ago, probably when he was about twenty. He was a bit unbalanced at the time and had been in prison – not because of Julia but for something later on. I know it's not much but—' Already the letter seemed silly and its meaning arcane.

'I'm afraid that it isn't really anything. I can't make sense of it. He sounds rather disturbed here. What's he on about, "made her body disappear"? That's not really something the police have powers to help with. It sounds a bit supernatural. No, we'd need a lot more than this to justify looking into it again.'

'I suppose you're right. I knew him well so perhaps I'm seeing things that wouldn't be clear to other people.'

'Do you have any more information? Run it by me, if you'd like to. Might as well think about it while you're here.'

'It's hard to put my finger on specific things. Owen used to follow Julia. She dumped him for someone else and he hung around, annoying her. Nowadays you might call it stalking but then he was just seen as a bit of a nuisance. She was his first girlfriend and I think the rejection was too much for him, too harsh. You could say he had a motive.'

'How old was he at the time?'

'Sixteen.'

'It's very unlikely that a sixteen-year-old—'

'I know, but not impossible. He was very strong too. He could have hurt her a lot without meaning to. Do you see what I mean? It could have been some kind of argument that got out of hand and then he didn't know what to do so he hid her body. He could easily have carried her to the reservoir. At night he could even have come back and—'

'Yes. That's quite a lot of conjecture.'

'All right, but I became his friend afterwards and he talked about Julia every day. He always wanted to go back to the place where she disappeared. We used to go with him – my friend Kath and I – but it was his idea each time. I know he went there by himself sometimes. I know it.'

'But at the time you didn't think he might have done any-thing to harm her?'

'It didn't cross my mind. This has taken me a lot of time and distance to work out. I know it doesn't sound like anything but I've thought about it often over the last few years.' Now I was beginning to feel shy. It occurred to me that her tone was more patronizing than friendly and I was not helping myself. 'Never mind.'

I shouldn't have discussed it with her, or shown her the letter. For the second time in my life I had made a fool of myself in this police station accusing someone. Last time it was

Mr McCreadie, the supermarket manager, who had boasted that he knew what had happened to Julia and I took this as an admission of guilt. Owen was on my side that time – now I see that it was in his interest to agree with me – but the policeman shouted me out of the building. He was right, I had no evidence, and this woman was right too. I still had no evidence. She thought I was unhinged. I could have told her that I was a journalist and knew a few things about investigating, but I wasn't sure that it would help, and it wasn't strictly true since all I do is write profiles on the lives of ordinary people. I don't know much about crime.

'Can I have it back, then?'

She passed the letter to me. She looked as though she was reaching for words of comfort or encouragement.

I knew that she wanted to be helpful but I had nothing more to ask her. I folded the letter and put it into my pocket. 'Thanks for your time. I just wanted to know if Julia was ever found. I realize that this letter doesn't mean anything. It was just a silly thought. I'm sorry to have brought it up.'

'Don't keep apologizing. It's fine. As I say, the case will get reviewed, and I'd be very surprised if we don't resolve it one of these days. You will get closure.' She gave me another kind smile.

I smiled back and felt tears under my eyelids. 'I'd better get going. It's Owen's funeral today.'

She threw me a slightly odd look. I suppose it seemed strange that I had just accused him of murder and was now on my way to mourn his death, but that was the way it was. I didn't want Owen to be guilty. I didn't particularly want him *not* to be guilty. I just wanted to know what had happened.

I thanked the policewoman again, apologized again, and left the building. I sat down on the bench in front of the police station and lit a cigarette. A police car was parked in front of me. How far I had come since I was last here. I leaned forward and touched the paintwork, ran my fingers along the car door. It felt fine, a little warm from the sun. Since it had no connection with my life any more, it was just a life-sized toy. I could have pulled it back with my whole hand, then pushed it forward down the road to see how far it would travel. I almost felt that I was the only real person in a charming toy village and, once I'd solved the mystery, I could sweep up the trees and houses, put them all back into their box and grow back to my normal height.

I sent a text message to Mete.

Arrived safely. All OK? Hug for Elif.

I missed them. I had missed them all day, since before I had said goodbye. When I woke in Istanbul it was dark. Mete walked with me to the centre of Yeşilköy where I would catch the airport bus. Elif was asleep in her buggy, head stretched to the side. If she had known I was about to abandon her, she would have screamed. I gave her the kiss of betrayal and stroked her hair lightly so that she wouldn't wake. Mete and I were both groggy and half deaf with tiredness as we kissed and promised to text throughout my trip. He went to a street

34

vendor and bought me a sesame bread ring to eat on the bus. I slept instead. Now it was the middle of the afternoon but I was no longer tired. The wind was fresh and scoured my cheeks. I looked out at the hills, pondered what I had learned in the police station. Julia was still lost, but I would find her.

I had forgotten the beauty of the moors. I had forgotten that it feels good to rest your eyes on them, to watch and feel as they change through the day, and wait for them to disappear at night. They simmer under the town, pushing the streets up and down, and they curve away into the horizon and pull you out of this dark little place when you most need them to. I used to walk on the moors almost every weekend, sometimes with one of my parents and sometimes with my friends, or by myself with the neighbour's Jack Russell. I knew the paths and trails well. If I walked alone there, I would usually meet someone I knew and we might go further together. Sometimes I went with schoolfriends to kick a football around or play with a Frisbee. We lost many. After Julia disappeared none of us walked on the moors alone. Most of us were not allowed to and would not have wanted to. They had to search the crags and fells for Julia, but there was too much land and Julia was tiny. She might have been lying under the paths we trod, under the grass where we ran and jumped and babbled about how the fresh air and open land made us feel free.

I took another drag from my cigarette and gave a gentle cough. I hadn't smoked since before Elif was born and I wouldn't smoke again after this trip, but at the moment it was the most natural thing to do. I used to smoke in the park with

Julia, and if the cigarette now didn't make me feel better, it took me a little closer to her.

Occasionally, when I've been at a computer, I've put Julia's name into a search engine and scanned pages and pages of missing people. Nothing meaningful has ever come up. I've tried the websites that help you trace people. I've become familiar with tales of missing siblings, abandoned children, lost grandmothers, ex-soldiers who never quite came home. Julia Smith must be a common name. At any given time there are bound to be a few lost or missing Julia Smiths, I expect, but in my local Internet café on an Istanbul back-street, I've never found any of them.

But who was *my* Julia Smith? It is hardly fair, now that I am in my thirties, to judge Julia on the person she was at fourteen or fifteen, yet that is all I can do. Julia was a confident and rebellious fifteen-year-old so I tend to imagine an exciting life for her but, had she lived, she might have settled for something ordinary, have stayed in the area and married here. It is impossible to say. I always remember the same incidents, from a few months before she disappeared. The one I tend to think of first occurred in the park, just around the corner from here.

Julia sat on one of the elm-tree stumps. Kath was beside her on the grass. Julia was slim and dark, Kath plump and fair. Both had short hair, fringes gelled, Julia's daring and fashionable, Kath's untidy, an unconfident and unsuccessful attempt to follow the trend. Kath's face had zones of orange where she had used foundation to hide her spots. Julia either didn't have spots or didn't care about showing them. I don't recall which but I remember her blue eyes and thin black eyebrows. People used to tell her she had beautiful long eyelashes so she fluttered them every time she laughed or smiled. Julia was reading something aloud. It was a warm day in late spring. It was 1982. We were in the park near our school. I was with a group of friends escaping from school for lunch and, as we approached, Julia called us over. She flapped a piece of paper up and down.

'I've had a letter,' she cried. 'I've had a letter.'

We knew who it was from: her neighbour's son who was in the army and had gone off with the Task Force to the Falklands. We crowded around the stump, dropped our plastic carrier-bags of books onto the grass. It was the fashion to have a supermarket bag that was tatty and snagged but not quite disintegrating.

'Read it, then.'

'What does it say?'

'Is it from the soldier?'

'Lucky cow.'

'Thought you was still going out with Owen Carr. What's his name?'

'Alexander. Alex, to me.'

We sprawled on the grass. There was a small pond nearby, and flowerbeds, but we never went there. We always came to the shady corner with the row of elm stumps. The sun didn't reach much of it so the grass was often damp but it was our spot and we felt happy there.

'I can't read all of it. It's personal, and I'll get embarrassed.' Julia giggled and spoke in a sugary voice that sometimes irritated, but we were too excited to care much that day. 'But I'll read the last two sentences. Listen to this. "Yes, Julia, I can read between the lines and I hope you can read between these lines too. I'll be back in a couple of months, I hope, and we'll see each other then."' Julia squealed. 'You can guess what was between the lines. I am in love. I am totally fucking in love.' She applied pineapple lip-gloss from a bright yellow tube, smeared her lips together and added, 'I hope he doesn't get shot.'

We knew she was rather hoping he would. We were hoping it too, of course. There could only be one thing more exciting than a hero boyfriend going off to fight in a war and that was one who was killed in battle. It wasn't that we wished for a real death – not at all – just a story death, and for us this was a story, or else we didn't know the difference yet.

We chattered away, asking questions. How old is he? How do you know him? Is he good-looking? Is he tall? Julia, we learned, had seen him once or twice at her neighbours' house when he was on leave but they had hardly spoken. Her love had blossomed only when he was already on his way to war. Then she wrote letters to him under her desk at school, used notepaper and envelopes with stars and moons in each corner. We never saw what she wrote, but after just three or four exchanges she had flirted her way into some sort of infatuation. According to the bits of his replies that we were allowed to see, Alexander encouraged her. The rest of us knew no one who had gone to fight and we were probably envious. We all knew that Julia's love was no more than a fantasy but we enjoyed the story none the less. Only Kath said, 'What about Owen?'

'What about him?'

'Are you still seeing him?'

'Not really.' Julia folded the letter, then unfolded it again. 'Owen's too young for me now. Have you noticed how he always waits to hear what other people think before he says anything so he can agree with them? Ask him if he likes a certain record and he won't say anything till someone else does. It's so annoying. I've tried, but I can't be bothered with him any more. He's boring and pathetic sometimes. I can't learn much from Owen, if you know what I mean. I have certain needs.' She said this with great wisdom but I had no idea what she meant. I'm not sure that she knew either.

'Have you told him? It's wrong not to tell him.'

'Hark at Kath. It's like having your mother with you all the time. I'll tell him when I tell him. He won't be bothered.'

'I'm not being your mother. I just wanted to know.'

'Why? Do you fancy him?'

'Of course not.'

'Cos you can have him if you want. Alex is going to send me a photo of himself in his Navy uniform. Owen's all yours, if you don't mind my cast-offs.'

Julia giggled again. Kath ran her fingers over the spots on her chin. We probably listened to Julia for the rest of the lunch-break, sitting on the grass at her feet. People passed us on the path that led from the shops, by the pond and down to the church. Normally we did our best to make them feel miserable, found something to whisper and giggle about – bad hairstyles, funny clothes – so that some people walked all the way round the edges of the park to avoid us. On this day we let them pass. We were more interested in Julia.

The soldier returned home a few months later, apparently, and set off again across another sea. But Julia had disappeared before he arrived. For the first day or two we thought perhaps there had been a row at home and she had gone off in a sulk. There were stories about her father's drinking. Or was it her mother who drank? I'm not sure. But days and weeks passed and there was no news. We wondered whether she might have run away, somehow hoping to meet Alex on his ship. The police contacted him but he was in a far-off country and knew nothing about her.

Owen and Julia lived on the same street. We'd see them holding hands, kissing at the bus stop or on a tree stump in the park, but never speaking. Owen was quiet. He did not have many friends. He might have been bullied except that he was tall, quite good-looking, so the bullies left him alone. He was the school sprinting champion but only shrugged if anyone mentioned it. Julia was garrulous, energetic. Some couples are made possible by contrast but it didn't help these two. It made them both like Owen. They were never laughing when we saw them in the park or by the reservoir, hand in hand, just plodding around. I should think, now, that if Julia tried to joke or start some fun, Owen would have cleared his throat or frowned. It was not surprising that she lost interest in him.

Julia informed Owen that he was no longer of interest to her. To make it clear she stuck two French-manicured fingers up, right in front of his face. He did not walk away. He began to follow her around before and after school, trailing along the streets with his sports bag over his shoulder. Sometimes he stood behind a car and watched her from a distance.

Julia always wanted to be older than the rest of us. She was always the first to wear the latest fashions – making ra-ra skirts herself or adapting them from charity shop clothes – and the first out of them. She looked like the girls in cities, not our village. She spent hours taping music from the radio and listening to it so that she could drop the names of bands into conversations, ones we'd never heard of. She talked about London as though she always knew what was happening there, though I don't think she had ever travelled so far. Sometimes it seemed she was ready to scream and pull out her hair because she couldn't grow up soon enough. That was why, when I was fifteen, it was so easy to believe she had run away. It is why, now, I see how her precocity made her vulnerable. She was only grown-up to the rest of us. To everyone else she was a daft teenager. If a man was friendly, good-looking, appeared to know about the world, he could have persuaded her to go for a walk. She would have said yes and not been afraid of danger, not known exactly what it was.

Another memory of Julia. Aunt Maggie was moving to London. The day before she left, Julia and I visited her house to help with the last of her packing and clearing away. Maggie was popular with all of my friends because she didn't have children of her own and seemed much younger than our parents. We loved her lacy clothes and sparkly earrings. We liked the way she swore, *Oh, hell's bells and buckets of blood*, and told us stories of her lovers, men around the world who seemed to fall at the sight of her. She was something of an aunt, something of a sister to us, always on our side and always interested in our lives. *So what's happening on Planet Isabel this week that we all need to know about?*

On that day Julia and I drank coffee with Maggie and helped her wrap glasses and plates in old newspaper, stacked them in boxes. I passed the window and noticed Owen outside. He was sitting on the wall of the garden opposite, tapping his feet against a pillar-box. His eyes were fixed on Maggie's house but I wasn't sure whether he could see me. I beckoned Julia to the side of the window. We hid behind the curtain and peeped out.

'Look who it is.'

'Stupid sod.'

Julia smiled to herself. She pulled at her fringe, made sure that it stuck out and fell over her right eye the way it was supposed to. She might call him a stupid sod but she enjoyed the attention. When it was time for her to go home, though, she went giggling and whispering by the back door. Owen waited another half-hour or so on the street. Eventually Maggie stuck her head out of the front door and told him he should be getting home for his tea. I didn't see what happened then, and Maggie didn't wait to find out, but when I went home an hour or so later, he had vanished.

'I can't believe that boy is Sheila's son,' Maggie had said.

'Why not?'

'Sheila's such a down-to-earth, sensible woman and she's produced a thing that's only good for mooning around in the street. What does he think he's doing, the silly boy? He won't find a new girlfriend, acting like that. Sheila's always spoiled him, that's the problem, and Julia's too good a catch for such a mummy's boy. That girl's a real livewire, Isabel. She's special. I think she's going places.'

'How can you tell?'

'It's a look in her eyes. She's hungry. You know what? She's the kind of girl I can use in my books. She's a female hero for a story I'm going to write one day. Can you help me move my typewriter downstairs? I don't think I can manage it on my own without scraping the wallpaper. Why I care about that now – a bit of woodchip paper – I don't know. It's what this town has done to me. Addled my brain. I'll be glad to be away from here at last. I hope you'll all visit me as often as you can, though. I don't want to lose touch with the good people.'

★

The police and everyone in the town searched each public space, each garage, each shed. They knocked on doors and visited the schools. There was a little attention in the local newspapers but it soon turned quiet and we never heard any more. The war finished and we were still waiting. We weren't used to problems that had no solutions, and were in a state of suspension. No wonder we kept looking around at each other.

Kath and I could not bear the waiting. We held a sort of séance, just the two of us, to see if we could make contact with Julia. We'd learned all this stuff at school, how if you stood in front of a mirror with a candle and said the Lord's Prayer backwards you'd see the Devil behind your left shoulder. I'd tried this once on my own. I was curious to know what he would look like. I imagined a very young, tall man with a wide, handsome face and a smirk, who would appear, scarlet, just behind my ear. I turned the lights off, shone a torch on a copy of the Lord's Prayer and recited it backwards, word by word, but he didn't show up and I was not surprised or particularly disappointed. Kath and I did not know how to raise the dead but were familiar enough with the rituals of church, the communion, the liturgy, to feel quite confident putting together our own dark ceremony. We guessed that candles were essential and a bit of chanting. How were we to guess, at the age of fifteen, what might work and what might terrify us?

★

I set off from my house carrying a box of candles and a couple of cassettes in a plastic bag. As I half walked, half ran in the dark I convinced myself that it was working already. The spirits of the dead or missing were looming at me from the leafy branches of trees, creeping out from beneath parked cars, from dustbins. I held the bag at arm's length. I tried to breathe silently so that they would not notice me. When I arrived at Kath's and she opened the door, she kept asking if I was all right. 'You look funny,' she said. I shut the door behind me and leaned on it, feeling safe for a while.

We placed candles in jam-jars around Kath's room, making sure the arrangement was symmetrical. We knew, without having to discuss it, that symmetry was important. I put the tape into the cassette player and 'Sunday Girl' came on. I knew immediately that it was the wrong music, too cheerful, too bouncy, though when I hear it nowadays it terrifies me. I said nothing. Kath turned off the light and we went around the room in silence and lit the candles. Then Kath had the idea of filling the air with Julia's favourite perfume. Julia liked Charlie so we found some that belonged to Kath's mother. It made our noses wrinkle and our throats itch. We sat on the floor, looked up at the ceiling and concentrated. I wasn't as frightened now that I was with my friend.

Occasionally I glanced at Kath but her eyes were fixed on one spot near the lampshade, mouth open, lips dry. I thought I could feel Julia's presence and we chanted some words we'd written to make her come closer. For a few minutes I believed it. I almost thought that we could talk to Julia. I saw the fervour in Kath's face – she needed to believe that Julia was there – and then I knew that Julia was only in Kath's imagination. In that case, the same must be true for me.

'Should we say something else, talk to her normally?' Kath whispered. Her eyes were small and black like raisins.

'Maybe. You say something. I don't know what to say.'

'Julia. Julia, can you hear us?'

Kath lifted her head as though she expected Julia to float down through the ceiling. For the first time, I wanted to laugh. The words sounded stupid. It was all right in our heads, but aloud it was silly. Kath believed it, though, and this made me more self-conscious.

If Julia was there, she did nothing to help us. I looked from candle to candle, hoping for a quick flicker of a flame, a sudden blackout or a new shadow creeping across the wall. Nothing changed. Kath spoke a few more times, trying to coax Julia into the room, but eventually she fell silent. One of us put the light back on and we blew out the candles. The music was still playing.

'What did you think?' Kath's voice was half strangled. She hugged herself and rubbed her neck with both hands.

'I don't know.'

I looked around the bright room, with Kath's books along the walls and shoes on the floor. Candle smoke mingled with the smell of the perfume. Behind them was the faint aroma of strawberry jam. I thought about the churchyard and how easy it was to pull ghosts from dark, empty air when you wanted them.

'I don't think she was here, Kath.'

'But she was. I could feel it. Oh, Isabel, I know she was with us. I think she's in grave danger. She's alive but she needs our help.'

I understood even then that this was the only possible answer for Kath. It was what she – we – wanted to hear. Julia wasn't dead but she needed us. No other answer could have satisfied us and that was why I knew it could not be true.

The air was cold. I should move on. My phone vibrated on the bench. A reply from Mete.

We fine. See you tomorrow.

I kissed the screen and put the phone in my pocket. Yes, I could wait until tomorrow. I was sitting in front of the old police station and nothing bad had happened. I had not been arrested, not taken away in a car. There was no sign of my parents anywhere. All fine. Good.

A beep and another message. It was Mete again.

Your English friend is here to visit! What shall I do?

He must mean Bernadette. She came from London a few days ago and spent a day with us. She went off to travel around the Greek islands but promised to return to Istanbul. I'd thought she meant in a couple of weeks – she had booked her flights and ferries – but what was it, four or five days? Her flight home was not from Istanbul but from Athens. She must have run out of money, or fallen ill, perhaps. I wondered what she would do with Mete and Elif. Mete liked her but he was too busy already and she might be expecting a bed for the night. I knew that she didn't have the money to pay for hotels. Bernadette is terrified of children and would not be good with Elif. She has often told me that she finds small children sinister. 'You don't know what they're thinking about you,' she says. 'How can you bear to be near them?'

I couldn't worry about that now.

Make her a cup of tea,

I replied, and pressed send.

I'd reached the end of my cigarette without noticing. I dropped the butt on the ground and crushed it with my shoe. The sight of my foot, delicate and feminine in a shiny high-heeled shoe, surprised me. I wiggled it around and admired it. There was still plenty of time. Where next? The scene of the crime, of course. I would head for the reservoir.

Maggie picked a russet from the bowl she kept by the fireplace. She took a chomp and began to chew as she followed the bookshelf along the wall to the window. She liked to crunch a russet or two on a slow day. The girl called Leila had started it, and she'd got it from Jo March, who liked to steal away with half a dozen russets when she read a good book. Leila always had an apple in her hand when Maggie passed her on the stairs or in the hall. She left little brown apple cores around the house, like snail shells, on the edges of tables, on piles of books. No wonder there had always been mice in the house. Maggie could hardly hear the birds in the garden for the apple-crunching inside her head but Leila had only made a sound with the first crunch. After that, she ate silently. She was a strange girl.

Maggie ate up the apple core in two large bites, dropped the stalk into the fruit bowl. Her eyes rested on the framed photographs of the girls. She stroked the glass of her favourite. This was the picture she always returned to, the two girls at the top of the path on the hill.

They both came to her at different times. You can't turn people away when they need you. Who would argue with that? It had all begun with a surprise telephone call. 'Hello, love. What is it?' She had pressed the phone to her ear. 'Yes, yes,' said the girl. 'You must help me. I seem to have disappeared but I'm not missing. I'm not missing.' How sorry Maggie was. I'm just a poor old woman. I didn't mean any harm. Dust blackened Maggie's fingertip and she wiped it on the underside of the shelf. Don't blame me.

She looked at the girl on the left, her hair a swishing sea anemone in the wind. The tendrils seemed to move even while the rest of the photograph was still. 'I've brought you back now,' said Maggie. 'You've been gone for too long. I'm giving you a life but I don't know how good it will be. I can't promise anything but life, and the chance to claim what should always have been yours. It's my job. It's all I can do.'

Maggie stood at the window, felt the cold glass at her face, watched the horse-chestnut leaves ruffle on the grass below. Conkers and prickly husks dotted the ground. The view irritated her. One was supposed to love the sight of autumn leaves, wasn't one? But there was nothing beautiful about this. It was as miserable as dirty tables in a fast-food restaurant. If only she could look down and see the old reservoir, but she was in the wrong time and the wrong place for that.

Two boys and a girl came along with knobbly sticks and poked them at the branches of the nearest tree. The conkers didn't fall so the children bashed the branches harder and the leaves made a noise like water rushing over stones. She peered down to see them crouching on the grass, searching with their fingertips. There was a man strolling between the trees now, along a sort of invisible curve, as though following an edge, trying not to fall off a cliff or into a pond, but there was nothing to his side, just more grass. He was tall and lean, rather handsome with short dark hair. He was talking to himself, or to some-one he thought was just behind him, for his head turned every now and then and his lips moved.

'Excuse me.' She had no idea why she was calling to him, only knew that she should.

He didn't hear her but the children looked up. The girl nudged the bigger of the two boys. They all had pale skin and toffee-coloured hair. They looked like sister and brothers.

'Excuse me, could you tell that man over there that I'm trying to catch his attention?'

The girl ran through the trees, over the bumpy grass, and tapped the man on his arm. This was wrong, of course. What had she done? Was she putting the girl in danger? There were witnesses around so he couldn't harm her but, all the same, she had sent a young girl of no more than nine or ten straight over to a stranger who was talking to himself. Maggie regretted calling out. She had nothing to say. If she were to talk to him, she'd have to go downstairs, open the back gate. He could be an escaped murderer. If she kept her eyes on the children and they kept theirs on her, then they should all be safe.

But the man was not interested in the little girl's message. He turned to her, smiled, but then walked on, laughing with whomever he thought was strolling at his side. The girl smiled shyly at Maggie and shook her head. Maggie realized that the man was walking as though at the side of a stretch of water. Yes, that was it. He thought he was by a pond or a lake. He was at the edge of the reservoir, taking a walk on an autumn's afternoon. Perfect. She had no need to ask him anything. All she had to do was watch.

— 2 —

A duck or goose quacked a peal of laughter. The sound had a muffled, bleak quality and I stopped for a moment to prepare myself. I approached the gateway that leads to the lakeside path. The masts of the sailing-boats clinked a busy rhythm in the wind. I began to feel excited. I passed through the open gate, closed it behind me and there I was. This was the place. The wind picked up and the clattering grew more urgent. Birds chirruped and cawed from the trees and reeds. I had always remembered this place as silent but now it was like stumbling on a clearing in a jungle. There were the rowing-boats, lined up together, shiny and complacent as they rocked. The small refreshments kiosk was still in its nook under the trees, closed today but with its price list and ice-cream menu on the outside wall, a sign for scones and tea at £1.50. I looked around for other people, children feeding ducks, or birdwatchers with binoculars. A youngish man was walking by the water's edge. Behind the kiosk, some distance away, was the short terrace of cottages that formed part of Julia's paper round. Bare rosebushes arched over the doorways. The gardens were neatly mown, as they always had been. I felt like a ghost from the future, come to view the present, 1982. I moved further towards the lake, staring and listening but I didn't know what I was waiting for. I approached the water, almost afraid to breathe now. Surely something was about to happen.

I watched the man, who was now standing near the sailing-boats. He was dressed in a stiff black suit – clearly for a funeral – and was feeding bread to a Canada goose. There was a whole loaf of sliced white at this feet. He must have bought it especially. He and the goose were engaged in a movement, almost a dance, back and forth. He looked up at me and smiled. He was probably in his early forties, was good-looking, with a sandpapering of dark stubble on his head, a strong jaw. His smile grew as I approached and I smiled back, slipped my hands into my coat pockets. The goose gave his ankle a jealous peck. The man bent slightly at the waist, backed away. 'Ouch. Hello.'

I nodded and cleared my throat. Five or six geese came out of the water to see what was in it for them.

'Want to feed the geese?' He held up a slice, pushed it towards me. His hands were waxy soft and his nails polished, perhaps manicured. He was well-spoken but with a twang of the south-east. I wasn't quite ready to converse with anyone but I needed to warm up a bit, rehearse for Owen's wake.

'Thanks. Why not?' I took the bread and backed away from the geese.

'I love them.' He tore a slice of bread into halves, then

quarters, then smaller squares and scattered them at the water's edge. 'They can be a bit sharp when they want to. They're not exactly cute, are they? Canada geese, but that's fine. Hey.' He shooed the nearest goose away with his arm. 'That bit wasn't meant for you.'

'Are you – sorry if it's rude to ask – going to Owen's funeral?'

I tore the bread and threw it, a piece at a time, as far away as I could. I have never liked the geese to come too close. I hate their pushing and pecking. It's not enough for them to get the bread. They have to act as if they want to knock you off your feet as well. Still, I smiled as they waddled back for more. When I'm with people who love animals, I pretend to like animals more than I do.

'Yes.' He chucked two handfuls of bread pieces into the air and watched them descend over the birds' heads. 'I came from Leeds and got here too early. I didn't want to take any risks with the buses. You never know whether you're going to be hours late or hours early. It's impossible to arrive anywhere at just the right time round here.'

Then he threw a whole slice of bread, spinning it like a Frisbee and calling, 'Neeoww,' as it went. Four geese put their heads together and squabbled over it. I watched as a small brown feather lifted into the air and wilted gracefully to the ground. The man held out his hand and I shook it.

'So, you're Isabel. I wasn't sure at first but now I can see it clearly. It's your eyes, I think, and your bone structure. It's good to see you.'

My eyes sprang wide open. I let my gaze run over his face but didn't recognize him. 'Sorry.' I stumbled over the word. 'Have we met?' I supposed we might have been at school together, except that his accent was wrong.

'No, but I've seen pictures of you. Your cheekbones are a little more prominent than they were but apart from that you've hardly aged at all. Lucky.'

'Haven't I? You are . . .?'

Haven't aged since when?

'Owen's friend. He used to talk about you a lot. I knew him years and years ago. We stayed in touch, on and off, though I hadn't seen him for a while before he died. I wish I'd made the effort to come up every now and again and take him out for a pint.' He sucked his lips together and let them go with a smacking sound. 'It's easy to say that, isn't it? But I'm not rushing round taking my other mates out for pints in case they all die next Tuesday so I suppose I'm not telling the truth. Then again, Owen was different.'

'Was he?'

'Oh, you know how he was, Isabel. Needed looking after, needed propping up a bit, didn't he? Poor old Owen.'

I hesitated before I spoke. It felt too intimate to speak like this about Owen, but it was what I needed to do. 'He didn't always get on with people, that's true, but I suppose it was only a lack of confidence. I didn't get that at the time. It was just annoying. Were you close to Owen?'

'When I lived near London, he would come and stay with me quite often, when he wanted to look for you, in fact.'

'Oh.'

'I suppose he found you then, eventually, since you're here.'

'No. He didn't.'

'You never replied to his letters? Never received them, perhaps.'

'I got them but there was no point in replying. They were a bit confusing, to be honest. I was never sure what he wanted to say so I began to ignore them. He went quiet after a while. I didn't think I had anything to say in return and I had no intention of coming here to see him. Did he really go looking for me?'

Owen could have found me, I think, if he had wanted to. It is true that I have moved around a lot but I have been careful to leave a trail behind me so that I don't disappear. I have a terror of disappearing and am always dropping white pebbles as I go, putting friends in contact with friends, sending messages and passing on my new addresses, one after the next, so that they can find me if they want to. Owen knew that I was staying with Maggie and, when I left, she would have been happy to give him my new address.

'Spent weeks on end trying to find you.'

'What for?'

'I don't know. He just wanted to be your friend again, I think. He didn't have many friends. He thought you understood him better than other people did.'

'I don't think I understood him particularly well.'

The man shrugged and I realized that his presumption was irritating me.

'Look, I didn't want any contact with him. I didn't know it was so important until his letters became strange and, frankly, incoherent. I thought it would be irresponsible to do anything that might encourage him to write more.'

'Good of you to come to the funeral.'

Was this sarcasm? His face was blank. There was something odd about the way he looked at me and I realized it was that he hardly blinked. His gaze was watery, blue and still. 'It was a small thing I could do.' I knew that I was not doing this properly. I needed to befriend this man, if I were to learn anything. I made my voice casual. 'So, were you and Owen very close friends?'

'Yeah. He was a good bloke, Isabel. He used to make me laugh. You know, I'll tell you about Owen. When he came to stay with me, he would decorate rooms in my flat and build shelves without asking if I wanted them. He started with the hall and wallpapered the ceiling, tiled the floor, put up a nice mirror. Then he worked on other rooms and it always looked good. Yeah, he was a great friend. I'd go to the pub and come home drunk, right, and in the morning I'd crawl out of bed and go into the bathroom or kitchen to find a new shelf or light-fitting. He liked gardening, too, and used to mow friends' lawns when they were out.'

He chuckled. The smile stayed on his face and in his eyes for a long time after he stopped laughing.

'He must have been very good with his hands.'

'He was.'

'Where was he living at the time?'

'He was up here with his mum and dad. I had a place near Watford, a flat. I believe that he liked to construct things as a way of atoning for past mistakes. Well, one day, about five years ago, he put a new shelf in an alcove in my bedroom. I stacked some books on it and he told me to take them off. It wasn't for books, he said. The next day he came home with a goldfish bowl and two little red fish. The expression on his face—' The man's voice crumbled. He put up his hands as though he was trying to frame Owen's face in the air. His fingers tensed, loosened, then dropped to his sides. He blinked, swallowed and waited a moment. 'They were sweet, the fish.'

'Did he stay with you for long?'

'Hardly at all.' He was steady again now and raised his voice to prove it. 'Just weekends, here and there. But each time he came he did something to my flat. Some people have to be doing useful things all the time, don't they?' He looked me up and down, then down and up. 'You look as if you don't like to sit around waiting for your nails to dry. You look as if you get up at six and go to the gym before breakfast. Myself, I'm pretty lazy. When I'm not working I'm sleeping. But it always seemed to me that Owen worked harder than he needed to.' He smiled at me. 'I've still got one of the fish. It's cute. A lot fatter than it used to be, but it doesn't seem to have grown much longer. Maybe I give it the wrong kind of food. I can't afford to buy the most expensive brand. I know fish food doesn't cost much, but anyway . . .' He looked out over the lake. 'A friend ate the other one.'

'The other fish? That's disgusting.'

'Yeah. I've always felt bad about it. I told Owen it died of fungus but actually it was swallowed alive to pay a debt in a game of poker. Poor Owen. I wonder, Isabel,' the man lowered his voice, 'maybe he's listening in now and learning about this for the first time.'

'Don't.'

'He might be.'

'If he is, do you think he's pissed off?'

'You know, Isabel, I'm not sure. I couldn't guess how he's feeling. What do you think?'

'I never knew this particular Owen you're talking about so I couldn't say. If I had to guess I'd say, yes, he's pissed off. He was very serious, even when he was being funny. I mean, I don't think he was the laughing-it-off type. On the other hand, I imagine he has more to be pissed off about right now than a goldfish. He's dead.'

The man looked up at the sky and rolled his eyes around to me in mock-fear. I let out a feeble laugh. He echoed it with a weaker one.

'It's all right,' I said. 'He's probably building himself a new bed and some bookcases.'

'I don't know if Owen believed in life after death.'

'I don't know either. It wasn't the sort of thing we ever talked about, though we did go to church together for a few years. I was brought up to think I had no choice but to live in heaven for eternity. I don't know whether Owen expected to be there too.'

'It's not very appealing, is it, heaven? Look at this beautiful landscape.' He waved an arm towards the trees, then beyond them to the moors. 'I tell you what, I'd rather have a day here than for ever in heaven. I'd be glad to do the exchange.'

'You'd sell your soul, then, for this place?'

'Everyone should sell their soul for their heart's desire, Isabel, if they have any integrity. It's the only thing worth doing.'

'You may be right about that. You like to use my name, don't you? It's disconcerting.'

He walked away from me. 'I'm sorry. I shouldn't have spoken to you.' He threw more bread at the geese. 'I'm bothering you.'

'No, no.' Now I felt bad. I quite liked this man and was enjoying our conversation. I worried that I was too comfortable with him, since I had no idea who he was. 'It's fine. Just a bit surprising that the first person I meet when I arrive here is a complete stranger who seems to know a lot about me.'

'Thank you for pointing it out. I won't use your name again.'

'You can use it as much as you like, but you haven't told me yours.'

'It's John.' He turned, mollified. 'Delighted to meet you, Isabel.' He held out his hand again. I shook it for the second time.

'It's nice to meet you too, John. Do you think we ought to be getting to the church now?'

'Yeah. Probably. We don't want to be late.'

But we were moving in the wrong direction. We were

walking along the lakeside path, away from the village and towards the rowing-boats at the jetty. John swung the bread bag by his side. Sometimes it hit my leg. I moved further away but then he edged closer. I considered turning back and going to the church alone, but John's connection with Owen was too powerful and I could not leave. I had to find out everything he knew about my old friend. The path narrowed and I was relieved to slip a pace behind John. His walk was loose and relaxed. He bounced slightly on his heels as he went. He was tall and skinny but not weedy. His head moved from side to side, registered every movement in the trees or in the rushes, alert as a meerkat.

I looked at the water but it didn't mean anything yet, not while I was with a stranger. It would not be mine again until I could reach in and touch it on my own. For now I decided to continue with my questions.

'So, how did you meet Owen?'

'We worked together in a kitchen.'

'Kitchen? What – round here or near London?'

'Neither. Somewhere else, a different part of the country. It just happened that we were both there at the same time.' John lifted his head and gazed at the moors he would sell his soul for.

Then I realized. 'Oh, sorry. Yes, I see.'

He meant prison kitchens, of course.

'Owen was a wreck the whole time he was inside. I tried to help him when we both came out. I really did. He often talked about that girlfriend of his who went missing. Watch out along this bit, there are roots sticking up. It upset him a lot. He talked about you too. I think he was a little bit in love with you, Isabel.'

'Do you? No, I'm sure he wasn't. I never thought that.'

John chattered about the colour of the bulrushes as I turned this over in my mind. Owen only wrote to me because of what we had done together, one stupid thing that left me connected to him for ever. I would not have said he was in love with me. I always saw him as Julia's boyfriend and I thought he only saw me as Julia's friend. I knew that we would never have spent time together under any other circumstances. Apart from Julia, I didn't see what we'd ever had in common.

'What did he do when he came out of prison? I mean, what sort of work? Did he ever marry?'

'He had a few relationships. One lasted three or four years but I think that was the longest. He didn't have any children and I don't think he wanted any. He worked in sales. Something to do with office equipment.'

'Sales? So he must have been quite good at talking, then, quite confident.'

'Oh, yes. His shyness wore off as he grew older. As far as I know, he was quite successful. He worked in Bradford, I think, but travelled all over the place. He liked driving. He liked having to spend half a day getting to another part of the country and then half the night getting home. It suited his temperament.'

'Was he in a relationship when he died?'

'No idea. As I said, I hadn't made much of an effort to keep up with him in the past couple of years. I don't know what he was doing. He didn't mention any remarkable changes, not in his last Christmas card. I imagine he was just ticking over when he had the accident. Just getting on with life.'

'Just getting on with it.'

'Muddy patch ahead. Careful, in your Sunday-best shoes. You're dressed very nicely.'

'Thanks.' I stumbled along, one foot on either side of the squelchy mud.

'And what about you, Isabel? Why did you go with Owen to set fire to a supermarket one night and almost burn the whole village down?'

I looked down at the mud. I had known that someone would bring this up but hadn't expected it to be a stranger. Do I have to dwell on this? I'm not sure of its relevance and it is still painful to recall. 'It's hard to remember now,' I muttered. 'I don't spend much time thinking about it, these days. We were just teenagers. Teenagers do silly things.'

I didn't tell John about the incident with Mr McCreadie, the supermarket manager. He already knew more than was his business and it had happened such a long time ago. I wanted to be the one to ask the questions but John continued, 'That's quite an understatement. And you had your own little holiday at Her Majesty's pleasure. How was that?'

He knew everything about me. Why would Owen tell him all of this? What had it mattered to Owen by then?

'You've gone quiet, Isabel. I can see that you're deeply uncomfortable with the fact that Owen shared so many stories with me. Don't be embarrassed. Everyone screws up sometimes. I certainly have.'

'Good for you. But, unlike other people, I don't need to talk about it.'

The path was wider here. John stopped for me to catch up and we continued walking side by side. I wanted to change the subject but could think of nothing else to speak about.

'It was a strange time,' I told him eventually. 'After Julia disappeared, none of us was really normal. I mean, not until we left the area. I'm sure it was the same for all of her friends, in different ways. We got up to things that didn't feel as if they belonged to us. Don't think I'm trying to deny responsibility for what Owen and I did. I'm not, but one way or another we were controlled by Julia – or her absence – for at least a couple of years. I grew out of it the minute I left this area. You see? I put it behind me and have been fine ever since.'

'Julia's ghost was leading you astray.'

'No, that's not what I mean. Not like that. Just that we weren't capable of understanding everything, not that anyone tried to explain a single bit of it. There was no counselling in those days, nothing like that. No one came to analyse pictures we drew, or to sit with us in circles and share memories of Julia. Nothing but a terrible silence around Julia's absence. Double nothing. It was bound to leave us – well – restless.'

'If only she could come back and tell you what happened.'

'Don't be ridiculous.'

Of course I had thought the very same thing myself, many times, but it was idiotic to say it aloud.

'Or maybe you know what happened?'

64

'How could I? No one knows.'

'It's beautiful here, isn't it? Look at all the colours. There's the blue of the reservoir, the exquisite green of the mallards, the brown branches of the trees. It's alive even in November. I can't imagine how beautiful this village must be in spring and summer. It must have been a lovely place to grow up. I bet you were always roaming over the moors or coming down here to feed the ducks. Did you have a bike?'

'Yes, an old one. I don't remember cycling by the reservoir but I'm sure I did. I suppose it wasn't a bad place to be, till Julia went. I didn't grow up anywhere else so I've nothing to compare it with. Yeah, maybe it was nice.'

'This was the sort of place I fantasized about when I was a kid. I always lived in cities. Never liked them much. There's very little wildlife, and even keeping a pet is harder in the city. I had an old bone-shaker I used to cycle around on but I wanted to be in the countryside. The woman next to me on the bus said that this is Eva somebody land, or some name like Eva. Eve? Ena?'

'Eva Carter.' I smiled. After many years here Maggie couldn't stand the village – just a clique of nosy, uptight Tories, she said – and sold her big house and garden for a small terraced house in London. The town moralists and gossips belonged in the 1950s, she used to say. It was impossible to feel anything with these stuffed mattresses. She craved passionate, wild-tempered neighbours, or some such thing, but she didn't find them here. She concluded that it was easier to be romantic in Hounslow than on the Yorkshire moors.

'Who is she?'

'A writer. Her books are set round here. There's one called *Goose Island*. I haven't read it but, look, see that little island? Over there.'

There was a small island with a couple of trees on it, and next to it a couple of tiny ones that were just bumps in the water.

'Is that where it's set?'

'I've never read it so I don't know for certain, but that's called Goose Island. It's sweet. There's not much room for anything to happen there. You could just about have sex.'

'Oh. Right.' He ran his hand over the top of his head.

I smiled. I had embarrassed him. 'No, no. Sorry. I only say it because that's what's most likely to happen in an Eva Carter book. Somebody will row or swim out there at some point, probably a dark, rugged man to rescue a beautiful woman, and they'll make love on the island.'

'Traditional stuff?'

'No. In Maggie's stories the woman always does everything she wants. She sometimes even murders a man or two along the way, but she still gets the glittering prize at the end. Usually a different man.'

'Cool.' We both looked out at Goose Island. Or was it Swan Island? Perhaps it was and Maggie's book had confused me. I couldn't remember. 'You could do it under the shelter of the trees,' John said. 'But there's something sad about it. It's melancholic.'

'Maybe it is. They had to search the whole reservoir area,

with divers and everything, so to me it's just bleak. Julia pervades the place but it must have been sad before then, if you noticed it too.'

'I'd like to buy you a drink after the funeral. We're both outsiders here, Isabel, and we need to stick together. When the locals see us coming along the main street, they might try to chase us out of town.'

I laughed. 'Why should they do that?'

'A pair of ex-cons showing up together, all dressed in black. Could be scary to some people.'

'I hadn't thought of it that way.'

'So, a quickie, then? A quick drink somewhere, I mean.'

'Thanks, but I'm on a pretty tight schedule. I've got a plane to catch tomorrow. I don't live round here, you see. I'm in Istanbul now. In the meantime I need to talk to some people who do live here still. I want to learn more about Owen before I go home.'

'Who are you planning to talk to?'

'I'm not really sure. I thought I'd see who's at the funeral.'

'How will you broach the subject?'

'I'll just see how it goes.'

'So you're leaving tonight?'

'Tomorrow morning. Tonight I need to pack, need to make phone calls. This and that.'

'Busy-busy. Why do you live in Istanbul?'

'Because that's where my job is and it's where my husband and child are.'

'What's your job?'

'I write articles for a monthly journal, and sometimes news-papers. Mete and I also manage a shop together, with his relatives.'

'What kind of shop?'

'Food, everyday stuff.'

'And you run it together? How romantic.'

'Yes, it is. It's very romantic, as it happens, but we don't get much free time to spend with each other and Elif.'

'How old is she?'

'Nearly two.'

'You don't seem like a mother.'

A white duck pushed its bill through the reeds and waddled alongside us for a while. I walked between John and the duck as we progressed around the reservoir. No, I thought. I don't seem like a mother. This morning I did, but now I do not. I wiped my foot on the grass to remove a lump of mud. 'I'm going to the church,' I told him.

A smile lurked around his face somewhere, almost in his eyes, almost his mouth, not quite in either. He thought that in making me indignant he had somehow wielded power.

'You're much too early. We've got plenty of time yet. Shame we can't go for a quick row. The water's so tempting. I don't know why I'm saying that because I can't even swim. It still looks like a big, glistening invitation, though. Don't you think?'

The boats were lined up with a pair of oars inside each one, but there was no one around to take the money. I had an idea. I didn't particularly want to spend hours in a pub with John, but a quick trip out on the water right now might prove useful. 'You're right, John. We have time.'

'Fantastic. You'll love it when we get out there.'

'We can untie one and leave a note on the jetty with some money.'

'You're so moral. I love it. I'm a good rower, you know. I used to row often when I was younger. Won't it be a nice thing to do? A little peace enjoyed together before we say goodbye to Owen. Just look at it.'

John sighed and gazed out across the reservoir. The wind had died down and the water barely rippled.

'But quickly. I really don't want to be late for the funeral.'

'There's still time.'

The reservoir was whitish blue, cold. It didn't look like the reservoir I remembered, which had been dark green and viscous. Goose Island (it *was* Goose Island) was smaller than I'd thought it, nearer, and with fewer trees. I didn't want to go out there again but it was the perfect way to remember Owen and, perhaps, learn something new.

Owen and I took a rowing-boat out on the day we committed our crime. It was a vivid, yellow day. The reservoir stretched out under the sun, stripes and shapes of silver covering most of the surface. The middle of the water was the only place where we could talk in secret and I had big news to tell. I ran down the street from the police station and told Owen to meet me at the end of the jetty. I called Kath, too, and told her to come, but she was studying hard for her A levels and stayed at home. I didn't mind. A crocodile of primary-school children slunk along the pavement towards the reservoir, armed with nature books and jam-jars. I ran past their bobbing heads to the jetty and waited for Owen. One of us paid thirty or fifty pence, whatever it was, to the old man who always sat there in the afternoon with his ham roll and copy of the *Sun*.

We took it in turns with the oars and rowed out near Goose Island. In the shade of the trees the day darkened and cooled. There were mallards on the island. We argued about which kind were male and which female. Owen would not concede that the brown ones were female and decided that they must be a different breed of duck. 'They must be moorhens,' he said, 'those dull brown ones, because mallards are colourful with bottle-green heads.' I had been visiting the reservoir with my parents since I was tiny and I knew which were mallards, coots, moorhens. We argued, I remember, for a long time and then we both grew irritated, so I began to tell him why we were there. Owen was eighteen and I was seventeen then. He was unemployed and I was on a training scheme at McCreadie's supermarket, taking dance classes in the evenings and at week-ends. It was a couple of years since Julia's disappearance and the rest of us were living on a strange edge that left us dizzy because we could not stop ourselves looking down. I was still inventing stories in my head, almost daily, that kept Julia alive, kept her life twisting forwards. I told Owen what Mr McCreadie had said to me that afternoon about Julia, and how we were the ones to do something about it.

When I'd finished speaking, we switched places so that I could take the oars. 'The ducks don't know what kind of ducks they are so it doesn't matter anyway,' Owen said – just because he was wrong and I was right – and trailed his hand in the water. I pulled the oars hard. I was not as strong as Owen but I could row almost as well. I liked to see how fast I could make the boat go. I liked to feel as if I were in a race against some imaginary boat just off to our side, rowed by Olympian heroes. I would make us speed along, then lift the oars to see how far we would glide before coming to a rocking rest. I liked the patterns in the water, the whorls and pleats I could make with the oars. Even that day I couldn't help but look. Then Owen stared at me with his black eyebrows furrowed. When I saw his face like this I knew he was still missing Julia. He never said how he felt but he used to go, with me and Kath, to the spot where she had vanished. We would stand there and look for clues – something that the police had missed – but we didn't find anything. Perhaps we were seeking something clear, like a bump in the soil, a scrap of school uniform, a gap in the bushes, but I think we knew that if there was anything, it would be less tangible. It would be an understanding. By staring at the place, feeling it underfoot, knowing the changes in light and weather, we would lead ourselves to the point of knowing what had happened there. Of course, the place never changed enough and we were frustrated. Now Owen simply stared but his expression was not empty; it was full, brimming with something I didn't quite recognize. What I know is that the fullness made me feel small. Somehow – I don't remember how words led us to it – we concocted our plan.

I often wonder how murderers who kill together find each other. How and when do they know that it is safe to tell the other one what is too terrible to share? There must be some conversation, some gentle play of words and gestures that builds up to a look or movement that says, *I am like you. Tell me what you want to do and I'll understand.* How does a lover confess and know that the other will not call the police? I still do not have the answer but, then, Owen and I were not murderers, or lovers. Our plan was to set fire to the supermarket, at night, when it would be empty. I remember one of us saying – it would have been me – that even if we were wrong about what Mr McCreadie had done to Julia it made no difference. He could have done it, might as well have done it, and what he had done in my head made him as good as a murderer.

So now I was on the jetty with Owen's friend from prison.

'I hope I don't push you off,' he said.

'I hope so too. Is it likely?'

'It's just something about being on a jetty, with water on three sides of you. The urge to push other people off is so strong. I can almost see my arms reaching forward and shoving you as soon as you turn your back. I'd never do it, but I can feel it, tingling in my fingertips.' He laughed. 'Don't worry about me. I'm not remotely dangerous.'

We were walking along the wooden slats, heading for the far end. I wondered why he had been in prison. I did not plan to ask. It was up to him to tell me, if he wanted to.

'Good. Right, then,' I said to John. 'Let's go if we're going. No time to waste.'

He jumped ahead of me, selected a boat. Its name was *Penelope*.

'Then help me get *Penelope* out.'

We untied the rope. It slipped from my hands and fell into the lake. I reached in and pulled it out slowly, enjoying the water against my hands. I clambered into the boat and John followed me. I perched on the bench and took the oars. I liked the feeling – it had never gone away – the heaviness of the wood, the sense of movement about to begin.

'Will we take it in turns? Can I row on the way back?'

'Yes, of course you can.' But already I had taken ownership of the oars and wouldn't want to give them up easily. 'What was Owen like when you first met him? I mean, was he depressed? Was he very friendly?'

'I always felt sorry for the guy. Smoke? Oh, you haven't got any hands. Have one on the way back.'

'Thanks.'

John took a packet of cigarettes from his pocket. He slid one out and lit it. I got a tiny breath of smoke before he moved the cigarette away and held it over the water's edge.

'This is cool. I like this. Nice ashtray, too. I haven't had much fun in the last year. I moved to Leeds to be with my girlfriend, and a month after I got there she left me for someone else.'

'That must have been hard. Had you found a new job?'

'I work in a pub at the moment. We were going to set up a business together, interior design and selling design products. She was good at all that stuff, you see. She had a degree in fine art. I'm good at driving and accounts so we could have made it work. But, listen, I'm single now. There are a lot of advantages to that.' He smiled at me, showing even white teeth.

I said nothing but looked behind to make sure we were not going to hit anything.

'If that girl – Julia – was murdered,' John said, waving a match around, 'what do you think the motive was?'

I began to row. I got us clear of the other boats and the jetty before I answered. 'Can you be so naïve as to ask that?' We were moving out into a clear space. There was less than half a mile of water ahead, with only Goose Island between our boat and the other side. 'Read the newspapers and find out what happened to this week's missing schoolgirl. Don't ask questions, John, but tell me some things instead.'

A picture was developing in my mind of Owen and John talking quietly to each other in prison and Owen was confessing to Julia's murder. I could almost hear him. I didn't know whether or not to take it seriously but I couldn't help imagining it. As the scene took shape, detail appeared in black, white and grey. Owen was on the edge of a bed and John was on the floor, leaning against the wall. Owen was holding himself, cuddling his chest with his long arms. He cast a faint shadow over John.

'I'll be as helpful as I can. What would you like to know?'

'Did Owen talk much about Julia? I mean, what do you know about her?'

'I believe she was Owen's girlfriend for a while, at secondary school, but they were both very young. Puppy love. I think it was all very sweet. By that I mean that I don't think he ever got his leg over.'

I cut the water with the oars and pulled extra hard. 'And why do you say that?' I was certain he was right. I realized that there was an inconsistency in my thought, though. I had always imagined Julia to have slept with Owen, but not Owen with Julia. Of course, that made no sense.

'He told me the name of the first girl he had sex with and it wasn't Julia and it wasn't when he was fifteen or sixteen but, you know, I think he was lying even then. I think he was a virgin when he came to prison. The story didn't ring true, you see. It was a fantasy about a woman on the beach somewhere like Benidorm but not Benidorm. I can't remember where it was now. Anyway, she was wearing a skimpy bikini and he was swimming quite near her. He was there on holiday with some mates, though he didn't say who they were. It was another thing that made me suspicious. So the woman kept smiling at him and then she beckoned him to follow her behind some rocks. And this is the funny part. The second they were out of sight, she got down in the water and started sucking him off.

Yeah, without even speaking to him. He came in her mouth and then, before he knew it, they were shagging on the side of the rocks and she was squealing. Her name was Jodie. *Jodie*, I ask you.' John shook his head with a smile. 'I reckoned he was making it up even as he told me. He probably thought something along those lines had happened to every other guy his age. I think he thought it should have happened to him. I can tell you, it didn't happen to me. Then another time he told me he'd never been abroad, so how could I believe him?'

My memory of Owen was a fragile thing and John was putting it in danger. I didn't know exactly how Owen's memory was going to exist for me in future. I wanted to know the truth about Julia, of course, but until then I had to be fair. Owen might have been innocent, after all. And even if he was guilty, was it still all right to laugh at something silly he had once said about sex?

'Well, it might have been true. We can't know every holiday he ever went on. Look, never mind Owen himself. Specifically about Julia. What do you know?'

'Nothing much. I know she was sixteen when she went off. Or was taken. Whichever.'

'Fifteen.'

'Fifteen, then. I don't know what she looked like. I know she was a gobby little thing. Owen once described her as a rum lass. Not being from the north I didn't really know what he meant. I asked Owen and he couldn't explain it to me. He just repeated it. "Julia was a rum lass."'

He said 'rum lass' in a parody of a northern accent.

'You don't need to do such a comedy voice as if we're both from Surrey and have never met anyone from Yorkshire. You live in Leeds now yourself.'

'Aye. And I sort of know what a rum lass is now. At least, I know one when I meet one.'

I avoided looking at him. Something about the way he talked, the way he watched me was forcing me into a sensible, bossy role with which I was not comfortable, but I felt that if I did not keep control he would somehow get the better of me.

'How did Owen sound when he talked about Julia?'

'Sad. Wistful. Is that any use? Would you like some more? Lonely. Thoughtful. Confused. Lustful, no, romantic, no, starry.'

'Starry? I don't know what you mean. I need to see and hear it for myself. Can you do an impression of his face? Imagine you're Owen talking about Julia. I want you to do his face and voice.'

'All right.' John shut his eyes and put his fingers to his temples. This was probably a stupid idea – I could hardly imagine the police using such a method – but I had no other way of getting to Owen. John narrowed his eyes and stared into the water. 'She was a right rum lass, that Julia.' His accent was still ridiculous but in a strange way his facial expression did make me think of Owen. 'Ran rings around us all.'

'That doesn't help me much. Wait, you used the past tense there. Did Owen refer to Julia in the past tense?'

John looked confused and shrugged. 'I don't know. I don't know why I used the past tense. I don't suppose it came from Owen. I probably put it in myself because I was thinking about her in the past. But I think Owen would have spoken about her in the past by then anyway, wouldn't he? A lot of time had passed. I don't think you can take it as a clue.'

'I suppose not. No, maybe you're right. John, I'm afraid I don't know how to do this properly. I'm not a detective so I'm just going to ask. Did Owen confess any crimes to you?'

'Yes.'

'What?'

'Breaking and entering, and arson. That's why he was there.'

'No, no. I mean, anything else. Any secrets.'

'You think he murdered Julia?' John's tone was casual.

'I don't know. Did he?'

'He didn't confess to it.'

'Good. So, that's a start, then.' I gave a nervous laugh.

'I don't know that he would have told me, though. Maybe he would but I would find it hard to believe that he'd done anything so serious. He was a kid when he was in prison, never mind when he was fifteen. Come on.'

'Sixteen. He was big, and very strong. He liked to brood.'

'He was soft. Violence wasn't his way of doing things at all. He steered clear of fights. He avoided confrontation.'

'Does the way an inmate behaves inside always reflect the crime he committed? I don't think it does.'

'You're right there. Murderers can be charming and fun to spend time with while tax dodgers can be plain nasty. You have a point, I'll admit, but it doesn't quite apply in Owen's case.'

'And the fire?' I was almost afraid to mention it again. 'That showed violent tendencies, no?'

'Perhaps that was your bad influence. Don't look like that. I'm joking. No, he shocked himself with the fire, I think, but that was the most he could have done. He was never going to hurt anyone.'

'It's a different kind of violence that we're talking about, though. It has nothing to do with getting into fights. Don't you see? It's not that at all. Well, never mind. You're appalled that I'm asking these questions. He's not even buried yet.'

'But you need to know. I understand what you're doing, Isabel. You think Owen killed Julia and, if he did, he might have been a danger to you, too, but at the time you trusted him. That makes you uneasy. In fact, you must have been frightened of him right until the moment you heard of his death. Give me a clear reason why you think Owen did it.'

'He had a motive. Julia had dumped him for a fantasy relationship she was having by letter with a soldier. But that's not the main reason. It's the way he behaved afterwards. Let me show you something.'

I steadied the right oar under my arm, took the letter from my raincoat pocket and shoved it into John's hand. It was warm, a little tattier than when I'd packed it in the middle of the night.

John read the page. He reached the end, frowned, and read it again. 'I'm not sure what he's trying to say. Suicide?'

'There's no way she killed herself. Owen's trying to justify her death, her murder. It's bizarre. Even if she did kill herself, how could she have taken her body with her? No, I think this is Owen saying she asked for what she got. What I don't know is why he thought that. It could be an admission of guilt.'

'Could be. I don't see how you can tell.'

'I can't. It's a feeling. I know there's more but I can't get to it.'

'Was the fire Owen's idea? That was a pretty disturbed thing to do.'

'No, I'm fairly sure it was mine.'

'But you had nothing to do with Julia's death.'

'No.'

'There you are, then. Why should Owen have done? What about your experience in the young offenders' institution? Didn't you meet more dangerous people there than Owen?'

'I don't remember.'

'You must. Of course you must remember.'

'I don't. I can't. It's not in there.'

'You just have to try and—'

'Shut up about it.'

The church bells were striking the time.

'We've come too far.' We were almost level with Goose Island and the shore was far away. 'Let's get back or we'll never make it.'

'You don't fancy stopping off quickly? Couldn't that be part of our adventure?' John grinned and glanced at Goose Island.

I looked at the scrub of grass and the trees, claustrophobic and pointless. Then I turned to John, still smiling. There was a time when I would have liked to see what kind of adventure I would have, but not now. 'It's a bit cold.'

'We could continue the conversation later, in the pub. It'd be nice to have a chat.'

'Maybe, John. It depends on who else I bump into. I haven't got long.'

'Of course. Can I row now?'

We switched places, the boat rocked then steadied. John rowed fast. His arms were thin but moved the oars like whisks through the water. We reached the jetty and I jumped out while John tied up the boat. There was still no one around to take our money. I remembered that I had no cash but John had already taken a couple of pound coins from his pocket and put them on the jetty, just beside the rope. He was writing a note on the back of a bus timetable.

I left John and walked to the water's edge. I picked up a handful of pebbles and chucked them in, one by one, to hear them splash but the sound was feeble. I was glad I had found a companion for the funeral. I had dreaded entering the church on my own, seeing Owen's family full of grief. When I looked at the water I still saw John's skinny arms with the oars. I felt as if I were still moving. I turned around to find John but he was not there. I couldn't see him on the path. I called his name but he didn't answer. He must have left for the church without me. I started to walk, quickly, almost a run. I looked at my wrist but I'd left my watch at the guesthouse. I looked at my phone but the time didn't make sense. I would be late for the funeral.

I passed a beech tree with what seemed to be silver birds fluttering around the trunk. This was not far from the cottages on Julia's paper round. I stopped, moved closer and saw that the silver birds were Cellophane around a bouquet of flowers. A card was nailed to the tree bark. It said, 'Safe in heaven now xx'. I looked for a name but there was none. The flowers were fresh so someone must have died there very recently. I ran for the gate, pushed it open and left the reservoir behind me.

In my head I saw myself asking Kath, 'Was there ever any news of Julia?'

'No. I guess she made a new life somewhere.'

'So, you think she's still alive?'

'I bet she's married somewhere with kids.'

'But you'd think she'd have got in touch.'

'You didn't. You've been missing for years.'

'I haven't, really. I didn't have anyone to come back to here. The people who would have thought me missing knew exactly where I was. I put them through too much, you see.'

'Nothing compared with what Julia's family went through.'

'No. You're right there. But I can hear her. I can hear her saying, "I'm here. I'm still here." I need to find her.'

'You'll have to stay longer.'

'No, you don't understand. I can only stay one night. That's all I have.'

The sky deepened. Purple-black clouds were pressing down on the moors. It would rain soon.

The curtain flicks the back of the mirror and a spray of cold water strikes my leg. It is raining. I squeeze behind the dressing-table, open the window wide again, pull back the curtains and lean out. My legs and feet are in the room, but from the waist upwards I am out in the dark sky. The wind tastes of the moors and the lake. Rain spatters my face and hair. I drink a few more gulps of the night, then pull my head inside the room. To keep warm I put my clothes on again, my funeral clothes as they are all I have here, but it is uncomfortable and oddly formal to sit in a skirt and tights. There is a large oak wardrobe by the door. I open it and reach inside to see what is there. I'm sure it will be all right to borrow something, just for the night. I pull out a large brown coat, a man's coat that will reach almost to my ankles. It will do me fine. It slips from the hanger and dust rises to my nose. I reach my arms into the long sleeves, shrug it onto my shoulders, sit on the stool and pull the duvet over my legs as fine rain hits the carpet.

I check my phone again, hoping that, somehow, another message from Mete has come through without my hearing it. Perhaps I'll call him soon and make sure Elif is all right. She will be unsettled and might not sleep. If she begins to cry and I am not there, she may fret through the night. Mete can calm her as well as I can but he has to be up early to open the shop. Elif is going to Mete's aunt for the day and I don't know if she'll be able to sleep there. Mete and I promised not to call each other but how can I not speak to him now? It's expensive but I must hear his voice. I've become afraid, worried that if I stay another night, I'll lose my balance. I won't want to get back to them, or be able to.

It is because the business with the supermarket and the fire came up. I had thought I could avoid recalling the whole episode as it is not directly related to Julia's disappearance. I would prefer to stick to Owen and Julia but John has shown me that I can't do this. All right, John. Is this what I met you for? But I am not going to go through every little thing. If something is too painful, even now, to write down, then I shall not write it. So, then, this is the time to set down notes on Mr McCreadie. After all, he was our main suspect at the time of the fire. We thought he was a murderer. I have since cleared him of all charges but now I shall go back to be certain. Why is it so hard to discuss the mistakes I have made, even with myself, and so easy to talk about Owen's when his were worse? I rub my face with my hands, take a pillow from the bed and place it on my knees for extra warmth. I shall not be afraid of this.

In the beginning, there was nothing wrong with McCreadie. It was my first job and he was exactly as I expected a boss to be: a bit like a teacher. He was middle-aged, balding, bespectacled and had the kind of posh North Yorkshire accent that people respected. He looked and sounded very much like all the local bank managers. I was one of the till girls so I didn't speak to him unless he spoke first. I left school at sixteen and went to work there on a training scheme. To everyone who knew me it seemed that I had given up all ambition, but I was vaguely hoping that by continuing with my dance classes I would be able to leave the village within a year or so and go to a dance college. But I didn't mind working on the till and I never considered it to be a boring job. When I took tea-breaks upstairs with the women who had worked at McCreadie's all their married lives, I did not think they deserved my pity, that I would go on to do better things. I looked up to them. I would stir my tea and listen with pleasure to their quick banter and their jokes.

The supermarket was busy, a focal point for the village since there were no huge out-of-town stores then. Mr McCreadie greeted staff and customers as he passed them. Beyond civilities, he didn't stop to talk about things that had nothing to do with work. But that changed, for me at least. Usually I worked on the tills. I was put on checkout number one most days as I was one of the fastest and the queue was always longest there because it was near the door.

One morning someone remembered that I was on a training scheme – that was why I earned about twenty-five pounds a week when older people worked the same hours for twice as much or more – so had better try some other departments. They put me in the butchers' room behind the shop. I spent the day putting cuts of bloody meat onto polystyrene trays and covering them with clingfilm. Stewing steak, sausagemeat, pork chops, globs of liver. I wasn't asked to butcher the meat. Men did that. I didn't mind handling it but I hated being stuck in a dismal, dark room away from the bright lights and action of the checkouts and aisles, away from the comforting piped music. There was no clock in the butchers' room and at the end of the day I went into the stockroom to see whether it was time to clock off. Mr McCreadie was watching me through the window of his office. No one else was around but this did not bother me for a moment. I trusted everyone I met. I saw him, went over to the door and said, 'Have you got the time?' I was pretty innocent back then. I understood innuendo and dirty jokes from other teenage girls but not from middle-aged men – I thought such language belonged to us not them – and it took me a few moments to understand his reply. He said, 'Love, you tell me when your time of the month is and I'll tell you when I've got the time.' Once I'd worked out what he meant I could think of nothing to say or do in response so turned away from him. As I moved, I noticed that his hand was burrowing in his trouser pocket. I felt cold, a terrible sense of danger, but still did not know what I was supposed to do. I managed to say, 'Fuck off,' under my breath. Mr McCreadie lurched forward, put his arm around me and lowered his cheek to mine, spoke almost in a whisper, 'Watch your mouth, treasure. You could end up like that friend of yours. We know what happened to her.' He leaned forward. I pulled away from him then, but he followed me and pushed his face right into mine. He tapped his nose, 'I know what happened to young Julia Smith,' and walked away, chuckling. I pushed past him to the door that led back into the shop. 'Don't act as if you're upset,' he called. 'You moved in on her young man fast enough, got your claws into him in a hurry. What a nice way to find a boyfriend.' As I walked away, I said, 'He is not my boyfriend,' which was the weakest and stupidest of all the things I could have said to Mr McCreadie at that moment, though later I had my revenge.

I went to the police first. The man behind the desk promised to look into it but didn't think I had any evidence. 'His car is light blue,' I pointed out.

'So?' He banged his mug of tea on the desk and I jumped.

'I thought there was a light blue car involved,' I whispered.

He shook his head and snorted at me. 'Half the cars in the bloody town are light blue, not to mention the ones that drive through every day. Don't spend so much time listening to gossip and daydreaming.'

'No,' I said, 'I'm not.'

He waved his arm towards the door. 'Get home and tell your dad from me you need a bloody good hiding.'

No, it is clearer to me than ever that Mr McCreadie did not kill Julia – he had an alibi for the day she disappeared and was talking rubbish for the purpose of taunting me – but someone did. I've read the story plenty of times since then; the girl has a different name in each story, town, country, and she may have left behind a bicycle, a shopping-basket or mobile phone, and I know that the missing schoolgirl is almost always dead.

Maggie insists on happy endings for her girls because that is what they deserve. They mustn't be punished, she says – as Celia or Jasmine or Roxy wins the man, the fortune, and gets away with murder – just for being girls and for wanting things. A girl or woman who seeks satisfaction must be shown to triumph. The more she attempts, the larger the rewards. Then it will be a triumph for all women. But I don't think that is the point. How does it help Julia? It is not a question of rewards or retribution but of noticing what happens. Still, I have not read many of Maggie's books carefully and in a little while I shall take a break from Owen and Julia to skim through *Goose Island*. Perhaps then I shall have reason to change my mind.

Elif will be sleeping now, curled up in her cot, her pyjamas wrinkled and warm. Mete will be on the bed under the window. If she has woken, perhaps he will be singing to her in his sweet, out-of-tune voice. The mobile of wooden fish is above his head, occasionally kissing his hair as it swings. His hand rests on the side of the cot, where mine should be.

Outside our flat, cars zip through the dark along the main roads, out to the airport and back. In the all-night soup café around the corner, a handful of people are tearing at pieces of fresh white bread, squeezing lemon juice into dark lentil soup, feeling the traffic's hum in their feet and legs. If they speak, their voices will be quiet, muted by the night.

I feel Elif close again, as if she is by my ankles, pulling herself up onto her feet, then slipping down again with a giddy laugh. I can almost touch her but I can't take her in my arms. If I try to imagine it, she slips out of my grasp and goes back to my ankles, wraps herself around my leg and holds on. A little spirit baby that has come with me in place of Elif. Even her name sounds different now. It sounds foreign and beautiful, nothing like me or my own name, nothing that I could have made.

I headed up the hill to the market-place, entering between the old Methodist chapel and a wool shop. The chapel had turned into a snooker hall before I left but now there was a large white board on the red brickwork: *Evolution: just a theory? The Rev. White discusses Creationism on Tuesday, 11 November at 7.30.* I looked above the door and saw that it was no longer the Methodist chapel or a snooker hall but an evangelical church. I couldn't imagine what local circumstances had conspired to bring evangelicals in and send snooker players away. I continued towards St Peter's, which I knew would not have changed.

The town centre was more or less as I'd remembered it but the remembered version had such a violent presence in my mind that this real place seemed ethereal, an uncanny double. People moved slowly but smoothly in and out of the shops. They tied dogs to lampposts, talked to strangers' babies in prams, paired up with others on the street to pass the time of day. There was nothing to say clearly that this was a new time. There was no Starbucks, no mobile-phone shop, no sign of an Internet café, no sandwich bar. Two old men with walking-sticks passed each other in front of the bank with a nod and, again, I had the feeling of being the only human in Toy Town.

There was St Peter's, grey and square, solid and separate from the ground like an ark riding on dark water. It cast a deep gloom over the street. I had a vague memory of Owen's mother, Sheila, running jumble sales in St Peter's parish hall. Sheila was one of the women who didn't go to work but managed things in the village, always organizing a garden party or a bring-and-buy sale. We'd see a couple of them on a summer's evening, walking up or down a street with a wheelbarrow of jumble, or bramble jam, or newly made soft toys. We lived in a rigid matriarchy. Men existed somewhere around the edges, coming and going by car, disappearing through the back door when there was a birthday party or friends for tea, to hose a lawn or rake up leaves.

According to the clock on the tower, I was still fifteen minutes early. I used to walk up here, on the other side of the road, to get to choir practice. On dark or foggy evenings we would hang around afterwards to creep around the graveyard and tell ghost stories. Behind the church, by the entrance to the crypt, there was a stretch of grass that was never lit. We would feel our way through the inky black, over and between the graves, sometimes grazing our hands or knees on the lichened stone. The younger ones held onto the sleeves of the older ones. We never talked in that place but scrambled quickly onwards, stumbling back into the lamplight to see each other again, to laugh and shout and show that we weren't scared.

A woman crossed the road ahead of me, hands balled inside the pockets of her hooded anorak, a heavy frown on her face. Her head shook from side to side as if she was in the middle of a tired argument. I knew her, had known her. Pauline had been the supervisor in McCreadie's supermarket. She trained new staff on the tills, marched up and down behind the row of us, helping when a price was missing or we typed the wrong number into the cash register. She brought bags of change to fill the compartments in the drawers. Pauline chatted with the customers, seemed able to keep four or five conversations going at once. Like Mr McCreadie, she was known to most of the village, a local character. When she had a day off, the place had no warmth and we missed her.

Pauline looked round, caught my eye, and I thought she recognized me. She started, a smile almost came, but then she tilted her head down and moved on. I was a ghost, apparently. I supposed they had built a new supermarket, probably in the same spot, but I was not going to visit that part of town. I didn't want to know.

I walked behind her almost all the way to the church. When she reached the gate she stopped, turned again and stared at me. She took a mobile phone from her pocket and began to speak into it. I lingered at a bus stop on the other side of the road. Who was she telling? *Guess who I've just seen. Guess who's had the nerve to show up here again.* The bus stop made me think of rain and, sure enough, as soon as I turned away from Pauline's plump, tired figure, a drop of cold water landed on the side of my nose. A small group of people in black clothes had gathered around the church gate and on the steps that led up to the path. More raindrops fell. I wiped my eyes and mouth, sheltered in the doorway of a hairdresser's called Images.

Behind me stood tall pyramids of shampoo and conditioner bottles. Someone had taken the trouble to fill the window with swathes of autumn leaves, brown, yellow and red. Above them hung polystyrene human heads. The heads wore wigs, highlighted with stripes of the same autumn shades. Deeper inside the shop, under a warm yellow light, two blonde women stood over customers.

The rain fell steadily now, slanted by a cold breeze. Small

rivers bubbled along the gutters and the drains gurgled and frothed. Fat sploshes dropped from the shop's canopy and I moved close to the window. Soft shapes in black came together near the church gate, some sheltered by drab, dripping umbrellas. From this distance their faces weren't visible but the figures were all in pairs, males matched with females, holding onto each other with an arm, a hand. They blurred into one another. If Mete were here, he would be standing to my left, his right arm around my shoulder. I would be holding Elif close to my chest, her forehead tucked under my chin, and she would protect me. But they were not here, so I crossed the road and joined the funeral crowd. Cold water slipped down my neck and under my coat. The group began to thin. It formed a bumpy line and moved upwards along the path to the church door.

The hearse arrived, followed by two more black cars. I recognized Owen's parents and sister as they emerged and came together on the pavement. Sheila was just as I remembered her. She was tall and slim with sharp cheekbones, short silver hair in the same cropped style she'd had fifteen years ago. Her shiny black coat skimmed her ankles. Dennis was a couple of centimetres shorter, plump, white-haired. He wore a thick, solid black jacket. His right hand reached upwards slowly and rested on his wife's back.

Sheila's expression was vacant, and although she held her head high, her eyes were slipping and rolling around like marbles, unable to keep still and focus. I thought that the family would move directly to the church and I planned to wait until then so that I could nip in at the back. However, Sheila's glance now rested on me, and she didn't go forward with the others. She waited until they had reached the door, then came to me, as I had known she would. Her steps were careful, as though she were picking her way through a bed of small flowers. I should have met her in the middle but I could not move. I was afraid of Sheila, for no reason that I understood. Her right arm extended. Her face was pale and the sockets of her eyes were pearly and swollen, like iris petals.

'Isabel. I thought it was you.'

'Sheila. I was so sorry when I heard—'

Sheila rested her fingers on my wrist. They were warm and clammy. She stood a little too close to me. Her expression was without either dislike or affection. 'Thank you for being here. It means a lot to have Owen's old friends around. And you've come far, I know. Your aunt Maggie tells me you live in Turkey now.'

She looked drowsy and confused, as though she was ready to drop to the ground and sleep at the click of a stranger's fingers.

'The flight only takes a few hours.'

'You have a Turkish boyfriend or husband, she said.'

'A husband, yes.'

'Is he a Muslim?'

'Yes, no. Well, not practising.'

'Mm.' She nodded slowly without explaining why she had asked this. 'I thought you'd passed away, Isabel. That's what Owen told me when I asked about you once. He said you'd passed away quite suddenly. It was a shock when Maggie mentioned you in her letter last week. I had to read it two or three times before the news sank in.'

I gave an awkward laugh. *Passed away?*

'Owen never said your name when he came back here – apart from the time he told us that you'd died – but I know he thought about you often. I did too. The past is very – broken. I mean it's— I'm glad to see you looking so well, Isabel.' She glanced over my shoulder at the road. 'Are you staying long? Would you like to come round one day for a chat about the old days and Owen? A cup of tea, just the two of us? For Owen's sake, it would be nice.'

'I wish I could but I have to fly back to Istanbul tomorrow. I'm sorry. I have family there and I can't stay any longer.'

A memory of something, something that had been sleeping in my bones, stirred and rested again. What was it? Just a light that flicked on, then off again. A familiar shape, like a kite against the sky, that I could not quite see in the brightness of the sun, and then it was gone.

'Yes, of course. Ah, never mind. It would have been nice, you know, to understand you better, the influence you had on my son. I want to know more about Owen than I shall ever have in my hands to know. Anything I hear is a kind of treasure for me to keep and polish, good or bad. I don't mind that in your case it's bad.'

I stood silent for a moment. Over the road, the door to the hairdresser's opened with a ting and a couple of women came out, chattering and laughing. They saw the funeral cars, clapped their hands to their mouths and shuffled off in silence. The street and churchyard were quiet now. A few people lingered on the pavement, listening to Sheila and me, but the rest of Sheila's family and most of the guests had gone into the church.

I could not quite believe Sheila's words.

'Influence?'

Sheila shook her head. 'You see, I often think, if he hadn't met you . . .' She was nervous. She was building up to say something I should not like. 'I find myself wondering, often. I wonder how things would have been different. If you had never been there to collide with him, if you had never existed in the first place. If the pair of you had been put in different classes at school—'

It would have been better to say nothing but my mouth opened and I was speaking. 'That applies to Owen and me equally. Sheila, if you'd rather I didn't come in, I won't.'

My voice was steady but my heart thumped.

'Yes. No. Not at all. I mean, I don't blame you, Isabel. You were very young. Just a girl. You probably had no idea how much power you had. I expect you were unaware of the things you could do to people just by being yourself, by talking and having thoughts. You were pretty too, and that's not your fault. I don't blame you, not entirely.'

'What kind of power do you mean? I don't think I had any power over anyone. Certainly not Owen.'

'The power that young girls have. I know what that is. Well. He isn't here any more. He can't speak for himself, can he? So we'll never know.'

95

There was a whisper of suggestion in her voice that I was to blame for Owen's death. And, of course, this was not the time to say it but I said it all the same. 'I'm not responsible for that. He was in an accident.'

Sheila widened her mouth into a tight smile. A thin tear leaked from her eye and engulfed a stray crystal of blue eye-shadow. It stopped on her cheek like a stuck-on bead. I wanted to reach out and smudge it away with my fingertip. I wanted to say sorry.

Dennis appeared in the church porch under a small carved figure of St Peter. He stepped down onto the path then stopped. 'Sheila, love, don't you want to come in out of the cold? There'll be time to talk to people later. It's warm in here.'

She seemed to hear the word 'cold' for, though she did not turn round to him, she pulled up the collar of her heavy black coat and shivered.

'Shall we talk afterwards, if you still want to?' I hoped she would go inside.

'There was blood on his clothes,' she said.

'Oh. I'm sorry.'

I assumed she meant the car crash. She must have seen him afterwards. Perhaps she saw his clothes in the hospital.

'You must have known. Was there blood on your clothes too?'

'What?'

'That day. The day she went. He would not have hurt a fly. No, he would not. What did you make him do? You were always together. What was it you did? I can guess, believe me, but I want to hear it from you.'

'Nothing.' My voice was louder than it had been all day. The sound of it surprised me. 'Sorry, I don't understand. What are you saying?'

'We couldn't go to the police, could we? It's always the boy and not the girl. We knew who'd get the blame and it wouldn't be you. You see? Owen would have suffered. It's always the boy and not the girl.'

'But I don't know why you would think this. What did Owen say to you?'

'He said nothing. Owen never said anything at all but he didn't need to. He was my boy and I knew him. That day, there was blood on his clothes. Some spots on the sleeve of his sweatshirt. Not many, but enough to notice. Whoever killed her would have been soaked in blood, you would think, but Owen wasn't. I think someone else must have come home much bloodier.' Sheila did not look at me but it was clear from the way she spoke, the wavering, high-pitched tone of her voice, whom she meant. 'I put it in the wash and it came out fine but it never went away, not in front of these.' She jabbed her index finger at the air in front of her eyes.

So I was right. Owen was guilty and Sheila had rinsed away the evidence.

'And then you got him into trouble again two years later and he was taken away from us. I can't get that time back again now, can I? I haven't even got memories from that time, except bad ones of having to visit him in that place. Those memories shouldn't have to count, but they do. I don't have enough to be able to discard a couple of years. Well, some time later you took your own life, or so Owen heard, Isabel. I would not wish to dance on anyone's grave but I was so relieved to hear of your death. So much pain and worry just evaporated at that moment. I even managed to feel pity for you. I allowed myself a few tears of sadness. And more fool me, because now he's dead and all of a sudden you're alive again. It doesn't make any sense to me.'

'Whatever Owen did to Julia – I don't know what that was or even that he did anything – it had nothing to do with me. I promise you.'

'He was my son. He was good. Why did you run away from the country if you didn't have something to feel guilty about?'

'I wanted to live somewhere else.' *And people like you made it clear I could not stay.*

'Rubbish. You had a good home here. I knew your parents.'

'It's quite normal to want to move around in life. People do. And I did not have a home here, not by then.'

'Oh, you would have stayed here if you could. You want to come back now, don't you? Now that Owen has died you think it's safe. Why else are you here?'

I narrowed my eyes. The rest of the mourners, the hairdresser's shop, the graveyard and the paved path up to the church door disappeared from the edges of my vision. There was just Sheila, a dreary apparition before a wet, grey sky, saying these strange things to me and I could not respond. She confused me. I wanted to defend myself but could not think where to begin. I decided just to start speaking and find out what I said when I said it.

'I wanted to be at the funeral, Sheila. It's why I came. I'm leaving tomorrow, as I told you. I have no intention of living here again. Look, I've upset you by coming and we shouldn't be talking about this now. I'll go away. I'm sure you just want to get on with the service. You don't need this kind of distraction now.' I turned to leave. 'I'm very sorry about Owen's accident.'

'You're not bloody well leaving.' She hissed this at me. 'You're coming in. You can sit with the rest of us and see my son's coffin. If I have to be there then so do you.'

I was about to walk away, frightened by the vehemence of Sheila's words, but when I looked up I saw Owen's sister emerging from the church. She left the huge oak door open behind her, half ran towards us, tottering in knee-length black boots and a tight purple skirt. She put her arm around her mother. 'Mum, you go inside with Dad. Come on. This isn't the right time for arguing.'

Sheila lifted her chin, turned her head to Dennis and did not look at me again. She put her arm through his and they moved into the church. I avoided the eyes of the crowd in the entrance and along the path. Some of them must have heard the whole conversation.

Owen's sister perched on a low headstone. It belonged to Eliza somebody who had died in 1879. I couldn't see the full inscription. The sister drummed the top of the greenish stone with purple nails. She had Owen's eyes. The long, sleepy lids that turned down at the outer corners. She regarded me coolly, her eyes closing almost to slits. 'It's Isabel, isn't it?'

I nodded.

She looked away with a frown, apparently making some sort of decision, then turned back, smiled at me. 'Isabel, will you come into the church and will you come to our house afterwards for a drink? I want to talk to you. Don't worry about Mum. She doesn't know where she is today. She has to blame someone for Owen's death and she saw you from the car. You've brought back bad memories, but you mustn't take any of it personally. None of that has anything to do with today. It's good of you to come.'

'Are you sure it's a wise idea? I don't want to be here if it will cause trouble. I don't want to get in the way of things or distract anyone. I can disappear just as easily as I came.'

'You won't get in the way. Just join in with everyone else and avoid my parents. I'll come and find you later.' She pulled an elastic band from her pocket and tied her long hair into a ponytail. Then she turned and marched up the church path, passing mourners on the way but not stopping to speak.

I thought of skipping the funeral and catching Owen's sister when she came out, perhaps returning to the Lake View guesthouse for a while, when I spotted safety. A dark prickly head moved among the soft, silvery ones. It was John. He saw me and waved. 'You got here before me, Isabel.' He smiled and kissed my cheek as though we were old friends. 'I lost sight of you.'

'I don't know how that happened but I'm glad to see you,' I said. 'I've just found something out.'

'What?'

'I'll tell you later.'

There is no reason for Sheila to think that it had something to do with me. I dislike Sheila so much now that it is hard to accept that she is any friend of Maggie's. I wish Maggie had dropped her years ago, out of loyalty to me. I know that is too much to ask, but Maggie was my closest friend and I cannot bear that she may have known all this and not told me. Then again, Sheila had thought I was dead and had believed this for some years, so perhaps Maggie had not spoken to her since I left London. I must confront Maggie some time and find out what they have said. At the very least, Maggie will be able to put Sheila straight. I never considered killing myself. It did not occur to me at any time that life would not get better. Maggie knows that. She has always understood me well.

But blood on his clothes. Could there be another meaning? I see Sheila standing in the front room, peering into the hall. She watches Owen as he turns his back, stooping slightly to reach the doorknob. She notices the blood on his sleeve, wonders what has happened – a fight perhaps? – but gets no answer from Owen. He grunts and passes her. That's nothing strange. That's how teenage boys are. So normal. He goes to his room and stays there for the evening. He plays his music loud. No, no, he does not. For once he does not. He doesn't play music at all so Sheila knows something is not right. The silence from upstairs rings in her ears like tinnitus. Something has happened to her son and it is something bad.

When the police come knocking on doors to ask about Julia, perhaps Sheila feels a kind of pinprick in her chest. It unsteadies her but she knows, of course, it is nothing. She goes to the laundry basket, finds the clothes and puts them through the washing-machine at a high temperature. All the time she will be saying to herself that Owen could not have done anything – she knows her boy – but still she must protect him from idle suspicion. People are gossiping already, swapping names over the supermarket checkouts and at the doctor's surgery. She will use more soap powder than is necessary. When the clothes come out of the wash she will run her fingers carefully over the fabric, holding it up to the light and scouring it for any faint shape of what was there before. Is the blood Julia's? It could be Owen's own blood, some minor accident that occurred when he was out. But the tiny pin has moved deeper between her ribs now and she repeats, under her breath, that she knows her boy, of course she does.

– iii –

Maggie had a little wooden box from Turkey. She kept some of her postcards and letters inside. Leila had given it to her and she had one the same. Maggie had been to Istanbul long before her visit to Leila, when she had her Turkish lover, the professor. They stayed in a hotel so that they wouldn't have to tell his family they were there. His brother was a wealthy plastic surgeon who lived in an old house nearby but they never saw him. They visited the Blue Mosque, the Aya Sofya, the Grand Bazaar and the palaces, Topkapı, Dolmabahçe. 'I'm a historian,' he'd say, 'so you're lucky. I'll be your guide to the world's most beautiful and important city.' She can't have paid much attention to his words, though, for now she couldn't remember even which palace or mosque was which any more. What she had was a picture in her mind of the city's curving skyline, with peaks and domes like a cream-topped dessert.

And random memories of things they did. He liked to eat oranges. He peeled them deftly, one after another, and pulled away segments to give to her, then licked the juice from his fingers. One hot evening they entered a dark shop and bought a bag of nuts, half a kilo, perhaps.

Could it have been a shop that sold only nuts? She couldn't remember anything but the glass-lidded containers of nuts and seeds by the counter, large sacks of almonds in the shop's shadowy corners. The man scooped up hazelnuts, almonds, pistachios, pumpkin and sunflower seeds, and poured them into a brown-paper bag. They left the shop and walked towards a restaurant but realized they had spent the last of their money on the nuts. The lover ran back to the shop and asked the man if he could return them. The man laughed him out of the shop. 'You expect me to stand here and separate all these? Get on your way, my friend.'

Most nights they ate out in cheap, simple restaurants selling kebabs, soup, stuffed vegetables and rice. They stayed in that night. They looked out on the Bosphorus from their hotel balcony and ate the nuts with cold beer. He knelt on the floor and rested his elbows on the edge of the balcony to watch the ferries come and go. When Maggie yawned he turned and lifted her feet to remove her shoes. With his fingertips he kneaded her calves and ankles. She could smell oranges in his hair. In the bedroom they undressed. He liked to take her clothes and fold them into a soft, neat pile on the carpet. He took her earrings last, always. He lifted them carefully from her ear-lobes, just the gentlest touch of his knuckles against her hair, so that her head tilted back and her neck tingled. Now she remembered the dark green bedspread and the grey-blue view of the water far below, as if there were never a wall or balcony between but the water was lapping right there at the edge of the room.

But she remembered little else. When she returned, years later, to the palaces, they weren't the same ones. Only their names were the same, as if new buildings had been put up but they had kept the old signs. The Dolmabahçe Palace was the wrong way round. She couldn't say what she meant by this, only that she seemed to be facing the wrong direction all the time. Topkapı was smaller. Perhaps it was simply that he wasn't there any more, so it couldn't be the same. This time she preferred the streets, the dark hilly passageways, the box-room grocery shops. She liked to stop at the window of a shop selling pastries, baklava or Turkish delight, and gaze at the soft, sticky jewels. She could have lived there, she supposed. She would have been happy. But, then, her lover had never wanted to. It was not exotic to him. He'd say, 'The water gets cut off all the time. The streets aren't safe after dark. Have you noticed when you walk through Sultanahmet that at least seventy per cent of the people you see are men? And when you see women, they are hardly ever on their own. You can't have a comfortable life here, Margaret Eva. You think you want this, but you don't.'

She had never wanted a comfortable life, but he did. That must be why they parted from each other, though she was not sure any more. Bess and her husband had been delighted when it ended. They never met him but were anxious, none the less. Perhaps they were worried that, somehow, he would exert a dangerous influence over young Isabel. 'Isn't he a Muslim?' Bess had asked. 'I'm not saying it's a problem but won't he want you to go and live there and be like him? If you've never believed your own religion, how will you believe his?' But he had gone to live in New York and Maggie found she didn't love him quite as much without Istanbul.

The walls and ceiling snapped and crackled again, as if someone in the attic had just woken and begun to stretch her feet. It was the other woman. It was the mad wife her husband kept hidden up there who never came out, who didn't know what 'outside' was because she knew nothing any more, except the dark room full of tea-chests and bookshelves. Perhaps the mad wife was standing just above her now, with a box of matches and a wedding veil. But she knew it was only the mice, eeking and scuffling in the walls. She didn't mind them – they were just playing – but it was nicer, she thought, to imagine a woman up there in the big dark room. It was not nice, of course, to think such a crime of her husband, who was a good man, but, still, she liked to imagine. They might as well use the attic for something.

Because everyone was changing. They were altering in shape and swapping faces. While she had been sitting at the table, standing by the window, as the sky outside had shrugged off its colour and the dog-walkers had come and gone, everyone had moved to another place. It was like musical chairs and – just as she had intended – one person was standing, out of the game.

— 3 —

On the day I told Mete about the funeral we had found drops of blood on the front doorstep of our shop, little cherries in the dust. We didn't know whether we should call the police but there was no damage to the shop or the street. There had been a couple of attacks on properties in the area in the previous weeks, minor burglaries and vandalism, but this did not appear to be an attack on us. It seemed to have nothing to do with us: someone had borrowed our step to bleed on, then walked away. In the end Mete had mopped up the blood and we looked out at the clean pavement all morning, wondering whose it had been and how it had come to spatter across our step.

I once thought I would be a dancer but I don't dance now, and Mete is a pilot who doesn't fly. I let my body grow lazy until I found I was so unfit that I was quite a bad dancer. My posture has slipped a little and I get breathless when I run upstairs. I'm thin but not skinny any more and my muscle tone is not as good as it was. But in the years that I was pirouetting and doing the splits, Mete was flying fighter jets from Izmir to Diyarbakır and Ankara. He was sleeping in the forests of eastern Turkey, parachuting into the Mediterranean and the Aegean and swimming miles to the shore. After an injury that damaged his eyesight and left him with a bad back, we married so that he could leave the air force. For now, he is running his uncle's shop. He will always be a pilot, whether or not he flies. He is always thinking about the sky, is always moving through it, and dreams of getting a commercial pilot's licence one day. It's a question of waiting, of saving money, of deciding what to do next. The grocery is borrowed from his aunt and uncle and it is temporary. We are just caretakers.

In the afternoon I took Elif to the outdoor market a few streets away. She likes to walk among the stalls, call hello – *merhaba* – to the headscarved women weighing carrier-bags full of vegetables, haggling and offering samples of fruit, cheese, fresh nuts. She stands on tiptoe to peer into barrels of green and black olives. Her favourite things are the shiny aubergines, round like pumpkins, which she knows by the Turkish name, *patlıcan*. She reaches to touch them, stroking and patting the purple skin.

We stopped at the last stall in the row. The table was heavy with plastic bowls holding chunks of soft white sheep's cheese. A pair of middle-aged women cut small slivers for customers to try and waited with narrowed eyes and pursed lips for their response. I bought half a kilo of the kind I always buy, the one they say is best for breakfast, and waited as one of the women wrapped the damp cheese in plastic and brown paper. We left.

Elif trotted beside me to the edge of the market picking up fallen leaves — she said she was tidying up — and occasionally bumping into the legs of other customers.

I dropped Elif off at Mete's aunt's apartment for the evening and decided to call in at the Internet café to check my emails before meeting Mete. There was just one and it was from Maggie. The title of her message was a cheerful 'Hello there!!' so I was not prepared for its content.

> Tragically, Isabel, Sheila's son Owen was killed in an
> accident on Wednesday. Were you still in touch with him?

There were details about the funeral, then some scraps of news about Maggie's life. I shut down the computer and set off to find Mete at the shop.

The sky was darkening and the call to prayer snaked into the air from four or five nearby mosques. Half of the street had been dug up and was turning to mud. I was not allowing myself to think about Owen yet. The information was in my head but I'd pushed it to the back.

I fixed my eyes on the muddy road ahead as the calls came from passing men. *Where are you going, lady? Hello, hello. How are you?* I have developed a way of walking that keeps the catcalls at bay. I keep my head down, wear an expression of aloofness, and move with a quick stride that shows I know exactly where I am going. It says that I'm not a tourist and I don't have time to talk. When I'm with Elif, they don't do it so I can relax and slow down, let my eyes wander about the street.

But then I find myself alone again and my guard is down so it is worse than ever.

It was beginning to rain so I had an excuse to pull up the hood of my long coat and become invisible. In this little dark space I was finally able to think about Maggie's email. I felt sick and cold. My feet dragged over the bumpy pavement and, once or twice, I almost tripped. Then tears were slipping down my face and my skin felt hot. I didn't know whether I was crying for Owen exactly. Perhaps I was, but I'd convinced myself a few years ago that he was responsible for Julia's death so maybe I was crying because now I could never find out.

A television or radio blared from a window and a couple of women shouted across the street at each other from their balconies *Asiye Hanım . . .*

Efendim . . .

Asiye Hanım . . .

Evet. Efendim?

Asiye, are you there? . . .

Yes . . .

Asiye? . . .

Yes, what is it?

I turned the corner at the *börek* shop, breathed the oily smell of pastry and stepped into the small back-street towards the light of our own place.

Mete was in front of it, laughing with an elderly woman. She gave him some money and walked away, still calling her good wishes to him. She disappeared into an alleyway leaving only Mete and me on the dark street. I could tell from the way he surveyed the pavement after the woman had gone that he was still thinking about the blood. He didn't notice me coming towards him and jumped when he saw me. 'Allah. You surprised me.'

I am afraid of the dark and I seem to make other people nervous of it too. 'Sorry.' I put my arm round his waist, tucked my hand under his denim jacket and rested it on the slight band of fat around his waist. 'I've come to help, if you need me.'

Riza, Mete's cousin, was on a ladder at the back of the shop. I waved to him. Mete and Riza look like brothers. They are both tall with round brown eyes, wide, friendly smiles, long eyelashes. They are in their thirties but look about twenty-five. Riza's black hair is cut short, almost military in style. Since Mete left the air force he wears his hair longer, lets it curl into the back of his neck. Every few weeks he plucks a white one from the mass of black, holds it up to the bedroom lamp, and shakes his head.

Riza called to me through his cigarette. 'Come in and get dry for a bit. Mete's taking you for dinner tonight.'

'Are you?' I pulled down my hood and went inside. Riza chucked me an orange from a box on a shelf. 'Good.' I cupped it in my hands.

'Yes. Do you want to? My back hurts and I don't have the energy to stand up any longer. Riza can manage for the rest of the evening. It's been quiet.'

'And my uncle and his brother are coming over soon.' Riza slid down the ladder and sat on the bottom rung. 'So we'll close up and take care of everything.'

Mete lifted a sack of rice into the shop and winced.

I rubbed his lower back. 'Here? Is that better?'

'Yes, just there. Perfect.'

'Come on, then. What shall we have?'

'Hey, have you been crying?'

'Oh, but it's all right. I'll explain when we sit down somewhere.'

'So let's go and cheer up. Somewhere nice in town, like Çiçek Pasajı? Or would you prefer the *pide* place round the corner?'

'The one behind the mosque with the hat man? Yeah, let's go there.'

The hat man is young and stands outside the *pide* house every evening selling navy woollen hats. Next to him an old man sits at a small table selling tickets for the Milli Piyango, the national lottery. The Milli Piyango man always has a small crowd of people around him, but the hat man never seems to sell a single hat. Even when it is snowing, he stands there with a hat on his head, another on his right hand, and a pile at his feet.

I took Mete's hand. As we walked along the main road, stepping around heaps of light brown mud, I looked down at our legs, two pairs of jeans taking steps in perfect time. Mete's legs were several centimetres longer than mine, slightly fatter. Our march was quiet, rhythmic. I moved my hand up and down his back, slowly making circles and letting my fingers find the flex of his muscles as he walked. Owen was in my head, sliding from one side to the other as I moved. This was my world, here with Mete in Istanbul, but I was slipping out of it.

Perhaps I should return to my hometown. Perhaps I should stay here.

The hat man leaned against the wall of the restaurant. He spun a hat on the tips of his fingers. When he saw us, he came forward and offered us two hats for the price of one but we declined. The Milli Piyango man sat at his small wooden table, licking his fingers and arranging lottery tickets. We passed them both and went inside.

The restaurant was long and narrow with eight or ten white-clothed tables. The brick walls were whitewashed and covered with photographs of Istanbul. Behind the counter there was a large photograph of Atatürk. Our favourite table was at the back, near the kitchen, where it was warmest. Two or three waiters greeted us. One stepped forward to pull back our chairs. 'Good evening. Welcome.'

'Evening, my friend.' Mete beamed at him.

The waiter splashed lemon-scented cologne over our hands. We rubbed our palms together and ordered *pide*, mine with eggs and cheese, Mete's with beef, and *ayran* to drink. When the waiter left us, Mete pulled something from my hair and laughed. 'Is this why you were upset? Did you fall out of a tree?'

He held out a small yellow leaf.

'Ah, that belongs to Elif. We must save it for her collection. I don't know what they're for but she chooses them very carefully.'

'Then I'll put it here.' Mete took his wallet from his pocket and slipped the leaf into the plastic pocket where he keeps photographs of Elif and me. 'But what's wrong, Isabel–Misabel? *Ne oldu?*' What happened?

'I went to the Internet café earlier to check my emails.'

'Was there a message from Bernadette?' Mete asked. 'I wonder if she got to Greece safely.'

Bernadette had left late the night before. I'd taken her on the bus to the airport.

'Nothing yet. She should be flitting around between islands by now. She'll be taking photographs probably.'

'Did she like Turkey?' Mete was anxious that his country had made a good impression on my friend from home. 'What did she think of Istanbul? Did you take her on the boat trip? I forgot to ask.'

'I did. And she loved all of it. I think she was sorry to leave. She was nervous of travelling by herself. There was someone with her on the flight, a friend who was visiting Turkey too, but she's on her own now.'

'If she was fine in Istanbul she should be fine anywhere. This is such a difficult city. I mean, I love it but, hey, it's Istanbul.'

'Did I tell you she used to be an opera singer?'

'Bernadette told me. I heard her singing in the morning when you went out to get the bread.'

'That's a good sign. I never once heard her sing when I was living with her. She refused to admit she could sing at all. She was in a pretty bad way. In those days she could never have travelled abroad. It was hard for her to get to the end of the street and back.'

'She was singing very quietly but she didn't seem to mind that I'd heard her.'

'I'm glad.'

'But one and a half days in Istanbul isn't enough. We'll have to persuade her to come back again for longer. I hardly had a chance to talk to her. Şey, Isabel, it's good for you to have friends from home here. Why don't you have more visitors from London?'

'It's a long way for people to come. And I'm not in touch with many people now. I suppose I could invite Maggie to visit us soon. She'd like to spend time with Elif.'

'Yes, that's a good idea. You should call her "aunt". It's more respectful.'

I laughed. 'I can't, not to her face. She'd hate it.'

'I don't know if I could live outside Turkey. I think I would die if I was away from home for long. If I didn't die, my parents would die.'

'Why would they die?'

'I just know they would. They have to see me often and talk to me every day. It's the way we are in Turkey.'

Mete's parents live far away in Izmir. He doesn't see them often but he calls at least once every day. We have to stop at telephone kiosks when we are out so that he can stop to say hello and tell them he loves them.

'But, Mete, I was going to tell you something else. I had some bad news in an email from Maggie. Someone has died.'

Mete stared at me. I had frightened both of us.

'Who?'

'It's all right.' I put my hand over his. 'I mean, it's not all right but it wasn't someone very close to me. A friend from years ago. I was at school with him. It was a car accident, apparently. I want to go to the funeral.'

'Yes, yes, of course. You must. And I'll come with you.'

'Oh, Mete. You don't need to.'

'It's all right. I don't mind.'

Mete could not come with me. Mete wasn't a part of my earlier life and I loved him for this. 'We can't afford it, can we?' I said, and it was true. 'Not for Elif to come too.'

'It would be expensive. I don't know how we would find the money.'

We locked our feet together under the table and I watched the waiters come and go through the kitchen door as Mete turned his eyes to the street. Our food arrived and we didn't speak for a while. I picked up the long strips of warm bread with melted cheese and chewed them slowly. I liked the feeling of Mete's feet around mine and I squeezed them tighter.

'Mete, I think I should go to the funeral, even if I go alone.'

'Do you really want to? You said he wasn't a close friend.'

'I only need to stay one night. Just a day to say goodbye to my friend, and then a night to get used to it all.'

'Are you sure this isn't because of Bernadette?'

'What do you mean?'

Mete watched the hat man for a few seconds, then flicked his eyes back to me. 'You've seen Bernadette and you're homesick. You want to visit your town, maybe live there again.

I understand it, if it's true. You don't have to make up a story about someone dying. We just have to talk about it.'

'Mete, I'm not lying.' I must have shouted this for other diners looked across. Mete blushed. 'It has nothing to do with Bernadette and I wouldn't make up something like that. For God's sake.'

I was astonished that Mete had invented such a sophisticated scenario, so quickly, and yet it was so far from the truth.

'All right. All right. I'm sorry. Don't get angry. How's your food?'

'It's fine.' The bread was hardening around the edges. I could never eat it fast enough. I frowned and drank a mouthful of salty *ayran*.

He has never been here, to the moors. Though we have had holidays in London together, he has never been north, hardly met anyone from my life before I knew him, just Maggie and a few London friends. He doesn't know much about me and he doesn't seem to mind, though he doesn't know how little he knows.

On the way home, he apologized.

'I feel bad, Isabel, because you've met everyone in my family. You've done so much to help us, looking after the shop with me when you could be doing something more exciting. I wish I could know your family, see where you were born.'

'We can go for a week or two later in the year, maybe even at Christmas.'

I said this knowing that, even by Christmas, it was unlikely that I could stand to take Mete back there.

'What about your parents? Why don't you even know where they are?'

'I lost them.'

'What does that mean? You always say it but I don't understand. Did they die?'

'No, I'm sure they're alive. They moved somewhere and didn't tell me where.'

'But why not? That's terrible.'

'We've been through it before, Mete. I get tired of talking about it. They just forgot and that's all there is to it.'

'I'd like to meet them and tell them what I think. Anyway, you're right. We don't have the money right now. I'll miss you, though, when you're there. Even one night.'

'Just one night. We'll sleep through it.'

'I won't.'

Mete sometimes says things like that, as if to tell me that he is determined to love me more than I love him, or that he doesn't believe that I can love him quite as much as he loves me. He commented once that I didn't carry photographs of him around in my wallet. I put a picture in to please him and then he complained that I had only one while he had several of me. There was Isabel on the beach, Isabel smiling in front of the Blue Mosque, Isabel holding a baby, a cat, a bag of apples, an ice-cream. Isabel and Mete dancing together at a party. I understand why Mete likes them but I have never bothered much with photographs. I know what Mete looks like but I have never found a picture that shows the face I love and keep safe in my mind.

'Was he a good friend once?'

I tried to think of Owen as a good friend, as I try now. It wasn't right. It was the word 'friend' that rang out of tune. Owen was more an estranged brother to me.

'I hadn't seen him since about 1985 but we were quite close before then.'

'I'm sorry.'

I put my hand on Mete's face, his cheek, and then his chin. I pressed it hard and kissed him. A passing car tooted its horn and young men's voices called out. The words were lost in the wind.

'Fuck off them,' Mete mumbled, into my mouth.

'Yeah. Fuck off them all.'

I'm still not sure how he will react when I tell him everything. He is a generous person, open-minded and warm. At the same time, he can be quick to judge and is worried by anything that might not be respectable. He reads the newspaper aloud, speaking harshly of all criminals. Once he told me to keep away from a certain customer who, Mete claimed, had been held in a military prison. We did not know what the man's crime was – even that there had been a crime – but the mere fact that he might once have been in prison made him too dangerous for me to speak to.

And now my visit is not only for one night, after all. I

wonder what he thought when my message appeared. He knows that there is no danger of my staying here, but he will be confused. It occurs to me that perhaps Bernadette is not there at all and he has mentioned her simply to make me feel insecure too. I remind myself that he said Leila and not Bernadette. Leila does not exist so either he is wrong or he is making the whole thing up. Mete has heard me say Leila's name in the past when I tried to explain my life at Maggie's house and the strange, imaginary friend I had acquired. He may have thought she was real. If he is lonely and wants to make me miss him more, I can forgive him that.

So we agreed that he would stay in Istanbul. We left the main road and walked through the park. The dark had lost its sharpness and now seemed blurred. We held each other tight as we passed under vague shapes of trees and along a stretch of grass we could not see but where stray cats prowled and sometimes screeched. We hardly breathed until we stepped out onto the pavement at the other side. Apartment blocks, cars, road signs slipped into place, clear and solid.

We went to Emine and Ahmet's place to collect Elif. They live in a small apartment on the edge of Yeşilköy. It's a narrow street where cars seldom go and children play late into the evenings. There are usually a few, boys and girls together, kicking a ball around. The apartment is on the fifth floor and that evening the lift was broken. We climbed the stairs in silence, apart from our breathing, which grew louder with each flight. The light in the stairwell didn't work properly. It would stay on for a couple of seconds but not long enough to reach the switch on the next floor so we were in and out of darkness all the way up to the top.

Mete called through the letterbox and Emine came to greet us. Lights were on in every room and the place seemed cheerful. We slipped off our shoes in the hall and stepped from the mat into the thick carpet. Mete kissed Emine's hand, pressed it to his forehead, then I did the same.

'How is Ahmet?' I asked.

'He's sleeping now. He's not in pain today. Tomorrow the doctor will come and tell us if he needs to go back to hospital.'

We followed her into the living room. Elif was on the floor, building a tower with red blocks. Emine offered us tea and sweets, but we both saw how tired she was, the watery pinkness of her eyes and the loose wrinkled skin around them. We exchanged glances, never sure whether it was better to stay and keep her company or leave her to rest. Elif hurtled at me like a rolling ball, shrieking about an *aaba* she had seen in the street. An *aaba* was a car, her pronunciation of the Turkish *araba*. I picked her up to cuddle her.

Emine laughed and explained that a car had got trapped in the street by a lorry that couldn't turn round. They had watched from the window, then Elif decided she wanted to go down to see so they had sat on the step of the apartment building until the problem was solved. Emine chuckled to herself, but I knew that Elif had worn her out and we should leave. Mete and I exchanged a glance. I sat Elif on my hip. Mete leaned in heavily to kiss her and the three of us stumbled and bumped against the wall. Elif laughed and Mete did a clown fall, backwards onto the sofa. I squeezed his toe and joked about his clumsiness. Behind us somewhere, Emine fussed around, making sure we had all Elif's bits and pieces, the stuffed blue horse she will not sleep without.

'İyi geceler,' we said to Emine as she kissed us. Goodnight.

'İyi geceler. Güle güle.' Go with a smile.

I climbed naked into bed. The white sheets were cold and I shivered. Mete took off his shirt, then leaned over, pushed back my hair and gently removed my earrings with his index finger and thumb. He stroked my neck at each side as he did so, kissed the skin beneath my ears. My head tilted into his hand. He ran his fingers through my hair to straighten it, placed the earrings together on the bedside table. Beads of pink quartz glinted in the weak street light. I unbuckled his belt and undid his jeans. He slipped them down and stepped out of them.

'Tell me about this boy who died. Was he your boyfriend?'

I sat behind him, began to massage his spine. I placed my fingertips on the sore part of his back, so light that he could hardly feel my touch. I thought of Owen and how he was not my boyfriend. I didn't have boyfriends then. The intensity of my friendship with Owen might have made it impossible. I don't remember caring much about boys, unless they were in films or magazines, certainly not the ones I knew. Until at least the age of fifteen I had thought that real boys were dirty and should not come too close. Perhaps at the back of my mind I had a sense of what Julia might have suffered but I cannot be sure of this.

I pressed my chin into Mete's shoulder, wrapped my legs around his. He scratched his leg then rested his hand on my thigh. 'No. No. Just a boy in my class. We stayed friends after school because a lot of other people left the town. We were bored for a while and used to hang around together. We both thought we would get away one day, see the world, whatever we thought the world was. We just weren't quite ready at the time. I thought we had lots in common but we didn't really, hardly anything.'

I gave his shoulders gentle squeezes, moved my fingers and thumbs down towards his elbows pinching skin and muscle all the way. Tiny pimples turned pink, then brown.

'But you must have been close. You're going to his funeral.'

'It's not him so much, Mete, as the time he comes from. I want to say goodbye to him but to all of that as well. I just want to touch it again, then let go. Is that better?'

'Much. Thank you. Shall I do you now?'

'No. Lie beside me.'

'Mm.' Mete pulled the sheet up under his arms and wriggled to get comfortable. 'He was lucky to have you as a friend. I didn't know any girls as nice as you when I was at school.'

I laughed. 'I don't know that I was very nice.'

'I think you were. What was your friend's name again?'

'Owen.'

'Owen. I've never heard it before. Owen was in love with you even if you didn't love him. I'm sure of it.'

'How can you possibly know that?'

'Of course he was. Of course he loved you.'

Mete was trying to hide the wobble in his voice by smiling as he spoke but he was not succeeding. He was jealous.

'Come on, pilot. We're wasting time. Elif's asleep.' I turned onto my side facing Mete, put one knee over his leg and tucked the other one under. I kissed the delicate skin just outside his eye. A few tiny black hairs straggled away from his eyebrow. I smoothed them with my finger and kissed him again.

'Is there a mosquito in the bed?' He opened one eye, wide and round. A comedy expression.

'Mm-hm.'

The words of Maggie's email flickered behind my eyes. *Owen was killed in an accident on Wednesday. Were you still in touch with him?* I sat up, kicked the covers from the bed to the floor. Mete stared at me.

My feet are icy. I pull the coat and bedclothes tighter around my body. My phone drops to the floor and I notice that I have a new message. I didn't hear it arrive.

She just wanted to meet you. It's no problem.
She can stay another night if OK with you.

I try to see what time the message came but, by mistake, I erase it. I massage my toes for a while and listen to the leftover rain dripping outside, from trees and the roof of the garage.

Fine. If Bernadette wants to stay another night, why should she not? It makes no difference to me. The sofa in our flat is comfortable enough, even for someone of her size, and there won't be a queue for the bathroom. Elif will have to sleep in the bedroom with Mete but he has probably put her there already since I am away. Bernadette is welcome to make herself at home.

I draw small spirals on the page with my pen. They turn into snail shells, then hats on the heads of sinister-looking old ladies who grow dresses and walking-sticks. I cover a whole page with these stupid pictures. Oh, for fuck's sake, Isabel. *Write* it.

Owen and I had arranged to meet at three o'clock in the morning. I knew that the action about to unfold had been precipitated by me and that what happened would change everything. I did not understand how but I knew that I was about to bring the world down from its suspended state and get it moving again. When we had taken the boat back, we both went home. I watched television, a gardening programme about roses, with my parents. I tried to read and picked up several novels but could not concentrate so went to my room, sat on the bed with the window ajar and watched the sky darken. My parents went to bed at ten or eleven. I usually listened to music and went later. That night I put my headphones on and played music until about one. Then I fell asleep. I woke with a start at half past two and got dressed in old clothes that I knew I would have to throw away, jeans and a cotton jumper, worn-out trainers. It was like getting ready to go on a trip or holiday. I wasn't scared, not at all.

It was a fifteen-minute walk from my house to the super-market but I passed no one. It had been a mild day but now I could see my breath in front of my face. I could smell trees and soil exhaling softly in the darkness. Owen was already there, a crouching figure in the corner of the car park, knees hunched, almost out of sight but for the firefly glow of his cigarette. We didn't speak but I padded over in my trainers and joined him. He gave me a Silk Cut and a lighter. We sat in the delivery bay with our backs against the door and smoked in silence. There were bread crates in a tower in front of us. The sky was clear. There were few streetlights and the stars were bright.

'You can see all the constellations tonight,' Owen said, and stretched out his legs. His voice was deep and muffled, as though his mouth and throat were stuffed with cotton wool. 'Look at them.'

'Yeah.' I could feel the metal door against my head, a cold pressure. I looked but, though I had once lain by the reservoir and studied the night sky with my father, I could not make patterns out of those dots and dashes. They seemed to move as I watched them.

When our cigarettes had almost reached our fingertips, Owen whispered, 'Come on, Isabel. It's time to give the murdering bastard—'

'Right.'

My voice was calm, I remember. I tied a scarf around my

hair. I'd thought of it before I left my house. I thought it might stop my hair smelling of smoke. We stood and turned to the door.

We hardly spoke from that moment. I remember the night in flashes and staccato sound. The smash of the window upstairs. Owen's body, moving up the outside wall, quick as a spider. Our voices, making sounds, not words. The fire blazing with a roar that rose quickly and grew still louder. Objects and furniture toppling around us and then our escape. I ran and ran. It had nothing to do with Mr McCreadie any more, not for me. It was something bigger, wilder. I heard the crackling as I ran, then a booming sound, like thunder. We might have brought the world to an end by morning, and it didn't matter. We didn't know yet and we didn't care.

I'm putting thoughts into Owen's head there. I don't know that he felt the same exhilaration but always believed he must have. There were patches of black on his jeans when he tumbled out of the building. He jogged away, head down, towards his house just outside the village on the edge of the hills. I waited until he had disappeared around the corner before I set off. The fire seemed to stretch up like an erupting volcano, miles into the sky.

My feet pounded against the soft Tarmac, bouncing off and returning with each step. I thought I could run for ever and not feel tired. I did not stop running until I reached home, and even then I had energy to burn.

I climbed through the dining-room window. I had left it unlocked so that I would not have to put the key in the door and wake my parents. My clothes stank so I wrapped them in plastic and put them at the back of the wardrobe. My skin was smoky too so I went to the bathroom and, as quietly as I could, soaked a sponge with water. In my bedroom I wiped my face, my neck and my arms, then the rest of my body because I could no longer tell whether there was a smell of smoke or not, and squeezed the sponge out of the window. I patted talc all over my skin, then sprayed perfume around the room. I sat cross-legged on my bed until morning, wide awake every minute, wondering if anyone had seen me and, if so, who. All night I retraced the route, thinking of places where someone might have been looking out of a bedroom window or driving home from a late night out. I heard Mr McCreadie's voice above the roar of the fire. *You tell me when your time of the month is and I'll tell you when I've got the time.* I wondered whether it had been Julia's time of the month when she disappeared. It meant nothing but was all mixing up in my head. Julia, Mr McCreadie and blood. I conjured shadows and figures behind fences and in street corners where there had been none. The darkness filled with eyes and cameras. I had to reassure myself many times that no one had seen me. I wondered what had happened to Owen, if he had got home safely and what strange momentum had carried us from a gentle talk in a rowing-boat to this. I couldn't hear or see properly. I wanted Julia. My ears were ringing with a metallic discord, my eyes were full of fire and smoke, and I wanted Julia.

Cold blocks of sky filled the spaces where the shops had stood. A whole section of the street turned to ashes. Some people went to hospital but no one was hurt badly, I heard. I did not return to the scene. We gave our reason in court but no one took it seriously and it would not have made any difference. Rumours that Mr McCreadie had kidnapped Julia sprouted up around town, then wilted. His alibi was fine. The police thought our stunt was a burglary that had gone wrong. They thought it was Owen's idea and I was an accessory, helping him because I knew the layout of the building. We glimpsed each other's faces one day, with a roomful of space and people between us, but we never spoke to each other again.

Owen passed within centimetres of my shoulder. I watched from the corner of my eye. The coffin floated along the nave above the shoulders of the four bearers. It was easier to imagine that Owen had been nailed up inside this shining box for the past decade and a half than it was to consider the truth, that only days ago he was moving around, getting into a car and fastening his seatbelt, his blood warm. Had I been here, I would have seen him talking. I might have seen him smiling.

We stood to sing 'When a Knight Won his Spurs'. Apparently it had been Owen's favourite hymn at primary school.

I thought of Owen and me – and Kath and our other friends – at primary school, cross-legged on the wooden floor with our hymn books open. I saw rows and rows of scabby knees and blue books. I remembered standing here in church singing the Creed and the Gloria and the Nunc Dimittis every week for years and years, not needing to read the words in the service book and not having a clue what they meant or minding about it. I once cared enough to ask the vicar what 'very God of very God' meant – How can God be *very*? Very *what*? – but, not receiving a clear answer, stopped worrying about it.

I wondered whether Owen had known the colour of female mallards by the time he died. I would have liked to finish that argument with him. I didn't want to say goodbye to him now. We could have been friends after prison if I had not been so stubborn. We had understood each other. I wanted him to forgive me for doubting him. I closed my hymn book and fell to my seat. My head dropped into my hands and I let tears run through my fingers.

The church air tasted of a damp cellar or castle dungeon. *No charger have I and no sword by my side, Yet still to adventure and battle I ride.* I didn't think whoever had chosen the hymn had thought about the words. They didn't make much sense for a funeral. *Though back into storyland giants have fled, And the knights are no more and the dragons are dead.* The funeral was almost over and I had barely heard any of it, just something the vicar had said about Owen, that he loved gardening and growing things.

*

We made a stringy procession up the hill to the Carrs' house, slumping along in ones, twos and threes, occasionally ensnaring passers-by, pulling them into knots, then releasing them. Some mourners passed us in cars, driving slowly, careful not to splash our legs with puddle water. A black and white cat followed us, jumping from gatepost to wall to hedge. The woman who used to work in the library was right beside me on the pavement but if she had seen me she had not recognized the girl who had come into the library sometimes to borrow books about boarding-schools and horses, and brought in the ten-pence fines for the ones her parents always forgot to return.

When we reached the cul-de-sac where Owen's family lived, I switched on my phone. Another message.

She's still here. Drinking more tea. She's funny.

What was Bernadette doing or saying that was so funny? I pictured Elif looking up, with her wide, dimpled smile. Perhaps she would stretch out her fingers to touch Bernadette's hand or face, and Bernadette would fold her arms tightly across her chest, staring at the wall in terror, and I laughed as if I were with Elif, picking her up and away from Bernadette, making Elif laugh too. The lady from the library turned and gave me a warm smile. I smiled back and reached out to stroke the cat, now just beside me on a low concrete wall. Was Mete simply trying to make me jealous? Mete feels jealousy with a pain I don't understand. He makes things up in his head and gets angry because of them. He can raise his blood pressure and body temperature with one irrational thought provoked, say, by my smiling at a customer. I get a headache trying to think of ways I can tell him he is wrong, but once he has thought it he can't let it go. Perhaps now I was doing it too. I stopped, rubbed my fingers around the cat's ears, listened to its deep purr.

Owen's parents lived in a 1970s brick house with net curtains at the windows and vases of flowers on the sills. It was called Oakdene. There was a porcelain windmill in an upstairs window. I recognized it from the past. The front door was open so I followed the others towards it. I had stood on this doorstep many times, rung the bell and waited for Owen to come out with his coat over his shoulder and we would go rowing or walking on the hills, but I had never been inside the house before. It was never an indoor kind of friendship; I realized that Owen had probably not been inside my house either. I had not seen his bedroom or where he ate breakfast or watched television. I stepped through the doorway and into the hall.

A circle of elderly people murmured on chairs in the big square kitchen. One stood at the sink, her back to the group, organizing blue china cups and saucers into neat rows on the draining-board. Three of the four women had hair of the same shade, off-white, like dirty snow, and noses with a bump on the bridge. They must be sisters – Owen's great-aunts or grand-mother perhaps – but I recognized no one and felt too shy to enter. It would be good to have John at my side. He had stayed in the church to talk to some people I had never seen before, but I did not doubt that he would appear soon. I crossed the hall and tried the living room. There were eight or ten people here and I scoured the room for Owen's sister, but she was not there. An elderly man offered me a cup of tea just as a younger woman held out a small, cold bottle of beer. In confusion, I accepted both. The cup rattled on its saucer and some of the tea sloshed out. I placed it on top of the upright piano and sipped the beer. At one end of the room, opposite the windows, there was a long table of food, one plate of triangular white sandwiches and all the rest were cakes.

I have always tended to associate funerals with cake. I think it goes back to my grandmother's funeral, the only other funeral I have been to. The day after Gran's death, my mother began baking in preparation. Butterfly cakes, parkin, Victoria sponges. Bowls of icing, lemon glaze, melted chocolate, silver balls. Cake tins piled up in the kitchen and then, the night before the funeral, people from around the village knocked on the front door with more, but theirs were dark, respectful fruit cakes and malt loaves. We picked hundreds and thousands and burned sultanas off the kitchen floor for weeks. When the cakes went stale, we soaked them in alcohol and ate them with cream. 'It's a crime to waste food,' my mother said, with a wink, and gobbled up more.

I smoothed my skirt and tasted cake again, sharp lemon cake.

'Let me cut you a piece of something.' The vicar was at my side, gesticulating over the display with a long, shiny knife.

But I was not hungry, after all. I could see a small version of

Owen sitting at the piano doing his practice, his feet stretching out for the pedals. He was playing 'When a Knight Won his Spurs'. His head bowed slightly over the keyboard and his fingers moved heavily from note to note, resting on a chord with relief before setting off to the next. I remembered that I had come here to find his sister. I left my beer on the table, headed for the door but stopped when I saw Sheila.

She watched me with her face turned partly away, as though afraid of what I might do. It would have been rude not to approach and speak to her. I tried to think what I might say, just to repeat that I was sorry for her loss ought to be fine. She smiled. It was a shaky smile, bruised around the edges by her melting makeup. Crimson lipstick glistened from the fine lines around her mouth, like blood in tiny paper cuts.

'Are you leaving too?' She lifted her fingers as though about to touch my hair but left them, curled, in the air. 'Bye-bye, Isabel love. Give my regards to your aunt. I thought she would be here today but I'm sure she'll come up soon. I understand that she's very busy with her latest book. I'm looking forward to reading it. I haven't seen her in such a long time, but we do write to each other at Christmas. She's been a dear friend to me for many years and I always think of her fondly. You've got a look of her, you know, Isabel. Something in the way your eyes are set. You remind me of her. It's quite strange. I'm sorry we had words outside the church. It doesn't matter any more. I know I'm right but I can't keep turning it over and over. It's not fair on Owen now and I have to put him first. I think he just wants to rest. And me. I've had a headache that has hardly gone away since the day the poor girl went missing. Now is the time to think of being peaceful. What does the rest of it matter? Goodbye, Isabel.'

Sheila glided away over the polished floor. I was not planning to leave yet but she had not given me time to tell her so. I watched her blend into the group in the doorway until only her head was showing, the silver hair, neat and smooth, curving her skull into a ball-bearing.

I am sure that Maggie had said she was coming today, but she was not in the church. I would have liked to see her. I know that the day would have been easier had she been here, and perhaps I would have told her all about Owen and Julia. We could have been investigators together. Maggie has an energy that I seem to lack today. She is inventive and fearless. She knows Sheila and could have asked questions that I would not have known to ask. We might have sat in a café with tea and cakes and worked it out together. I would have had more success with Maggie at my side. I could also have asked her about someone else too, her other friend, and what the hell she is doing now with my lover and child in Turkey.

Why is Bernadette in my flat in Istanbul? How is she being 'funny' when I know that she hates children and, indeed, is uncomfortable with anyone she does not know well? I have been away for less than twenty-four hours. Mete and I haven't been apart since we married and no long-lost friend has ever shown up on the doorstep before. Surely she cannot have planned her visit to happen this way. It seems an extraordinary coincidence. When she stayed with us last week, she did not know that I would be away now, though she could have found out since then, I suppose. It is true that I had not noticed any spark between Mete and Bernadette. They hardly saw each other. To dream up some subterfuge would be irrational on my part. Indeed, I have never known Bernadette to be interested in men, apart from her ex-husband whom she has not seen for years since she gambled away their house and ended the marriage. That is not to say that she shouldn't be interested in men. She has found work and a home after years of unemployment and homelessness, why should she not now look for love? But I cannot think that she would go to Mete, of all people, for it. She doesn't know him. He is too far away.

I had to find Owen's sister. In the churchyard she had told me to wait for her. Surely, after years of being forced into silence by Sheila, she was about to tell me the truth. This was what the policewoman had meant when she said that, even years after a crime was committed, a witness could step forward from nowhere. But Owen's sister was not in the kitchen or living room. I looked out into the back garden. John and Dennis scratched the tops of their heads under a windswept cherry tree. They circled a big old lawnmower, gesturing at the grass. There was no one else around.

★

And why is Mete still awake? He needs to sleep to be ready for work in a few hours' time. He has to drop Elif with Emine and open the shop in time for the first delivery of bread. I stare at the reflection of my hands in the dressing-table mirror. There's soil under my nails. I washed and washed my hands when I arrived in this house but the dirt is still there, fine black lines curving round my fingertips. Well. I am here now and it is all about Owen and Julia. I don't know how much I want to return to Istanbul. I am not sure that I believe there is such a place after all. I pick at my nails but the dirt is packed tight.

− iv −

The park was quiet now. There were no children playing or dogs walking. A young couple had passed under the window, each holding a large kite, but had left without flying them. The drug-users may come soon. On occasions she had found a syringe or two in the back garden, thrown over the fence after dark, but not often. Still, she always kept the curtains open, even at night, for she liked to know what was happening outside.

She was trying to think of Isabel but Leila kept seeping into the fabric of the thought, like blood through a bandage. She was always there, always the centre of attention. Look at me. Look at me.

A key in the lock. 'Sweetheart, it's me.' Feet on the stairs.

Now that she had done a day's work, she was free to pack for her journey, but all she wanted was to touch and be with her husband. She put her arms around him, let her legs tip forward so that she was leaning on him, sinking into his soft chest until her ribs were bumping into his. He held a clump of her hair. 'What is it, eh? Are you all right, my love?'

'Yes, I'm glad you're here.'

'I've told you, I don't mind coming with you tomorrow, if you'd like the company.'

'Oh, I'd love the company, but I have to do this on my own. It'll just be a few days. We'll both survive them. My old friend needs me.'

'You're a good person. Remember to come back again, though. Don't run away from me.'

'As if I could. When I was a little girl, I ran away once.'

'Did you? How far did you get? What were you running away from?'

'Away from the village and on a bus to a city, I don't remember which. Leeds, perhaps, or York. I went back of my own accord because I had no idea where to go. My sister screamed the place down. She went to church and told God to bring me home or she'd have a fit and die. But she was the one who made me run away. We were walking home from school the day before and suddenly she was picking out houses for us, one on either side of the church, and we would get married and live in them. I thought it was a joke but she was serious and, for the first time, I realized she planned to spend her whole life there. I thought I had no choice but to run away, even if I knew I would fail.'

'But in the end, you did. You did escape.'

'Yes, but it has caused me no end of trouble. I don't know that I ever got away, really. Well. I'll find out tomorrow.'

'Have you sorted out somewhere to stay?'

'It's all taken care of.'

'You'll be lonely. Won't you?'

'But I won't. I'll have my old friend. I'll be sad, I know, because of the past, but I shan't be lonely. It's a sad place for me, but still . . .'

'Poor old Isabel.'

'Don't. You'll make me cry. I feel on the edge of tears every time I think of her name. I don't miss her any less, you know, even now. I don't know how many years it's been. I don't like to count. Do you remember her well? But I suppose you never spent much time with her.'

'She was like a mouse when I was around. So sweet, but we hardly spoke. She was too frightened of me and, you know, I hate to frighten anyone. I thought it best if I just sort of stayed in the background being inoffensive and sort of bumbling. I had to work at being bumbling, you know, always losing my spectacles and the like, but I think it made her less scared. She wasn't much like you, was she? Not much family resemblance there.'

'Oh, but I think you're wrong. I think Isabel and I are very similar. I don't know how it seems to an outsider, but from the moment she was born, I was sure that I had known her all my life. Were you eating oranges this morning?'

'Oranges? I don't remember. I may have had a couple last night. Or was it the night before? I'm sure there are still one or two left, if you want one.'

'Look, it's gone dark outside. I didn't notice it turn. Someone just pulled a lever and the day went.'

'Let me cook for you this evening. Let me cook us a meal that we can enjoy, since you won't allow me to come with you tomorrow. Pasta, perhaps? Tagliatelle in a cream sauce with a bottle of cold white wine.'

'I'd prefer meat. Red meat and red wine, if it's all right with you, sweetie. I have a strong craving for thick, red meat that I can sink my teeth into. I'm not sure why but tonight, it seems, I am bloodthirsty.'

'I'll see what I can do.'

He kissed her. She let her hand hold his until he was almost out of the door and she couldn't reach any longer. She was a homebody, at heart. She liked to be here with her comfortable husband. She didn't look forward to staying in a strange bed.

But there was packing to do. She would have to climb the ladder to the attic to find an outfit to take. She had forgotten all about this but it was important. She would need to take something black.

— 4 —

Cigarette smoke leaked like steam from the bedroom at the top of the stairs and I peered round the door. It was a boy's bedroom with a worn, air-force blue carpet, bedclothes and curtains of faded navy. Rough wooden shelves covered two of the walls and were lined with encyclopedias, faded exercise books, and piles of yellowing *Shoot* magazines. A desk lamp with dinosaur stickers on the shade leaned wonkily over the bed. But there were also touches of the present: an ironing-board and a pile of bedclothes in the window, a laptop on the desk in the corner. The room seemed freshly vacuumed, dusted. The window was open and I could see right down the main street to the reservoir. It was shiny now, a blurred mirror in the winter sunlight.

Owen's sister crouched on the floor beside the fireplace. She wore a tight lilac top with her purple skirt. Her hair was loose again and had a purple tinge. I could not tell whether this was dye or a mirroring effect of the clothes. She was slender with bones that jutted out and she had the poise of a ballerina.

She held a brandy glass containing a puddle of liquid. The bottle stood in the empty hearth, next to a small ashtray. Although she was slight and Owen had grown tall, she was the one in her family who most resembled him. I was excited to see those eyes again, to watch as they flitted around the room, then landed on me with a smile. They reminded me that once I had liked Owen very much.

I wished I could remember her name. Owen must have used it sometimes when we spoke. I saw her around at school and she might even have been at my dance classes too, with the older girls. She seemed to know me well enough. In the church-yard she had called me by my name. She lifted her hand and gave a lazy wave.

'Come in, won't you? Join me for a little drink.' She lifted the bottle, shook it at me. 'You're not driving, are you?'

'No, I'd love a drink.' I crossed the room and settled beside her on the floor.

'Good for you. Here we are. You'll have to have it in my water glass, I'm afraid.' Owen's sister poured brandy into a small tumbler. The fumes reached my nose before she handed it to me and I flinched. 'Grab a cushion. You know, this was Owen's bedroom from when he was about five, but it was mine before that. The walls were yellow then but Dad made everything blue for Owen. I wonder if I get it back now.' She slapped herself lightly on the cheek. I realized that she was slightly drunk. 'I must stop saying inappropriate things. I can't help it, though. The worse it gets, the funnier it is. God. I got the giggles in the service when that phone went off. I thought it might be Owen.

I really did. Was I the only one?' She shook her head. 'Keep me away from my parents, that's all. They don't see the funny side and I can't seem to see anything else.'

'I've never been in here before. It's a big room. Strange to see it now.'

'Bloody unfair, though. It was my room until Owen got big enough to leave toys around and then we swapped because, for some reason, boys need bigger rooms than girls. Why is that? Is it the same in every family? Boys get bigger rooms than girls. Fuck it. I can hold my drink better than Owen ever could.'

I lifted my glass. The brandy was too strong to sip straight away so I let it touch and burn my lips first. I inhaled the fumes as if warming myself at a fire.

'Thanks for coming, Isabel. We do appreciate it. I'm Annie, Owen's sister, in case you weren't sure. I don't think we really knew each other before. Did we?' She gave me a broad smile and her narrow eyes disappeared, leaving a black curve of eye-lashes.

'Annie, of course. I recognized you as soon as I saw you in the churchyard but I'd forgotten your name. You're a couple of years older than Owen, aren't you?'

'Yeah. I was. Not much of an age gap, I suppose, but it always seemed more. Weird day, today. I mean, obviously it is, but still . . . Have you come far?'

'From Istanbul.'

'Blimey. To be honest, I didn't even know you were still alive until I saw you. It's amazing you're here. I'm so pleased to see you.'

Once again, the fact of my existence had caused surprise. I almost felt it myself, as if my time away from the village had not been life at all but a form of death and this morning I had performed my own miracle and resurrected myself.

'I wasn't sure how you – your family would feel if I came, but I wanted to.'

Was I not supposed to be the questioner now? Here was a person who knew things and I must make a connection quickly. But I couldn't remember my questions.

Annie said, 'Look.' She poured a slosh of brandy into her glass and drank it, not in one gulp, but continuously, in sips, without pausing for breath. 'See? I can't taste it any more. I can't feel how strong it is. I know it but I can't feel it. But what shall we talk about? We're strangers, really. I don't want this to be awkward. You know, they say that we're all going to have huge parties this year, for the millennium. We're supposed to have organized them already. The whole world is going to be booked up and you won't be able to get through to the next year if you don't sort something out now. What have you decided to do?'

'I don't know. Maybe we'll invite friends around for dinner.'

'That sounds all right.'

'Why? What are you planning to do?'

'That's the thing. I'll probably spend it here with my family. They'll want me to. It's much easier for me now that I don't have to plan anything. I've got my answer to give people. We'll probably have a walk on the moors, watch some fireworks and go to bed. It'll be nice. It'll be cosy. I'm looking forward to it.

I was dreading the New Year, having to treat it with respect and having to care about it, but now I'm off the hook. Thanks, Owen, for dying this year.'

She took another cigarette from the packet, lit it from the first, still between her lips, handed it to me.

Sometimes the smell of cigarette smoke repels me. Today I breathed in hungrily, let it unfurl inside and arouse me. I put the cigarette to my lips, inhaled and felt certain, immediately, that Annie and I could become good friends.

Annie continued, 'I'm glad it happened quickly and he didn't know he was going to die. That's all.'

'That's something,' I agreed. 'He never knew what was coming.'

'The worst thing must be a lingering death where you know what's happening and you watch yourself disintegrate, start to disappear, where you feel all the pain of dying.'

'Yes, I suppose that's—'

'He set off in his car expecting to come home that night. The police said his death was instant but I don't know how instant it could have been, or how they really knew. I'm not a physicist so I don't know about velocity and impact and stuff but, look, he must have seen the other car coming towards him so there would have been at least a few seconds where he knew something, maybe more. But they said, "It all happened very quickly." Quick must be better than slow or they wouldn't have said it, but it's not very helpful to me. It doesn't seem fair that we know what happened to Owen but he doesn't, didn't. He wouldn't have had time to think that he would never see this room again. His life might have flashed before him but only the past, not the future he wasn't going to get. He wouldn't have had time to think, A week from now my sister will be sitting in my bedroom smoking a cigarette and I won't exist any more.'

'But he had a flat in the village, didn't he? He didn't actually live here.'

'He moved out a long time ago but this was always his bedroom. My room became the guest room but he kept his. Owen was the younger so that's probably why it never changed. And he was round here all the time. He was very close to Mum.' Annie sucked air through her teeth. 'At least today has given us the chance to tidy things up.'

'That's good.' Was this an opportunity to prod further? It didn't feel like one but I tried all the same. 'Were there many things to tidy up?'

'Oh, you know. The kinds of things that always get left undone.' She sniffled and used the back of her hand to wipe a dewdrop from the tip of her nose. 'I only wish I'd known Owen better. When we were teenagers he was just my brother and we didn't really speak to each other because, I suppose, brothers and sisters don't. There was some rule about it that we must have learned somewhere. Have you got any brothers?'

'No, I'm an only child.'

'You're lucky. Unlucky. One or the other. I suppose it depends. Anyway, then I left home and never spent much time with him again. Just some Christmases or summer holidays when I came to visit. It's strange. I could count the times I had a long conversation with him on both my hands, if I tried. The only communication I remember having with Owen is when we were both in front of the telly, talking half to each other and half to the screen, but always looking straight ahead. That must be why I find it hard to picture his face with any expression sketched in. It's just an outline that won't keep still when I try to look at it. I probably never really saw it. When he went to prison I was angry with him but so sorry for him too. I was more sorry than angry, I think.

'It was so painful *here*,' Annie pressed her hand against her heart, 'that I never visited or wrote to him. He must have thought I hated him but I didn't. I had a calendar with cats on.' She laughed. 'And I counted the weeks and months of his sentence. Each night I blanked out the square for that day. I did it with incredible care. I took a pencil and shaded it in from side to side, then top to bottom and diagonally.' She held her finger and thumb in front of her eyes and made quick, deft movements. 'It was a way of living through the sentence myself. I think I felt guilty and that it would help, somehow, if I was there too. I never told him that. I didn't know him well enough, you see. It seems like a contradiction that I could know him so little and care so much, but it's true. Maybe you knew him better than I did. I was only his sister. You were in his class at school.'

Annie was now staring at me with intense curiosity. When she finished speaking, her head and shoulders lurched drunkenly in my direction for a moment, then retreated. I looked directly into her eyes and saw Owen in his prison cell but not with John or even with Annie. He was with me. Owen was lying on his bed and I was looking down on him from the top bunk. I was holding the grey metal bed-frame and leaning over, not quite on the mattress and not quite off it. I looked down and was able to move my eyes around to take in his body, the folds and wrinkles in his heavy cotton clothes, dark patches of sweat under his arms. His forehead glistened. His eyes stared straight up but, unlike Annie's, did not seem to see me.

'Annie,' I said, 'it was too long ago. You know, I barely recognized the person they were talking about in church today, and I'm not sure that my memories are particularly reliable. I thought it would be different and I'd be able to share the things I remembered but I've realized that I know nothing. Sorry—'

'No, no. You can't get away with that. You've come all the way from Turkey for this. There's more to it. I'm drunk but I'm not thick. I know that the two of you were really close for a time. I remember seeing you wandering around together at the weekends. You both walked with your heads bowed like you were in some weird cult or you were acting in a science-fiction film. You must have known each other's secrets.'

And I understood. Annie believed that I knew something about Julia, that I knew more than she did. We were dancing around each other but we had the same intention. We both wanted information.

'I don't think that's how we walked. I don't remember it, at least, so I don't think we can have done it on purpose. You're reading the weirdness into it with hindsight. We were just a couple of teenagers. That's what they're like.' What Annie had described was the exact picture I had of Owen and Julia together a couple of years earlier. 'I probably talked to Owen a lot but he never said much back to me. We liked doing things together, not talking. That was the kind of friendship we had. We went rowing or walking, or playing on the fruit machines in the arcade. But we didn't even pick machines that were side by side. We showed up, made our way to different corners and left together. That was all. I think we were keeping each other company but I don't believe we knew each other, not to any depth. If he had talked more, perhaps I would have understood him better, but I'm not sure that it would have made a difference.'

'But you must have had conversations sometimes. What were they about?'

I knew the answer but I thought for a moment before saying it.

'For a few months, after all our friends had left town but before the fire, we spent a lot of time talking about Julia Smith.'

'But that was years after she'd disappeared, wasn't it?'

'A couple. That was what we had in common, though. Owen was the one who always wanted to talk about her.' It was an exaggeration but I needed to see Annie's reaction.

She turned away. There was a long pause. We stared into separate portions of space. An engine revved below the window, then purred. The car drove away and voices moved from the hall to the kitchen. Cups chinked and a chair scraped. Annie spoke first.

'I always wondered what you knew about that.'

'What could I have known?'

'I don't know. She was your friend. You might have known something.'

'I don't, didn't. Why? Do you think Owen knew something?'

'Anything you two knew, you would have told each other, wouldn't you?'

'I don't know that we would have. We didn't talk much, as I said.'

'But the two of you used to talk about Julia. You must have said something.'

'We just wondered together what had happened to her and whether there was a way we could find her. Of course, there wasn't.'

We stopped for a moment. Downstairs, people called, 'Goodbye,' and slammed doors. Annie shook her head, giggled and whispered something that might have been 'Sorry'. She cleared her throat and spoke quietly.

'Look, Owen was devastated by what happened. He liked her a lot. In fact, I think he might have been obsessed with her even before she went missing.' She gave me a slow, feline blink.

I nodded but tried to give nothing away. 'Where was he on the day she disappeared?' I asked.

'God knows.' Annie pulled the hem of her skirt under her toes and hugged her knees. 'There was an answer to that question but I can't remember it after all these years. We told the police whatever it was at the time. I think we were all at home together, decorating the house or something. I remember painting the walls in the kitchen. I'd left school by then but I still lived at home. I've lived abroad too. Funny how some people have to get away and some have to stay. I'm a nurse. I've worked in different parts of Africa and now I live in London, but I'm ready to move back here for good now. I might take Owen's flat, I think, if the rest of the family don't want it. I think that would be a good thing for me to do. You should move back here too, Isabel. We'd get along with each other, I reckon, and you can't stay away for ever. I'd be happy to be here again, if you were around.'

I suspected that Annie's affection for me was a side effect of the brandy but I was still touched. 'Annie, did you hear your mother talking to me outside the church?'

'I saw her face but I didn't hear everything she said.'

'For one thing, she didn't exactly make me feel that I would like to live here again. But, more importantly, she said she found blood on Owen's clothes on the day Julia Smith disappeared. She washed it off.'

'Oh, that's probably bollocks. She was saying that to get a reaction from you.'

'You think so?'

But I knew that Annie did not mean this. Her voice was breezy and light but a shock had crossed her face for just a second before she spoke. She smiled and relaxed her features. I wondered whether she was as drunk as she appeared to be.

'The woman's mad. She thinks Owen killed Julia and she blames you. She blames you for the fire too, but that was Owen's idea, wasn't it?'

'No, it was mine.'

'Oh. Was it? I'd never thought of it that way. I always felt sorry for you, having the misfortune to be with my brother on that day. Maybe I shouldn't have. No, I'm just joking. I wouldn't blame you for it. I'm sure you had your reasons.'

'Annie, why did you want to talk to me today?'

'To find out what you know about my little brother. I don't know if he's guilty of some horrible murder, manslaughter, whatever. I've never wanted to think about it for very long. Okay, I'll be honest.' Annie dipped her finger in the brandy glass and licked it. 'Here we go. My mother thinks he is. Was. She has never said so to me, not in clear sentences, but I know that's what she believes. He wasn't at home when Julia disappeared. He had come in from school for about five minutes — just long enough to dump his bag — then gone straight out again. That was normal for him at the time. He used to say that he was meeting Julia on her paper round to keep her company. It seemed sweet to me. We didn't know that it was a lie. She'd dropped him by then, you see. Maybe he was watching her from a distance.'

'Julia never told me about that. She would have, if he'd said anything, if she'd known he was there.'

'He pestered her a bit, didn't he? Poor girl. I bet she didn't have the faintest idea what to do about it. Who would, at that age? I don't know what he wanted from her. On that day, he went out at around the usual time but we only found out later that she wasn't his girlfriend any more. Then he admitted that they hadn't spoken for weeks.'

'So, even if he had done nothing wrong, he might have been a witness to whatever did happen. If he had seen something, why wouldn't he say so?'

'He claimed that he didn't go near Julia that afternoon. He said he'd been by himself, having a smoke behind some building. Mum panicked and cooked up a better alibi that included the smoking but had him coming home sooner. She made us all stick to it but she never explained why we had to. I think I knew there was something sinister underneath the lie. Otherwise I would have asked, wouldn't I?'

Owen's story of going for a cigarette was consistent with what he had always told me, though I had never believed it.

If I hadn't gone off on my own that day, it never would have happened because I would've rescued her, he often said. *I just wanted to sit by myself for a bit.*

'Which building was it?'

'I can't remember. I knew but I can't remember now.'

'Was it the bingo hall?'

'It might have been. Yes, you're probably right. It would have been that patch of grass where people used to congregate in the evenings. I used to go there sometimes myself. I think you're right.'

'Good. That all makes sense. But were there any witnesses?'

'There was one. A neighbour noticed him and mentioned it to my dad. He made some joke about not wanting to grass Owen up for smoking, but since everyone had to say where they were that day, he felt he had no choice.'

'The bingo hall is only fifteen minutes or so from the reservoir, maybe less. Owen could have gone to both places.'

'It's not out of the question.'

'It's not out of the question at all.'

So, Annie's thoughts mirrored mine. I took another sip of brandy. Annie pulled herself heavily to her feet and put the bottle on the floor.

'Let's have some music on. It's too quiet.' She pulled an old record-player from under the bed, then a pile of vinyl. It took her a few minutes to connect up the speakers and get it working. 'See what he kept down here.' She blew fluff from the sleeve of a record, placed it on the turntable, turned up the volume before the music started. The floor shook when the guitar began to play.

'Is it a bit loud, perhaps?'

'Oh, I can't do with all this sitting around in black. You'd think they were at a fucking funeral.' She let out an empty laugh.

We danced to music I did not recognize. We closed the door and kicked off our shoes. The people beneath us, talking in the kitchen, must have heard. The thud of the drums and of our feet through the ceiling. It felt good.

An arm grabbed my waist. I swivelled to see John at my shoulder.

'Hey, Isabel. Been looking everywhere for you.'

'What were you up to in the garden?'

His face was close to mine. He felt cold.

'I was chatting to Owen's dad about things. Stuff Owen used to do. Dennis is a great bloke. Did you know he's done six parachute jumps for charity? Hello, Annie. How are you bearing up?'

Annie smiled at John and twizzled on her toes. She lowered her heels and stepped forward. They embraced each other with a peck on the cheek. She darted from the room and returned seconds later with a camera. 'Can I take a picture of you both? It's a special day, kind of. I'd like to have a souvenir.'

She stood in front of the window and screwed up her face behind the camera. John and I sat on the bed.

'Get a bit closer.'

She fumbled with the lens cap, the focus lever, trying to work out how to use it.

'We should all go downstairs and gather round the coffin,' John muttered in my ear. 'If she wants a good photograph.'

'Ssh.'

'Why are you getting so involved?' He spoke to me without looking.

'I just came to see what I could find out.'

'Why now, all the way from Istanbul?'

'You know why. I'm here to find out what happened.'

Annie took a step back. 'Perfect. OK, keep still.'

'Don't believe you, Isabel. That's not why you're here. You're going to get sucked in again and this time you won't be able to escape. Smile.'

'It's a fucking funeral.'

He grinned at the camera. 'I know that. Smile.'
I smiled at Annie. I would deal with John later.

We sprawled on the floor, the three of us, sipping brandy and listening to music, one song after another. I didn't know the music and barely heard the words. Sometimes a phrase drifted into my ears but it didn't contain any particular meaning for me. Annie stared at a spot on the ceiling for long, silent periods, squeezed out slow, heavy tears. John lay flat on his back for a while and shut his eyes so I couldn't tell whether he was sleeping or awake. I fell into a reverie.

It was not true that Owen and I did nothing more than skulk around together like a pair of zombies. Annie was wrong about that. Owen and I bought a kite, once, and took it up onto the hill. We saw it in the window of the local toy shop. We were a little embarrassed about buying it and giggled as we paid. It seemed childish to want to own a kite but we thought it would be fun, or funny. It was purple, a traditional kite shape. We raced each other out of the village and into the countryside. On top of the moor we unravelled the string to see what would happen. It was a windy day in early spring, perfect for kite-flying, but all the time we were telling each other that it would never work. We laughed about the disaster it was going to be, how it was certain to crash straight to the grass, or the string would break and it would fly away, how we hoped no one would see us. I suppose we were talking ourselves out of enjoying it too much, preparing ourselves for disappointment, but when I ran with the kite, it rose into the sky and soared.

'That's ace, that is.' Owen shielded his eyes and tipped his head back. 'Bloody ace.'

Soon it was his turn. He took the string, leaned back and held it steady as the purple diamond swooped and twisted, not like a bird but like a child playing with us.

'How amazing to be that high in the sky,' he said. 'We should have bought two and made them dance together.'

I followed him as he took the kite further up the hill, over rocks and a stream. 'Can I have it back now, for a bit?'

'Not if you can't catch me,' said Owen, and ran along the ridge of the hill. He was a fast runner but the kite slowed him. I caught up and jumped on his back. We fought for the kite string and fell together to the ground. We lay there, panting, on our backs, and watched as the kite flapped in the sky. Occasionally it dropped down and my stomach lurched as though I were falling too, but then the wind would catch it and send it high again.

'You coming to the Snack Bar for a drink?' Owen asked, when we sat up again.

'Can't. Got a dance class.'

'Skip it.'

'But I like it. I'm doing an exam next week. I can't miss a class.'

'You might be a famous dancer one day.'

'Might be.'

'Will you still speak to us then, here in the little village where you grew up?'

'No.' I laughed. 'I won't. Definitely not.'

'But you'll speak to me because I'll be a big theatre producer and you'll need my help.'

'Will you? First I've heard of it.'

'Might be.'

Eventually the album came crackling to an end, the needle lifted and moved itself back to its resting-place. Annie and John pulled themselves up and we looked at each other in the silence, blinking. It was as if a sleeping potion had worn off and the three of us had woken up together.

John cleared his throat. 'So, what are you going to do?'

'I think,' I said, 'it's all about place. We should go to the grass behind the bingo hall and have a look round. You never know what might come to us. Let's walk down there and see. John, you're coming too.' I stood to find my coat. 'Wait, does the bingo hall still exist?'

Annie flopped onto the bed and rubbed her feet. 'I think it's there. Something's there. It's the same building anyway, and that scrap of grass is too small to have been turned into anything more useful. I wouldn't mind getting out of the house for a bit.'

'Aren't you going to the crematorium?'

'No. I can't be arsed. That's not the most important thing right now. Don't look like that, John.'

'You might regret it later, Annie. You won't get another chance.'

'I said my goodbyes in the church. He's not really in there, you know. It's just a dried-up pod he used to live inside. It makes no difference whether I'm there or not to see it go off to burn. That sounds callous but it's not. I know what I'm doing. I have to be very practical about all this. Otherwise I can't keep track of what's happening.'

Annie picked up the brandy bottle and put it under her arm. We set off downstairs.

Sheila and Dennis were putting on their coats in the hall. Dennis mumbled about his posh shoes being too tight. Then he noticed Annie and his face softened. 'Come on, Annie. Let's get it over with. Auntie Joan will hold the fort here. Almost everyone's gone now, anyway.'

Dennis held out a black jacket for her. She put the bottle on a stair and slipped on the jacket. Dennis patted her shoulders. Annie then took a black lambswool scarf from Sheila and tied it neatly around her neck. John and I waited behind her. She retrieved the brandy and held it tight.

'Mum, I'm only going out. I'm not coming to the crematorium with you.'

'But don't you want to?'

'I'm too upset. It won't do me any good.'

'Oh. Oh, well, if you feel that way.' Sheila stroked Annie's hair. 'I understand. Don't worry, love. Just do whatever you feel like doing today. Are you going out with your friends? That's a good idea. Yes, that will probably do you a lot of good.

I'm glad you have your friends here. It was nice to hear your music playing just now.'

Dennis said nothing but stared, bemused, at John and me. We filed into the front garden and closed the door.

We walked in silence towards the bingo hall, speaking only once or twice to haul John back when he started to take a wrong turning. All these years I have been thinking about what happened in 1982, as if I remember every detail so well, but I had forgotten about the bingo hall and the dirty rectangle of grass behind. I went there occasionally with Julia. We used to sit on the grass and talk about – I don't know what. I didn't remember Owen liking it but that is not to say that he didn't. He once told me he'd been there on the day Julia disappeared. I could see now how he might have met her after she had said goodbye to me, followed her as she delivered the papers, and persuaded her to accompany him there. Perhaps he claimed to have news, a secret to tell. Perhaps he went there on his own and she followed, begging him to stay away for good. She might have taunted him with a letter from her soldier.

'I still find it hard to believe that Owen could have hurt someone,' John said. 'Not that he wouldn't have wanted to – I don't know whether he would or not – but he wouldn't have been able to do it. You need either a violent temper or a very calculating mind. He had neither.'

'You knew him in prison but by then he wasn't the same person. The trial broke him, I'm sure of it. I don't think he was a wimp before that stuff happened. He was calculating. For that matter I think he might have had a temper, not that I ever saw him hit anyone.'

'So why do you think it? That's not fair.'

'I think it because of the way he looked sometimes, when he didn't get his own way. His face would turn white, so hard and angry. I remember him walking out of school once because someone had hidden his PE kit. It was just a stupid joke and they would have got it back for him, probably, but he turned quiet and got this strange look on his face. He walked out of the room, along the corridor and out of the entrance in full view of the entire school. Even the teachers didn't call him back. They saw him go but they just watched. Isn't that weird? I thought it was weird at the time, but I knew from their faces that they had no idea what to do.'

Annie put her arm through mine as we walked. 'I remember that. Two kids came round to our house with his sports bag to apologize. He sulked all night. He was a real sulker. But, you know, it's not as if he spent his weekends dissecting neighbour-hood cats on the kitchen table. He wasn't making bombs in the garden shed or hiding behind a tree to shoot an airgun at passing toddlers. I'm not surprised he seemed like a wimp in prison. He would have been terrified. What was it like where you were, Isabel? The young offenders' thingy place.'

'Oh, it was pretty bad, I suppose.'

'She doesn't like to talk about it.'

'Why? Is it too painful?'

I thought about that. 'Maybe,' I conceded, 'but there's another reason. I can't remember it very clearly. It's strange because I have a good memory but I just can't separate the bits and pieces of the experience into things I remember. It's a cloud, a very thick cloud that I can't see inside. I sometimes think I must have made it all up one day.'

'I'd like to do something destructive that causes a lot of damage but doesn't kill anyone. Just like you did. It would make me feel good.' Annie swayed into a privet hedge as she spoke, then bounced back as John pulled her arm.

'It wouldn't.' I put my hand on Annie's shoulder to steady her.

'It would feel good at the time.'

The bingo hall was just ahead of us at the end of the street, but not yet visible. Five or six teenage boys walked towards us on the pavement, talking and spitting. When they noticed us they fell quiet and crossed the road. They began to speak again when they reached the other side, as though John, Annie and I had done something to frighten them. I felt bad for whatever it was we had done.

John moved ahead of Annie and me. He began to whistle, a sharp, piercing sound like some kind of insect shrieking in the rain.

When Owen came out of prison, I'd been free for months already and was living with Aunt Maggie in London. That is partly why I never wrote back to him. We were treated so differently I didn't know what to say to him. I was a juvenile and he was an adult but there were only a few months between us. He was right to feel unlucky. But I was not having such a great time during those months. For the first few weeks after my release I had no home or job. I was waiting for something to happen. I wandered around the streets, avoiding talking to anyone but being fed up that I had no one to talk to. I remember following people around, hoping they would notice me, but ensuring they did not, groups of young women especially. I used to sit near them on the tube, in parks, and listen to their conversations of work, of boyfriends, of going to parties and to the cinema. If they carried bags of shopping I tried to see inside, to catch a glimpse of clothes, or books, or chocolates and perfume. I wanted to know how I should be living, how not to live like a ghost.

I was not planning to languish like that for ever, and did not believe that I would, but I had little thought of doing anything to change my life. Every idea in my head was a vague one. I might have wandered for ever – or collapsed to the ground and fallen apart – if change had depended on me. Fortunately it didn't. I was rescued without ever having to scream for help.

I was in a day centre in London checking notices, I don't know what for, jobs perhaps. I saw my own name and photo-graph on the missing persons' board and at first it didn't make sense. I'm not missing, I thought. I'm here. I looked behind me. People were milling around the building's entrance. Two girls shared a bag of chips in the doorway and another squatted at the bottom of the stairs picking at loose skin around her nails. She was crying silently.

I was eighteen and homeless. I lived alternately in the hostel

I'd been directed to, and an allotment shed I had found one evening on my own. I was alternately too much alone and too much in company. The allotment shed was freezing and too tiny to lie down in. The hostel beds were dirty, often noisy. People stole your things if you didn't sleep on top of them. My post-office account was almost empty. I had no plan other than, somehow, to forget the last year. I had acquaintances but no friends. It was January and every day was colder than the one before. The tears of the girl on the stairs chilled me and my shoulders shook. How could I be missing?

The photograph had been taken in my parents' house. Behind my hands were the edges of the crimson crocheted shawl on the sofa. There was the silhouette of the television, the glass slipper from my parents' wedding cake on top, and yet I knew my parents were not looking for me. I could not remember who had taken this picture. I was in my bottle green school uniform with short hair, permed and bleached into a sheep's fleece. I wore triangular pink earrings. No one would ever recognize me from that, I thought. I looked into it and felt nothing. I blinked into the eyes of the photographed me. I didn't like her. So far off in the past, so deeply buried under time, what right had she to be using my name any more? What was she doing here? I read the message underneath. It said, *My niece is lost.* At the bottom was a London telephone number.

So Aunt Maggie was searching for me. It was a miracle. I'd looked for Maggie's house during my first week in London but did not know her address. I had visited her a few years earlier and knew it was a terraced house in or near Hounslow with a small park or green nearby. I'd studied maps of London and walked the streets of Hounslow till my feet were blistered and sore. The sky was black by five and I was scared of the dark so I had given up. It was as if Maggie wanted to hide from me, as if she had picked up her house and tucked it away in a pocket somewhere. *My niece is lost.* I was not lost. Maggie was lost. I was not missing, since missing meant to be trapped in the place where Julia had gone. The missing lived in a watery nowhere just outside and in between the frames of other people's lives. I knew all about it. They couldn't breathe but didn't die. I was certain of this and I was not in that place.

Even so, I was not in any place worth being. I longed to sleep in a bed in a house with someone I knew on the other side of the wall. I longed for a light that I could leave on all night. I hardly dared hope that Maggie would let me stay with her but then why else was she looking for me? Maggie had never written to me or visited me since I'd gone away but she might not have known where I was. I had no idea what my parents had told her. I joined the queue for the phone box on the street. I remember feeling sick as I dialled the number, almost put down the receiver when I heard it ring, but then Maggie's deep voice came curling up from the earpiece, as strong and seductive as cigar smoke: 'This is Maggie speaking. Hello?'

'It's me, Isabel,' I told her. 'I'm not missing.'

★

Within an hour Maggie had arrived. She smelled of sweet perfume and looked just as I remembered her. Her auburn hair was cut short into her neck and high on top, like a pineapple. A large amethyst dangled from a chain and nestled in her cleavage. Close up I could see the freckles on her face and chest. Mascara was smudged around her eyes. She cried as she hugged me. I breathed in her perfume and coughed. I can't think of her today without tasting that heavy, flowery scent.

Maggie sniffed and ran a damp hand over my cheek. 'Why didn't you come to me? I would have taken care of you. I didn't know that you were in trouble. I would never have judged you.'

I was so tired I could hardly speak. I shook my head and tried to find my voice. 'I didn't have your address.' I rubbed my nose like a small child. 'I couldn't ask anyone. I tried to find your house but I didn't remember it clearly. I could see bits and pieces but only like a dream. I didn't know where it was.'

'Well. Well. You're here now. Whatever you do, Isabel, don't go back up north to your home. Were you going to?'

'I thought about it. I wasn't sure what to do.'

'Well, don't. I can't tell you how important that is. You must stay here with me.'

Then Maggie turned and began to pace down the street. Her feet moved quickly and I was afraid she would run off to the horizon and disappear again. I scuttled to keep up but there was no energy in my legs and I wanted to fall flat on my face and sleep. She noticed and slowed down but seemed to find it hard to walk at my speed. The pavement was crowded but somehow we steamed ahead, somehow missing the people coming towards us. As Maggie slowed, her speech became rapid to compensate and she hardly stopped for breath.

'That bloody sister of mine told me you were travelling in Europe. France, she said, the liar. George and I were going to Paris and thought it would be fun to meet up with you so I asked for your phone number. You'll meet George later. He's my boyfriend and a wonderful man. But by then, apparently, you had moved to Spain. Spain, I ask you, and I believed it. She made up some daft story that you were picking fruit and studying the language. I never knew she had such an imagination. I never knew she *had* an imagination.' Maggie tapped my arm. 'I mean, that's elaborate, isn't it, for her?'

I could see her quite clearly, this other version of me, travelling around Europe, climbing ladders to pluck scarlet apples from trees and dropping them into wicker baskets. Or bunches of purple grapes from vines. And it might have been possible. It was so much likelier than what did happen that I wanted to believe it. I still do, and sometimes tell people that I spent a year picking fruit and travelling in France and Spain. I'm not lying exactly. It has been part of me for so long now that it has almost become true. It is one of my pasts, if not the one I know best.

'How did you find out I hadn't gone anywhere? I mean, I hadn't gone—'

'No postcards.' Maggie began to go fast again. I hurried along, just a pace behind. 'I went up to see your parents for the weekend and to catch up on the village gossip. Not a single

postcard on the walls or mantelpiece. I asked for your where-
abouts but they wouldn't tell me. Not that I could have guessed
the truth in a million years. I was afraid you had a fatal illness
and your mother was keeping you hidden in the attic. You
know what she's like.'

I didn't know what Maggie meant by this but it was true
that my mother liked to get her hands on invalids. She was a
retired staff nurse and now, or at least the last time I'd seen her,
did voluntary work with the sick and elderly. They tended to
fear her. She liked to pray for them, they said. She prayed for
them a bit too hard.

'But I winkled it out of the neighbours, piece by piece. I
put all the bits together and bingo. There you were, locked
away in the dark. Sheila came clean and told me the whole
thing, and about Owen going to prison too. We'll get a cab
straight to Hounslow, if that suits you.'

Maggie hailed a taxi. I climbed in after her and sank into
the corner, looking out at the road, feeling safe and distant from
the people and buildings I was leaving. The allotment shed was
already part of another story. A couple of hours earlier I had
been stuck in that life. Now I was in a new one.

'Maggie, is it all right for me to stay with you for a little
while?'

'Yes, love. It's not all right for you to stay anywhere else.
I haven't had time to get your room ready but I think it's in
a reasonable state.'

'Thank you. It doesn't matter what state it's in.'

'Perhaps at the weekend we could get some green paint and

decorate it for you. I know green is your favourite colour. The walls are white with a hint of apricot at the moment.' Maggie looked at me in apology and patted my arm. 'I'm sorry about that.'

'That's all right. I don't mind white with a hint of apricot. It's fine by me.'

For the rest of the journey it bothered me. I didn't know that green was my favourite colour, or that I even had a favourite colour. I didn't see how I could. It depended on what the thing was. I was as sure that it was as impossible to have a favourite colour as Maggie was certain that my favourite colour was green. Perhaps someone else liked green and Maggie had confused me with that person. No wonder she still loved me.

The taxi pulled up outside a terrace of Victorian houses, just like the one I had searched for. There was the parade of shops I remembered – still a hairdresser's at the end – and there was the park. Someone had returned them to their places while my back was turned. I thought I saw a curtain twitch in the front bedroom of the house next door.

'You won't tell people, I mean the neighbours, about me, will you? I don't want anyone to know what's happened.'

'You're my niece who has come down from the north to try life in London for a little while. What could be wrong with that? Oh, by the way, I have a lodger. Don't worry about her. You'll get on fine.'

I stood behind Maggie on the step as she unlocked the door. I could hardly wait to get inside. She told me about her shop. It was a second-hand-book shop in Richmond. She always used to say, 'Rare and antiquarian, no tatty paperbacks. We sell to very reputable collectors, as well as ordinary readers on the street.' She ran the shop with George. She said that I could work there for as long as I wanted. This would cover my rent and give me some spending money.

I climbed the stairs. The house smelled of perfume and polish and cinnamon. It smelled of people, of women. I stepped into my new bedroom. I had slept here before when I had visited with my parents. I was about fifteen then. Maggie had just moved in and it was exciting. My parents kept looking out of the windows to see the bright lights of London. They didn't mind that it was Hounslow and not the West End.

The room was neat and tidy. Beside the bed were two books. I sat on the bed and looked at them. *Jane Eyre* and *Little Women*. I had read parts of *Jane Eyre* as a child but usually stopped when Jane left Lowood. After that Jane became an adult and, though I sometimes tried to read on, I found her love for Mr Rochester boring and couldn't understand the point of it. Now I held the book in my hands and believed that perhaps I was ready to read the rest of the story. Perhaps I should like to read about love.

There was a washbasin in the corner with a round mirror above it and a vase of dried flowers on the window-sill. I slipped out of my shoes and put them in the corner. The cream carpet was soft under my socks. All this for me? I walked around the small room, one corner to the next, letting my feet sink into the carpet. Maggie knocked on the door. I waited for a moment, then realized I was supposed to open it. I had to force my hand to turn the handle and I was still afraid as I pulled the door back.

Maggie beamed. On her arm was a pile of neatly folded pea-green towels. 'Do you like it? You might want a bookcase, I suppose, or a desk, but I can get them if you need them. Have you looked out of the window? You've got a view of the park. See?'

Maggie drew back the curtains, gazed out with an expression of wonder, as if she had never seen the park before. My father and I had strolled through the horse-chestnut leaves on our way to the station at the other side, talking of autumn and cold weather. The memory came to me for the first time. I'd picked up a conker and put it into my pocket. I liked the feel of it and kept it there for the rest of the trip. I couldn't see the park clearly now, just a gap where there was nothing else. I saw the string of lights along the road, the tops of houses, traffic-lights. I felt as if I ought to be able to walk into the park and find my younger self with my father, crunching through the leaves.

'It's lovely.' I turned to the books. 'Were you reading these?'

'No, they're Leila's.'

I assumed Leila to be the lodger.

'Will she want them back?'

Maggie seemed confused for a moment. Then she laughed. 'Leila isn't real. You must excuse me. I have a few imaginary friends.'

'Oh, I see.'

'Leila's a character I'm writing about in my new novel. I

gave her this room and put some things inside so that I could get to know her better. She was very distant for a long time but eventually she came in. I know it sounds batty and it probably is, but it's just like having a doll's house, only life-sized. That's why I chose a pale colour for the walls in here, even though it's not to my taste. I thought it would suit Leila.' Maggie fingered the doorframe thoughtfully. 'A brighter colour would have frightened her.'

'Has she gone now? I mean, is it all right for me to have this room?' I'd had a few imaginary friends before I started primary school. My parents put it down to the fact that I was an only child and I always believed them. Now I wondered if the tendency might be hereditary.

'Certainly. She just came here as a refugee – a bit like Bernadette and you – but soon grew tired of it so a few months ago I packed her off to New York. She became a journalist. She's really blossomed and will soon be on her way to other countries. The room is all yours and you can do anything you like with it. Of course,' Maggie nudged me with her elbow, 'I'm not mad. You could have had the room even if she was still here.'

I imagined the spirit-like Leila sleeping in this pale room, twisting under the white sheet, in fear of bright colours.

'My lodger is real, though. Her name's Bernadette. You'll meet her later on. She comes and goes but she won't bother you. She's homeless – well, she was until I persuaded her to move in for a little while. She was sleeping in the doorway of our shop for months. George or I would bring her breakfast or a coffee but she didn't have much to say for herself. Then we had a cold snap in winter and she got the most terrible cough. I'm not a soft touch. I wouldn't let in anyone I found on the streets but I felt I already knew Bernadette quite well by then. Her story is very sad and, to tell the truth, Isabel, I can't see it getting any happier.'

'Does she have any friends or family?'

'I suspect she does but she doesn't want to talk about them. She has very specific problems that she can't solve. No one can. I'd help her if I could but I can't – not beyond giving her a room with a bed. She doesn't stay every night, just two or three times a week. I have no idea where she goes on the other nights. To be honest, I'd never ask her, in case she told me. I'd rather remain in the dark. At least I know you'll be no trouble.'

I sat on the bed, dizzy from Maggie and all these people coming and going. Maggie's house was beginning to seem like an institution, like the places I had come from. Bernadette and Leila sounded like the Ugly Sisters. I was frightened of them both.

I smiled at her. 'I really won't be any trouble.'

On the mantelpiece in the front room there was an old photograph of my mother and Aunt Maggie as children, sitting on a wall eating ice-cream cones. Next to it was a picture of Maggie when she was about eighteen, tall and beautiful in a black ballgown. There were also postcards of cities, Venice, New York, and others I didn't know, of domes and towers.

'I'm going to have words with my sister about the way they've turned their backs on you. I shall call her now and tell her I've got you in my house.'

I grabbed Maggie's arm. 'Please don't tell them I'm here. Did you tell them I was coming?'

'Not yet. It was going to be a surprise. I thought I'd invite them down, and when they saw you again, they'd realize how stupid they've been. They'd be able to see you again but I'd be here to keep things safe.'

'But they don't want to see me. I don't want to see them.'

'Isabel, it's not as simple as that. You don't have to like them any more but we need to make sure your future is secure. You know, your parents have got quite a bit stashed away, in premium bonds and savings, and probably other pots of money I don't know about. The house won't be worth much but it will be something, and it's your entitlement. I'll be damned if you don't get that when they go.'

Maggie clamped her jaw shut and her nostrils flared.

'I don't think I want their money. I'd rather find a job and earn my own. I can look after myself, or I will be able to when I've decided what I'm doing.'

'You say that now but you won't in a few years' time when it turns out they've left it all to the donkeys on Bridlington beach. You might go to university one day, or have kids of your own, and they've got the money to pay for it, damn them.'

'Please don't invite them.'

I don't know why I felt this so strongly, only that I did.

One day I might want to see them again, but not now. I was empty. I had nothing to show, nothing to give them. I didn't want to go back to the town again or have anything to do with the people who lived there. If that included my own parents, it was too bad.

'All right, Isabel. I've kept secrets before and I'll do it again. You can always change your mind later. Why ever did you drop out of school and go on that slave-labour YOP scheme thing? You didn't really want to work in a supermarket, did you?'

'It's YTS now. It's a bit different.' I didn't know what the difference was. 'I didn't want to go to college. I didn't pass many exams, anyway. The supermarket seemed like a safe place to be. A girl in my class had disappeared – you remember Julia – and things seemed very dangerous. I just wanted to be somewhere normal and safe.'

'You can do better than that now. Wouldn't you like to go to university and become a teacher?'

'I don't think so.'

'What about some kind of catering course? You could end up with your own restaurant or hotel.'

Maggie prodded me as she said this. Clearly she was pleased with the idea so I tried to show enthusiasm. I opened my mouth but the right words didn't come.

'There isn't really anything I want to do.'

'So you want to do nothing?'

'No, I don't want to do nothing either.'

'Well, if you don't want to do anything and you don't want to do nothing, what are you going to do?'

'I don't know. Something. I used to dance. I think I might like to dance again.'

'Professionally? You'd have to get moving. I'm sure it's not too late, though.'

'No, maybe not professionally. Just something to do.'

'Leave it with me.'

I was a little worried that she had too many plans for my life. I wanted to have adventures and do wonderful things. I just didn't know what they were yet. It would be easy to be swept away by Maggie's energy and ideas but I must try to hold fast.

Maggie hit herself on the forehead and tutted. 'Hell's bells and buckets of blood. I've just remembered I promised to meet George and he's not on the phone so I can't cancel him. He lives round the corner so I'll pop over and explain the situation. You help yourself to anything you need and I'll be back in an hour at the most.'

And then Maggie left.

When Maggie lived on the moors, a few streets away from us, people considered her eccentric. Her house was different from other people's. It was more colourful, and she filled it with fabrics and sculptures from her travels. She had moved back to the village after years abroad, not to be near us but because she loved *Wuthering Heights* and had romantic ideas about the countryside. She didn't try to fit in. Some people in the neighbourhood thought she was a bit above herself. My mother always said it was a good thing that Maggie moved to London. There was more space for her to roam.

The front door opened and shut. No one spoke and the footsteps didn't sound like Maggie's. I swallowed, rolled over and pressed myself into the back of the sofa. 'Hello?'

'Hello?' came a female voice in return. A tall woman with long, drab hair stood in the doorway. She was about forty. She raised her eyebrows at me.

'I'm Isabel,' I said. 'Maggie's niece.'

'Right. I'm going to my room. It's just through there.' She pointed to a door beyond the kitchen that looked as if it ought to lead to a utility room.

'Oh.' Tears welled. I kept my eyes open until they subsided.

The lodger stopped in the kitchen to put the kettle on.

'I was thinking of having a cup of tea,' I said, trying to be brave. I hovered in the kitchen doorway. 'If there is any.'

'I have my own food in my own cupboard. I suppose you'll be sharing Maggie's stuff.' She didn't look at me as she spoke but put a teabag into a cup.

'Where does Maggie keep her teabags?' I looked around at the cupboards and jars. The kitchen was neat. There were long shelves with matching spice jars. Above them were white china pots that might have contained tea or coffee.

The lodger reached above my head, pulled one from a shelf and put it on the counter in front of me.

'Thanks.' I opened it and took out a teabag.

The electric kettle began to boil. I opened the fridge and found a carton of milk. 'Is this Maggie's?'

'We share the milk – it goes off too quickly otherwise – but we don't share anything else.'

'So I can use this milk, then?'

'But I've only put enough water in for me.'

The lodger made her own tea, then put the kettle down, showing some consideration by turning the handle towards me. I noticed that her hands were ingrained with dirt. Her right index finger was black from the nail down to the knuckle. I refilled the kettle and made myself a cup of tea. The lodger disappeared into her room.

I went back to the sofa and waited for Maggie. My head ached and I sipped the tea slowly. Then the lodger's door creaked and a shadow appeared in the kitchen. She began to scrub her hands at the kitchen sink. I could see her elbow going back and forth. She scrubbed with vigour and for some time. She huffed and muttered under her breath. Then she dried her hands on the tea-towel and came to the doorway. Her face was hard and scaly. Purple lines spread from her eyelids to her leathery temples. I wanted to take a pumice to her skin and slough off layer after layer till a real face emerged, raw and pink.

Bernadette continued to wring her hands. I found myself rubbing my own hands gently together.

'I'll sit here with you for a while,' she said.

'Thank you.'

'I've got nothing else to do.'

'Me neither.'

'Did Maggie say when she'd be back?'

'Not really.'

'How long has she been gone?'

'I'm not sure. Maybe about three-quarters of an hour.'

'I'm Bernadette.'

'I know. I'm Isabel.'

'Yeah. You told me.'

'Have you lived here long?'

'A couple of months. Actually, I don't live here. I just come for a couple of nights a week to keep warm and dry. I won't stay for ever but there's no alternative so I'll be here as long as your aunt will have me.'

'I've come down from Yorkshire.'

'Me too, a long time ago. I'm from Doncaster.'

'You don't have an accent.'

'No. I went to a posh school. I used to be posh.'

She laughed. Her mouth opened wide and a drop of blood appeared on her lower lip where the skin had chapped.

I had run out of things to say. I listened desperately for Maggie's car but she didn't come.

'Don't be scared of me, Isabel. You needn't think I'm dangerous.'

'I'm not.' I smiled, to show that I was not scared, and folded my arms. 'Are you really in hiding?'

'Yes, sort of.'

'Why?'

'I have debts, you see. I didn't become homeless because I had no family or friends, or job. I had the lot.' Bernadette put her hands on her thighs and gazed at her nails. 'I was married and we had a nice house with three bedrooms and a big garden. We had dogs too. But I lost everything. Gambling debts, and we're not talking about a few thousand quid. I'll never be able to pay that money back. The people who want it will always be out there. If I reappear, they'll kill me.'

'That's awful.'

'My own fault.'

'Do you have a job?'

Bernadette shook her head. 'Not any more. There's no point. I used to be an opera singer.'

'Really? Can you still sing?'

'I don't think so. I mean, no. I haven't looked after my voice and I wouldn't want to. I don't even sing in my head, these days. Not hardly at all.' She took a swig of tea and dabbed her fingertips at the corners of her mouth. 'What about you? Are you just visiting or what?'

'Yeah. Wanted to experience life in London for a little while.'

'It won't be worth it. You'll wish you hadn't come.'

'I'll make the most of it.'

'If you think so. How old are you? Fifteen?'

'Eighteen.' It sounded like a lie to me because I wasn't used to it yet. 'It was my birthday a couple of weeks ago.'

'Happy birthday. I'm off to lie down. My back's bad tonight.'

I went upstairs and ran a bath. On a shelf a glass jar was filled with balls of oil. I dropped a red one and a green one into the water, then wondered if I was allowed to use them. I reached in and tried to take them out again, worried about upsetting Maggie, but they were soggy now and fell apart between my fingertips. I climbed into the deep, oily water and stared into the jar, the winking spheres of colour. For the first time in more than a year, I wondered what had happened to Julia Smith.

Maggie returned with a Chinese takeaway. We sat together on the sofa to eat.

'So, sweetheart. Did you meet Bernadette or has she been in her lair all evening?'

'She came out for a little while and we had a chat. She told me about her gambling debts.'

'It's such a mess. Bernadette isn't her real name. It's just one she uses to get round. I think it was her grandmother's. I would have chosen something nicer if it were me. There are so many to choose from and people almost always get it wrong. If I could choose my pen name again, I wouldn't be Eva. That's my middle name because I had to choose in a hurry. I'd be Sophia or Anastasia. Now, Isabel, what name would you like to have?'

'Julia,' I said, before I'd had time to think. I sipped cold water and wondered why I had said that.

'That's a nice name. Still, Isabel's better.' Maggie pushed rice around her plate with a fork. 'What we need to do is get you a nice boyfriend.'

'Is it?'

'Leila was younger than you and I found her a lover very quickly. That was how she got her confidence. She never looked back once she'd met Tommy. It only lasted a few months but the miracle had happened by then.'

'What was he like?'

'A very handsome man, the first one. There were a few others and then, maybe seventh or eighth, she met a man from – another country and went to live with him. Her personality returned, you see, with the right man. She was a live-wire, all right, just needed a little help to get going.'

'But I'm real. It will be harder.'

'Not necessarily. Not if you use Leila as an example to guide you. You two have more in common than you think.'

I had my first good night's sleep in more than a year. Not that I slept right through the night. I woke several times to feel how warm the bed was, to run my fingers over the vase and clock on the bedside table, to hear the traffic on the main road and know that I was safe.

Leila had moved to New York to get on with living another chapter, but her presence was strong in Maggie's house. I slept in her bed, read books in the shop that had her name scrawled in pencil inside the cover. Maggie persuaded me to do things I was scared of doing – going out and making friends – always by telling me that Leila had done it first so of course I could do it.

There was a pink mug in the kitchen with big black letters that said 'Leila'. It became my own.

As I noted before, I did not tell Maggie that I would be here today as it seemed too complicated. But there was another reason I did not tell her. Maggie and I fell out a couple of years after I went to stay with her. It was not a terrible fight and we have always stayed in touch but are not as close as we used to be. I am sure that this was at the back of my mind when I decided not to tell her that I was coming today. Now that I look back, I see that I was wrong to make such a fuss over a small disagreement. Her behaviour seems perfectly understandable now. She knew I had no one else and she wanted me to be all right.

At the time, though, I found her enthusiasm oppressive so I ran off to Turkey. Before I left, I accused her of lying about Leila. I thought she had been playing games with me, creating the imaginary girl not for her book but as a way of telling me how to live. Maggie didn't argue, she let me believe what I chose. I can only be grateful for that now, and if I see her, I should like to apologize. I know that she will tell me straight away that it doesn't matter at all. I was young, she will say, and my feelings were easy to understand. But we are in the same country now, for a day at least, so why should I not talk to her? I will call her in the morning and apologize. And in a minute I'll take a break from Owen and Julia to read one of Maggie's books.

It's funny that Mete has mixed up Leila's name with Bernadette's. I have sometimes done it myself – I met them on the same evening, in a sense – and for me they share the same space. I must have conveyed this to Mete when I told him about them both. Perhaps it was I who confused their names, for when I told him, just last week, that Maggie's old lodger was coming to visit us, he said, 'You told me about her before. Her name was Leila.' I got the giggles as I tried to explain in Turkish and then English how the mind of my aunt works, and who Leila was, or was not.

I remember other people's words better than I remember my own. I still hear Maggie speaking. Here and there I remember my replies quite clearly but mostly I am reconstructing my words from what I believe I was thinking. Perhaps I make myself sound too weak. Perhaps I was not such a weakling as I tend to think I was. For example, I also remember myself as being very small, about five feet tall. But I am now nearer five foot five or six. I can't have been six inches shorter at the age of eighteen, can I? I am misremembering, possibly because of what happened afterwards. Where Maggie is concerned, everything is confusing.

— v —

She couldn't sleep. She lay on her back, straight and rigid as a dart, and felt the muscles in her arms and legs twitch and niggle. Beside her, he was curled up and soft.

'Can you hear that?' She nudged him.

'Eh? Can't hear anything. I was almost asleep.'

'We need to fix the tap in the bathroom. It's dripping.'

'What's that?'

She couldn't understand why he didn't hear it tap-tapping. 'The drip. I said the drip's tapping.'

He laughed.

'What's so funny?'

'Did you hear what you said? You said, "The drip's tapping." You mean the tap's dripping.'

'Oh, so clever. Well, it's the same thing anyway. I wish I had some earplugs. And this lumpy old bed is so uncomfortable. I should probably sleep downstairs on the sofa.'

'What? Is it the pea under the mattress, Your Highness?'

'Ha.'

'Sweetheart, you're very tense. Are you sure I can't come with you tomorrow? You'd be more relaxed. We could take my car and share the driving.'

'This is something I need to do alone, if you don't mind.' She had never told him the full story. He knew about Isabel, the main part of the tragedy, but not her own role in it. 'Did I ever tell you about my Turkish lover?'

'Yes, you did.'

'I wonder what happened to him.'

'What makes you wonder that now?'

'He wanted me to live with him in New York. I could have gone. I could be living in New York now. Isn't that strange?'

'But you didn't want to. If you'd wanted to go, you'd have gone. We make these choices for ourselves, even if later we wonder how.'

'No. I'm glad I stayed here and I'm glad I met you but, still, it's a life I could have had that I didn't.'

'I'm not sure I need to hear about your ex-lovers, especially while we're lying in bed together.'

'No. You don't. I was just thinking. One of my girls ended up with a Turkish lover, and all because of me and mine. She found her passion with him. I found mine with you. When I was young I thought I was destined for a life circumnavigating the globe, but actually I think I was never suited to going far away. It was a fantasy.'

'You always call them "your girls" but they're not yours. Why do you do that?'

'Well, they always came to me when they needed help. I was important to them. I was younger in spirit than any of their parents, and I'm not saying that I had any magical powers but I think they *wanted to be a little bit like me. I gave them the confidence to be unlimited. Small-town life tried to teach them otherwise.'*

'I can't stop thinking about your Turkish lover now that you've brought him up. It's as if he's sitting on the end of the bed, watching me. And he thinks I'm a dull, bespectacled old man.'

She saw him too. He was peeling an orange. 'You bring your old lovers in sometimes. I don't mind hearing about them. I don't mind at all. Brenda, she's my favourite. Tell me about Brenda again.'

'Ah, now, Brenda. She was as different from you as a woman could be.'

Maggie liked to have the company of their ghosts. She had been alone all day. She wanted a full house.

– 5 –

I drag the man's coat and the duvet to the bed and pull them over me. I reach up to the top shelf of the bookcase and take down *Goose Island*. Two of Maggie's other books slip to the floor. For now I leave them there. In a moment I shall look at those too. *Goose Island* has a photograph of a bigger reservoir than ours. It is more beautiful and yet more sure of itself. Perhaps it is a real lake. It looks as if it never changes. I run my fingers up and down the cover. Not yet. I am becoming nervous of what Maggie has written. I can't help but associate Julia with the title of the book, yet I know that Maggie would never have written about her, even if it were known that she had been anywhere near Goose Island that day. Maggie always says that she is not interested in writing about real people. More than that, Julia's story is not the kind she likes.

It was a patch of grass the size of a large living room, usually empty during the day but in the evenings it belonged to teenagers. As children, we saw them leaning against the high breeze-block wall of the bingo hall, even in winter, apparently doing nothing. I wondered how they could sit there, night after night, not interested in doing anything, not laughing or playing games. Later we took over the land for ourselves and were just the same. The patch was shielded from the wind, and when Annie, John and I entered the space from the road, it was almost like stepping indoors.

We separated and walked around. There was no particular point to this but we could think of nothing else to do. The ground was bumpy and gnarled, slightly tacky with mud. After a couple of minutes the three of us were standing in a row, reading the graffiti on the bingo-hall wall, as if we had reached a particularly interesting exhibit in a museum. The scrawls reached from the ground to just above eye-level. Mostly they were names, Kelly, Katy, Callum, the authors too lazy to announce love, to abuse their enemies, to give any date beyond the hints at age in their names.

'I suppose these are the teenage offspring of the teenagers who came here in the eighties, of our lot,' said Annie. 'If I'd known back then that nothing ever changes, I don't think I could have faced the rest of my life.'

'There's broken glass on the ground. Watch out.'

I put out my arm to stop Annie walking onto the smashed bottle.

'That's why I never liked it much here. If you came at night you'd get cut by some old cider bottle. There were always a couple of stray dogs around too, an old brown mongrel that we used to pet. Spastic. That was what we called it, poor old mutt. I guess we were horrible back then.'

'The glass might explain the blood on Owen's clothes, if he was sitting down here somewhere.' John was prodding at the broken pieces with his toe. 'Or, at least, it reminds us that there are ways of getting a bit of blood on your sleeve without having to murder someone.'

'Good point.' I knew that John wanted to convince us that Owen was innocent. I was not going to argue with him yet.

'It wasn't dark, though.' Annie was muttering, to herself, not us. 'It was summer so it would have been light and he ought to have been able to see. I guess he could still have cut himself. It's not so likely but I suppose he could have done. Would it look like this on a summer evening? How would it look? Prettier, of course. There would be more leaves on the trees, thicker green in the gardens. Not that pretty makes any difference.'

Annie sat down by the wall, hunched forward over her knees. She looked as she had when I saw her in Owen's bedroom. She pressed her fingers into her temples and continued to mumble.

I walked away from her, took an angry swing at the breeze-block wall with my leg. My shoe fell off.

'That hurt.' I tottered on one leg as I put the shoe on again. My skirt tightened around my legs and I wished I was wearing more suitable clothes. 'Well, we're here now. What do we do?

There's nothing on the wall that says, "RIP Julia, 1982," or "Owen Carr woz a killer here." There's nothing to help us. It's hopeless.'

'But what were you expecting? Of course there's nothing here. What could there be?'

'I don't know.'

'Her body?'

'Yes. I know it's silly but maybe that's what I was hoping for. Or some sign that it was once here.'

'Even if you murdered someone in this spot, what would you do with the body? There's nowhere to hide something so big. You couldn't just dig a hole in the middle of the grass and cover it up again.'

John took a tube of wrapped sweets from his pocket and popped one into his mouth without offering them around. It smelled of blackcurrant, of colds and winter days. It rattled around his mouth as he spoke.

'You could carry or drag a body into one of the gardens, if you knew that the owners were out. But you'd have to be strong to get it over the fence and you'd need to bury it quickly when you got there.'

'Has anything about the gardens changed since those days?'

'Not that I've noticed. The trees would have been lower so it would have been easier to see from the houses. It was a good spot for a smoke or a drink because it felt fairly secret. But half the school was in on the secret so it wouldn't have been an ideal place to get stuck with a corpse.'

Annie stood, brushed dirt from her skirt. 'They could have

been involved. You know, if there was a gang of people and they took against Julia for some reason or were in the mood to bully her. Look at all those names on the wall. Imagine what might have happened if they'd wanted it to.'

I could see her point. How often had a crowd at the bus-stop grown into a mob at the sight of some minor spat that could not be allowed to lie? Kids had their clothes pulled off in the park and thrown into trees. Schoolbags got chucked into the reservoir. When groups formed, things happened that no one had meant to happen. I turned a full circle, absorbing the atmosphere. Silhouettes of boys and girls seeped from the wall, from the black-pen names, the broken bottles on the grass. Not Kelly and Callum and Katy now, but Wayne, Kerry, Gary, Hayley. Thick voices bayed and taunted. The damp air had a tang of blood. I concentrated hard until I could find Julia's face at the centre of the group, hard and pretty, clean. And then the others fell away and the voices quietened. A dog barked, and a couple of motorbikes sped past. I felt safe again.

'Owen didn't have many friends,' I said. 'But everyone loved Julia. People didn't pick on her. She was too strong. It wouldn't have happened like that.'

Annie nodded and turned back to the road. 'You knew her better than I did. Even so, I want to get away from here now. It's hard to breathe, isn't it? The air isn't getting in properly. I don't know why.'

John and I followed and the three of us set off back uphill towards the market-place. Annie was right: there was more air out here on the road. Although we had learned nothing useful yet, I felt that we were making progress. We were closer to the past and we had eliminated certain theories. We were almost thinking like detectives.

'Has it jogged any memories, Annie?' I asked. 'Anything that might help?'

'I don't know. Lots of things are bubbling around in my head, things I'd forgotten. Owen threw away loads of stuff when he split up with Julia. He chucked out all his schoolwork from the previous months, most of his records and lots of diaries. He just left them in the front garden in plastic bags and didn't tell us what he was doing. Dad tried to persuade him to keep some of it but in the end they drove off to the tip together and dumped it all. Then, after Julia went, Mum decorated his room.'

Annie fell quiet. She bent down, gathered a handful of grass and scattered it, a few blades at a time, as she walked. I thought she had forgotten that she'd been speaking. Then she continued: 'None of us knew what she was doing but suddenly Owen's room had to be spring-cleaned and repainted, in exactly the same colour, though. Mum was always watching us, but especially Owen after that. She'd finish his sentences for him. We didn't have people round so much, you know. We'd always been a sociable kind of family, with friends visiting in the evenings and staying at weekends. There was just a very clear change but I didn't understand what it was. I was leaving home anyway that summer and was only here in the holidays after that so I wasn't very involved. Owen went along with whatever Mum wanted, most of the time. Occasionally he blew his top about some stupid thing, like Mum talking to him when he was tired, but he'd calm down again. I don't remember what Dad was doing or thinking. I have no idea if he was in on the secret too. I don't think so. Mum encouraged Owen to leave school at sixteen. He could have stayed on but I think she wanted him to get away from school and all the people his age who had known Julia. Dad wanted him to go to college, I think, but it was obvious Owen was never going to be much of a student.'

I nodded. It all made sense. 'Are you sure he never mentioned the bingo hall when he was in prison, John?'

'Never. He didn't talk about specific areas of the village. Had no reason to. He only vaguely mentioned the place at all, sometimes the moors. Why don't we go up there? We could follow the route from here and see where on the hill it would have brought them out, had they come this way. It'd be a nice walk anyway. I prefer the countryside to streets and pavements.'

We stopped in the market-place and bought bags of chips from Bobby's. I'd forgotten how hungry I was and how cold. I cupped both hands around the warm paper until the heat seeped through and burned my fingers. We ate our chips as we walked, hardly speaking. We followed the road that led to the nearest hill beyond the village. On the open road, with the wind blasting our hair across our faces, I felt less exposed than I had in the market-place.

'The clue could be anywhere,' Annie said. 'Even in chips.'

'In chips?'

'What clue, though?'

'I don't know. I'm just saying, I don't know what to look at or what to think but I seem to be in a situation where I need an answer. It might as well be chips as anything else. I must have been starving. This is the first time in my life I've managed to eat a whole bag.' She screwed up the wrapper and crammed it into her coat pocket. Then it began to rain, a whitish mizzle that thickened up the sky.

We left the road and climbed the stony path up the hill. A few metres up, the track widened out to a viewing-point with a bench and a litter bin. We stood in the wind and gazed down the grassy slopes, wiping water from our faces every now and again. We were not far enough away for the village to be picturesque in miniature but the buildings had shrunk a little and we could see their tops in silhouette, the streets zigzagging among them. Stone walls mapped the land from the village to our green spot and sketched lines across distant dips and hills.

'If he had already killed her, he couldn't have brought her here, could he? It would be impossible.'

'Not without a car,' said John. 'Even then it would have been hard getting her away from the road. He'd have had to bury her nearby.'

'Can't you remember anything? My brother was sixteen. He couldn't drive.' Annie clutched the brandy against her abdomen as if it were a hot-water bottle.

'Did he know how to drive, though, Annie? Could he have stolen a car, or used your parents'?'

'It could have been him in the light blue car that was seen by witnesses.'

I pushed my chip-wrapper into the bin. There was still a trace of warmth in the paper. I licked a few grains of salt from my finger.

'That's ridiculous. There's no way he would have known how to drive, or had the balls to take someone else's car even if he did. But he could have lured her up here while she was still alive, suggested taking her for a walk, maybe.'

'No,' I said. 'She wouldn't have come all this way in the middle of doing her paper round. The Grimshaws always kept an eye on our time-keeping. She would have waited till the end. And she would never have dumped her bag on the ground and left it like that. Besides, they would have been seen, walking all the way through the village and out here. There would have been plenty of witnesses. I don't think she ever got far from the reservoir, not while she was alive.'

'Annie.' John put his arm on Annie's shoulder. It was a tender gesture. 'What colour was your parents' car?'

'For God's sake.' She stumbled away from him on the pale, uneven grass. 'It was white.'

John and I nodded. I took off my shoes and scraped mud onto the grass. I narrowed my eyes to see the buildings better. 'That's the bingo hall there, isn't it?' I asked Annie. 'That's where we've just come from.'

'Yeah.'

'What's that big building near it?' I asked.

'That's the new supermarket, CostRight, or something. It used to be McCreadie's.'

'But it's not on the same site as the old one, is it?'

'Yeah. It is. It's bigger than the old one but it's in just the same place. They used the space that belonged to the little shops before the fire.'

'Oh.' I gazed down on the long, low red-brick building that had swallowed up not only the old McCreadie's but also a sewing shop, a baker's and a sweet shop. The car park was half full. The cars were in rows and clusters, like blanks in a cross-word puzzle. 'It all looks different from up here. It's hard to make sense of.'

John smiled at the view, put another blackcurrant sweet into his mouth.

'And if it wasn't for you, Isabel,' he said, 'it wouldn't be there. Think of that. All because of you, that jaunty sloping roof, the thick fluorescent lights, the trolleys, the lovely money cascading into tills. Ping, ping, ping. Look at those cars queuing to get into the car park. They'd be going to the shabby old supermarket that was too small and dark and didn't sell anything interesting or exotic. Be proud of your contribution to the land-scape.'

'I am, actually. I am.' And I was. The sight of the new building gave me a tingle of pleasure.

John pointed towards the edge of the village where a patchwork of tiny green and brown rectangles had caught his eye. 'And is that where he had the allotment that the vicar was talking about at the funeral? Is that where Owen was tending his vegetables?'

'Yes,' said Annie. 'It's only a small plot but he managed to grow quite a lot. He'd bring boxes of stuff home with him, different kinds of beans, carrots, squash. Fruit, too, but it wasn't so good. I had to pretend to like rhubarb every summer. At least I won't have to do that any more. There's a silver lining to every death, isn't there? I think he taught himself to garden. He liked having his own bit of territory so he didn't mind learning slowly. He was very private, as you know.'

'Not much chance of privacy in prison so, no, I wouldn't know. Don't most people round here have gardens?'

'Yeah, but the allotments are still popular. Owen had his name down for years, I think, to get that particular plot. Our granddad used to have it, a long time ago. Owen was determined to have that one and no other.'

We stared in silence again. Pictures moved around in my mind, the picture that I could see of the allotments and the setting sun, and others that had been stuck inside my head all day. I think John and Annie were seeing them too.

John bent down, picked something out of the grass. It was a tennis ball. 'It's waterlogged.' He held it up for us to see. 'We can still throw it, though. Come on.'

He lobbed the ball at Annie, who threw it to me. Annie and I both pulled faces when we touched the wet old ball but we formed a triangle and continued to chuck it to each other. I suppose we were all aware that we had just learned something important, but none of us knew what to do with the information. I threw the ball to John, he to Annie, Annie to me. Droplets of water fell as it flew through the air.

Annie dropped it. Her fingers were so wet and cold that each time she tried to pick it up again, it slipped back to the ground. She began to swear, a mumbling of curses, *fuckingshitt-ingcuntingstupidbastard*. Finally she grasped the ball in both hands and held it up in front of her face. 'I don't want to play any more. We need to talk about what I just said.'

'What's that, then?' John asked, but I knew that he had heard it. We both had.

'About Owen wanting that particular plot of land. It's obvious, isn't it? I'd never thought of it before but now I think we have to.'

'Do we have to talk about it now? This minute? Let's mess around a little longer.'

'No, we can't. It's a fact and we've all got to face it. The allotment is very close to the bingo hall.'

'But how do you get from one to the other? I didn't see any kind of path when we were down there.'

'You'd have to cross the road.'

'With a body?'

'No, no, no. Julia was still alive then. They would have gone to the allotments together from the bingo hall, or even met there before Owen went on his own for his cigarette.'

'Ah.'

'Let's not think about it yet. Chuck the ball over, Annie. Isabel's piggy-in-the-middle.'

'No. We can't do it any more. It's disgusting. It used to belong to a dog. Look, there are toothmarks in it.' Annie threw the ball, overarm, down the grassy hill. It bounced off a bump in the slope and disappeared. We stared at the bump.

I realized that the sky was darkening and the rocks and hills were falling into grey shadow. 'We have to hurry now. We need to go down and look at the allotment.'

Annie staggered towards me, put her arm through mine and leaned on me as we walked over the grass to the track that led back to the village.

'You don't have to come,' I told her. 'You probably should have gone to the crematorium with your family. I feel bad that we distracted you.'

'No. This is a better way of settling things and I'm glad I'm here. Come on.'

We stumbled down the hill, slipping sometimes on the mud. Annie planted the brandy bottle in a bush and walked away waving to it. 'Bye-bye, little friend.'

'You'd better pull yourself together. This isn't going to be easy. If you're not up to it, we'll walk you home first and you can get some rest.'

'Stop worrying about me. I'm fine. We'll need spades,' she said, 'and a pickaxe Where will we find them?'

'There must be plenty of tools on the allotment site. We'll break into one of the sheds if we have to.'

'Owen had a spade and a fork. And rakes. All that stuff. And a hoe, no doubt, whatever they're for. But we'll only need the pickaxe and spades, I should think.'

And we descended, following the same route but feeling different. We were closer to finding the answer and this made the short journey clearer, more detailed. I noticed every house name from Dale Cottage to Lower Heights, the red, green and blue front doors, the distance people parked from the kerb. When we reached the back-streets that led to the allotment site, we linked arms for a while, walked side by side, our strides as one.

'I wish I hadn't drunk so much.' Annie was in the middle, supported by John and me. 'The fresh air and chips have helped a bit but not enough. It's getting a bit dark now, for my liking.'

'I'm not keen on the dark either,' I said.

'Don't worry about danger.' John patted Annie on the shoulder. 'I'm sober.'

'Yes,' said Annie, 'but you're a convicted murderer.'

We slipped from the main road into an unlit tenfoot, let go of each other and proceeded in single file. Annie was now at the front, John in the middle, and I was at the rear. I watched John's silhouette as he bounced silently along.

'Are you?' I tried to sound casual but my voice was tight.

'She's exaggerating.'

We passed the backs of gardens, stepped around puddles and pushed aside thin, prickly branches that poked out between fences.

'What did you do?'

'I planned to kill someone. It never happened.'

'Because the police caught him first.'

'Were you going to do it?'

'Yes. The gate's locked.' John rattled the padlock, wiped his wet hand on his sleeve. 'We'll have to jump over it. Can you two manage that in your skirts?'

We didn't answer him. Of course we could. The gate was

chest-high but with metal bars across so it would be no harder than climbing a ladder. I'm not sure that Annie was listening. She followed John and me over the gate. We jumped, one by one, into the mud below. I had never been here before. I knew there were allotments, of course, and had seen them from the street, but I was surprised by the size of the place, the sense of life and order among the rows of sheds, the greenhouses, the squares and lines in the land.

'Owen's patch is down there. When he got the allotment he put up his own shed,' Annie said. 'But not in the place where the old one was. He laid a concrete foundation at the other end of the plot and put the new shed there. It's only tiny. There was no need for concrete at all. Not for such a small shed. What do you think, John?'

John was leaning against the gate. His face drooped and his skin was grey-green. 'Let's just tell the police. I don't see what else we can do now. I don't want to see some young girl's skeleton. Who's got their mobile with them?'

'We can't do that. They won't help.' I told them of my visit to the police station earlier in the day. 'We need some evidence first. We need to find something.'

'I don't feel good about it. I don't feel good at all.'

'Then why have you come with us?'

John shook his head. 'Never mind. Let's get on with it.'

We squelched along the main path to Owen's shed. It wasn't locked. A torch lay on the floor just inside the door. I switched it on and shone it around the wooden walls. There was nothing apart from tools, and an old blue mug by the window. We found a cobwebbed pickaxe and John lifted it outside, gave it a cautious swing. I was pleased to see that he was still committed to the plan. We took out a spade, too, then went to neighbouring sheds to find a couple more, and another torch.

John and Annie pulled the shed down. I couldn't watch. It was almost an attack on Owen himself – though they did not appear to mind – and I wanted to hide away until it was done. John and Annie seemed perfectly calm. They didn't gasp or cry out when wood hit the ground. They spoke occasionally: *This bit here. Try again but harder.* Once the shed was in pieces and kicked out of the way, I joined them to hack up the foundations. The concrete was not thick. Owen must have laid it in a hurry. It was brittle, uneven and cracked easily when John swung the pickaxe. Annie and I lifted the pieces out of the way, made piles of concrete next to the planks.

'Let's not talk any more,' I whispered. 'Let's not say a single word until we know, one way or the other. We need to be able to think all our thoughts as we do this.'

So we dug in darkness, in the spitting rain, and in silence. It took some time to forget ourselves and each other but we fell into a rhythm and worked carefully. The soil was lumpy and damp. Small stones clinked, every now and then, against our spades. As the hole deepened, a wall grew around us. I thought that we might never get out, that something would come up from the earth, make the walls fall in and bury us alive. Every so often, I tilted my head back and took a long gasp of fresh air.

All the time, Julia's face – blurred, grey – danced circles inside my head, somewhere near my eyes. Sometimes, when I became afraid that my spade would touch and damage her, I worked with my fingers, pulling with tenderness at a piece of stone, dusting soil away, loosening small pebbles and feeling the texture of the earth.

John scooped a large heap of soil onto his spade and chucked it over his shoulder.

'Go carefully,' I said. 'She might be in pieces.'

John froze, leaning over the hole, then sank his spade into the ground and began to lift the earth in small, delicate movements as if he were skimming hot soup with a spoon.

Julia, crying and crying. She wouldn't stop. Tears sluiced down her face, drenching every bit of skin. That winter the snow was heavy. The school heating had packed up, or perhaps there was a strike and fuel hadn't got through. It may have been 1979, the Winter of Discontent. We'd arrived at school in the morning and were sent home before assembly. We ran, skidding on the ice to see how far we could get in one slide, Julia, me and one or two others. I don't think Owen or Kath was there, just girls whose faces and names are vague now. Julia slipped on the ice and crashed to the pavement. Her bag flew out onto the road and a biology textbook slid all the way to the other side. We laughed at first, since she did not seem badly hurt. Julia was never a cry-baby. It was the kind of fall we all knew, so we laughed. But Julia would not get up. She pulled herself onto her knees then leaned forward and cried. It must have been the shock of the fall but she did not stop crying. We looked at each other, uncomfortable, not understanding what was so badly wrong. We had the day off school, didn't we? A fall on the pavement seemed a small price to pay. We picked up her bag and sat with her until the tears had stopped and her sobs were dry echoes of the ones before.

'We should have stayed at school,' she said. 'What right do they have to fuck up our day because of some radiators?'

I don't know why she cried so hard. Perhaps it was nothing. We were only eleven or twelve and would cry or laugh at anything. I remember things about her family now, the rumours of alcoholism, of parents who weren't interested. Sometimes I knocked on her door at the weekends and I remember the smell from the hall. I couldn't identify it at the time and probably didn't try. All my friends' houses smelled different, unique, things you couldn't put your finger on, mysterious combinations of pets, food, cleaning fluids, cigarette smoke. But later when I spent time in hostels, when I got to know Bernadette, I found myself inside the smell of Julia's house again. Old alcohol, alcohol sweated, excreted, exhaled, spilled, left for days in old cups, soaked into carpets.

Sometimes her mother flopped through the hall in her shrimp-coloured candlewick dressing-gown, said hello to me, then disappeared into the back of the house. The dressing-gown was all I remembered. Julia was so independent, making her own clothes, able to cook her meals, that she didn't seem to need parents. Years on, I couldn't help guessing why Julia cried that day. The mild shock of tumbling on the ice might have caused it, but perhaps the reason was that she couldn't stand to go home.

I had no idea whether I was anywhere near the truth but I could still hear her sobs as I dug deeper.

'The soil.' John's voice, half whispered, half choked. 'It smells so clean. It's beautiful, but there's nothing here to find.'

Bumps that would soon become blisters were forming on the insides of my fingers. Annie had sat down for a rest. She put her head on her knees and wheezed. John looked down on the area he had been digging. He ran the edge of his spade gently over the soil, then in the other direction, a soft caress. He crouched beside Annie. I noticed that the rain had stopped.

'It's not there, is it?' I could not speak of Julia's body as *she* any longer. I would throw up if Julia was *she* again. 'Is it worth carrying on?'

'No. If he'd done it by himself, it would be a shallow grave, a little dip in the earth, effectively. He would have done it quickly.' Annie lay on her back on the ridge of earth. Her head sank a little way into the soil but she did not seem to care. 'Should I be relieved? Now it goes on. At least if we'd found it and had to tell the police, it would be too late for them to get Owen. But there isn't anything. That's good. Yes, it's a good thing.'

'It doesn't have to be under the shed. It could be under the vegetables.' I looked around. I remembered Owen's letter and how he had suggested that Julia had taken her own body away with her. There was a whole city here, of sheds and little roads, of human design and natural life. Julia could be living in any part of it.

'No, no,' said John. 'This would be the best place. If it's not here, it's not anywhere. We've been going for more than an hour.'

'I was sure,' Annie murmured. 'You two convinced me of it. I don't know if I can trust you both any more. I feel as if I've just pulled my insides out and buried them in this hole for nothing.' There was no anger in her voice. She sounded surprised, and tired.

We lingered a little longer. John stood and began to shovel earth back into the hole. Black clumps tore apart and luminescent worms wriggled out.

Annie patted John's arm.

'Don't worry about the mess. We can leave it. I'll just tell the council it was me and I'd gone a little mad, or something. I'm his sister. It'll be fine.'

We laid the tools on the ground and moved away, past neat rows of vegetables, sheds with gingham curtains, glinting greenhouses. Though we had failed in our task, the air between the three of us was peaceful. I looked back at the mark we had made, a sharp, raw gash in the earth.

John waved a hand in front of my face. 'We tried, Isabel, but we were wrong. We need to stop looking now. I think it's time to let Owen rest. He didn't do it.'

'We don't know that yet. I can't give up until I'm sure.'

'I don't want to do this any more, Isabel. Owen was my friend. I want to think well of him. Let me tell you something.

When I came out of prison, Owen met me on the Isle of Wight. He came all the way down from Yorkshire to meet me and we went to the beach together to set off fireworks. It was his idea. He turned up with a plastic bag full of rockets and we watched them shoot up and explode, one by one, into the night. I can't explain to you the sense of hope he brought me that day. I was terrified but he made me feel okay. That's the kind of friend he was, but I had forgotten about it until a moment ago because of your relentless obsession with murder. What I want to do now is go to the pub and have a pint, drink to the good times we had and the jokes we shared. I want to look at the sky and remember the rockets flaring and falling. I want to say, "Goodbye, Owen, old mate" – that's why I got on the bus this morning – and I haven't had the chance yet.'

'You've been happy enough to go along with everything so far. Why have you been following me all day? I didn't ask you to.'

'I find you very attractive. Sorry. I hope you don't mind.'

'Oh.' I had no answer. This had nothing to do with my plans. I was only disappointed that, apparently, John had not been serious about finding Julia.

'Yeah.' Annie dusted soil from her skirt, pulled off a boot and shook out dirt and a couple of stones. 'I'm tired. What a long and weird day it's been. And how much weirder it would have been if I'd gone to the crematorium and seen all that as well. Maybe this was therapeutic but I'm not sure how it'll feel when the numbness wears off. I'm ready for the pub. Let's go up the road to the Crown.'

'All right.' John's words had touched me. I was almost crying and I could not argue with him now. 'Do you two mind if I have a moment here, by myself? I just want to try and remember Owen a bit. In the church it was hard to concentrate. I'll follow you soon.'

I stepped into the nearest allotment, knelt down, reached for a lump of soil and crumbled it between my fingers. It was hard on one side, soft on the other. Julia was not here. I knew now that we could not have found her body for I had given up believing that she had ever had one. I took more of the wet soil in my hands. John was right. It smelled clean. I let it run around and through my fingers like water. I rubbed it over my face. I shut my eyes for a moment and found myself back in Istanbul. I could see the domes and minarets, the Galata Bridge crossing the Golden Horn. I saw the fishermen in their woollen hats, the mussel-sellers on the corner at the end of the bridge. Mete was weaving slowly between them and I was following close behind. Why was there a gap between us? Why could I not remember how Mete and I had ever found each other in the first place? I wanted to remember. We were in Izmir. Mete was in his air-force uniform, in a café with his friends, and I was there too. That was as far as I could get. I opened and shut my eyes again. I was on a wet allotment with dirt all over me. This was real. Istanbul was better in every way, but this was my home and I had to be here. I still needed to know what had happened to Julia, whether or not she had left her body behind.

For Kath, the disappeared Julia had been a spirit in the air who could be drawn back to us with music and scent. For me she was a lump in the guts, hard and knotted. The lump was poisoning me. It wasn't Julia's fault but the poison had been leaking out for years. I could not return to Istanbul, could not be a mother to Elif until the lump was cut out and the poison drained away. I staggered to my feet. I couldn't find my balance and I had to stand still for a moment. I felt the ground under my feet sway a little. Then I moved on.

I still believed that I had been right when I first arrived and that I would find the answer at the reservoir. Divers had searched the water but they might have missed something. I wanted to retrace Julia's steps. I have sometimes imagined that Julia and I had taken each other's paper rounds that day, that we said, 'See you back at the shop,' then Julia took the route through the housing estate and I went down to the cottages by the reservoir. If Owen had been the killer, he would have followed Julia along the other route and perhaps nothing would be different. But if the killer had been a random stranger, then it is likely that I would have been the victim. I like to tell myself that, when faced with danger, perhaps I would have reacted quickly and been able to save myself. This is a fantasy. I know that Julia was stronger and smarter than I and, if she could not survive her attacker, I would not have stood a chance. If I had been in Julia's place that day, I would be in her place now. So I had to find her. The others could drink without me.

It was not so dark on the road to the reservoir. Streetlights cast a thick, yellow haze and the windows of the cottages were bright, but now the sky itself appeared to be lightening, as if the day were slipping back from evening to afternoon. I could feel the sun's glow, from low in the sky. My legs carried me past the row of cottages, and then towards the spot where Julia's newspaper-bag was found. A car engine hummed close behind me. I had not noticed it before. I glanced over my shoulder. It seemed to be about to park, or the driver was pulling up to speak to me. I ignored it but the sound came right up close behind my legs. I turned again. The driver reached across the passenger seat and rapped white knuckles on the window. For some reason I expected to see John at the wheel – he had a strange ability to appear from nowhere at any moment – but the figure was smaller, quicker, and not at all familiar. I jumped back on the pavement, pressed into the hedge. The car passed under the beam of a streetlight. It was light blue. I screamed.

I ran through a gap in the hedge, along a passage and out onto a pavement. Cars passed in both directions but the blue one wasn't there. It was a main road and was familiar to me, but I couldn't think where I was. I walked towards the brightest light I could see. It was vast, glittering and appeared to be swinging slowly from side to side. I blinked and squinted, then sneezed. People pushed past me with heavy loads in their arms. I was standing before the automatic doors of CostRight, the new supermarket.

The doors opened and closed as customers emerged with bags and boxes. I stepped back, confused. A large white sign with black letters was taped to the window just beside my head.

It said, *Vacancies, part-time and full-time checkout positions, application forms within – M. McCreadie, Store Manager.*

The sign moved in and out with the doors but I kept my eyes on the words. *Vacancies.* I stepped inside the store. The aisle ahead of me was a bright corridor of shoppers and signs with enormous red and black letters. No one looked at me so I continued. I pushed past trolleys and baskets to get to the nearest till. I joined the short queue and waited my turn. The girl behind the checkout whizzed products over the scanner in graceful, sweeping movements as though moving a shuttle back and forth on a loom. When I reached the front of the queue she greeted me with a crescent-moon smile and 'Hiya'.

'I'd like to speak to Mr McCreadie, please, if he's here.'

'Can I ask what it's regarding?' The girl spoke in a high-pitched sing-song voice, as though this was the only line she ever delivered.

'It's about— No, you can't. It's personal.'

She shifted a heap of white carrier-bags, pressed a bell under the till. I tapped my foot as we waited. It was crucial that I saw Mr McCreadie immediately. I'm not sure why I thought I wanted him, perhaps to punch him in the face as I once should have done.

'Hello?'

A young, gangly man stood before me with greasy black hair and a gummy smile.

'Hello?' I said back.

'Did you want to see me about something? Something personal?'

'Oh, I see.' I saw his name badge: *Mike McCreadie*. He was the son. Of course, the old Mr McCreadie would have retired years ago.

He continued to smile at me, bemused. 'Was there something you wanted?'

Yes, there was something I wanted. What was it? I blinked under the striplights, moved back and then forward to avoid customers passing with trolleys and toddlers. But what *was* it? I looked at the shelves stacked high with shiny packets of biscuits in different colours, the big signs above pointing to offers and bargains. I wanted to stay here a little longer. I had worked here once, not this exact building, but this place. I wanted to come back.

'I'd – I'd like an application form, please. I want to apply for a job here.'

Surprise popped up in his eyes but he blinked it away and gave a vigorous nod. 'Of course. I'll get you one now. Do you have any previous retail experience?'

'I do, as it happens. I have spent much of my life behind shop counters. It seems to have become my vocation.'

'We don't have any senior positions going. You'd be doing something like shelf-stacking or working on the tills. Does that meet with your expectations?'

'Perfect.'

'Are you sure?'

'Of course I'm sure.'

I chatted to the girl at the till as Mr McCreadie went to find me a form. Piped music snaked pleasantly around our voices.

'It's bright in here. Those lights. I'd forgotten how hot it gets when you're right under them. It's making me see spots.' I put my fingers out and looked at them with one eye shut, then the other.

'You get used to it.'

'And the music as well, I suppose. I don't recognize that tune. It's very cheerful. What is it?'

'Not sure I know. It's one of the ones we have every day, not too fast and not too slow. I don't tend to think about what the tunes are. I s'pose you're not really meant to.'

'I've never used bar codes before.'

'It's dead easy,' she said to me. The name badge on her beige overall spelled *Amy*. 'You'll pick it up. We just scan stuff in and that's all there is to it. You'll be fine. Everyone's really friendly. If you like I'll take you up to the staff room and introduce you. I'm clocking off in five minutes.'

'Thank you. That's very kind. I'd love to.' Then I remembered that it was dark outside and I had things to do. I wanted to see the staff room, hear the language again and belong – I knew I would – but I was not quite ready yet. 'Perhaps I could do that tomorrow. I need to sort a few things out this evening.'

Young Mr McCreadie returned, handed me the form and I filled it in. I put Doreen Fatebene and Sheila Carr as my referees because I knew their addresses. Under previous retail experience I detailed my shop work in Istanbul. Beneath that I wrote that I had worked at the old McCreadie's. Something about writing in small boxes next to typed prompts gave me an enthusiasm for unadorned honesty. Where it said *Reason for Leaving*, I wrote: 'I burned the building down'.

I sucked the end of the pen and showed the form to the young Mr McCreadie. He was looking at my hands.

'Should that be "burned" or "burnt"? I'm never sure. Well, I'll leave it as it is. I used to work on the tills, you know. I'd like to do that again, if possible. I don't think I can remember all the prices now but I suppose that doesn't matter, what with the bar codes—'

I noticed that my coat was smeared with dirt and that there was mud under my nails. I felt fresh, as if I had just taken a blast in a cold shower, but I did not look so clean. Mr McCreadie blinked, lifted his eyes to my face. 'Don't worry about that. We're looking for people to start immediately so I'll contact your referees and get back to you within the next day or so, if that's all right with you.'

'Lovely. I look forward to seeing you again, Mr McCreadie. And, by the way, how *is* your father?'

'He's fine. Thank you very much for asking, um, Isabel. Obviously he's getting frail, though, the age he's at now. He's as alert as ever but his eyesight and hearing are very weak.'

'I'm glad to hear it.'

And so I planted the application form in Mr McCreadie's hand and stepped into the street. I could have a job at CostRight within days, if I wanted it.

John found me looking into the window of an estate agent's. I saw his reflection over my left shoulder but didn't turn.

'Can you afford one?'

'Hello again,' I said, to the eyes of his reflection. 'How are you? This is nice. It's like talking to the hairdresser. Not really. I probably could if I wanted to.'

'Do you want to?'

'It would be an idea, in the short term. I'm not making much progress today, but if I lived here longer, I could probably do it. Some of these are to rent. I'm not so keen on the dark little terraced houses in town but a flat on the hill with a view of the reservoir might be pleasant. Where's Annie?'

'Gone home. She had a vodka and tonic, then started falling all over the place. I think she had a bit too much brandy. She needs to get a good night's sleep.'

'Poor Annie. I'm glad we met her. I like her.'

'Me too. You really plan to move back here? What about your Turkish family?'

'Oh. Well, they can join me in a little while. It's not impossible. I can work something out if I decide to do it. I think it will be better for all three of us if I can sort out these things – these Owen and Julia things – now, however hard it may be. There's no point in getting worked up about details at this stage. We don't have to live in Turkey for ever.'

'It's what you want, isn't it? To come home again and belong. I could tell, as soon as I met you this morning. Finding out what happened to Julia was only one part of it.'

'I didn't want it then, John. I needed the day to come round to the idea. With your help, I've been able to understand some things better.'

'Glad I could be of assistance to you. I'll give you my address in case you ever want to get in touch.'

'When are you leaving?'

'About now. There's a bus in half an hour.'

I wasn't prepared for this. I wanted John to stay too. It would be lonely on my own. 'I'll miss you, John. I suppose I'll have to get used to it. Well, there's Annie, of course. She talked about moving into Owen's old flat.'

'Annie won't stay. Not when she's spent a few more days in the village with all her relatives. She'll wake up one morning soon and know that it's time not to be here.'

'But I can't stay here without either of you.'

'Of course you can, if you want to. Isabel, I've got to get going soon, find the bus station.'

'It's round the back of the market-place. You'll see signs.'

Just half an hour ago, my plan was brilliant. Now it was fading and my limbs were cold from the skin through to the bone. Without John and Annie, it would be no fun to live here, and what if I never found out what happened to Julia? I could live here until I died and not know.

John kissed me. It was a peck on the cheek but he let his face rest against mine. I put my arms around him and placed my fingertips on his shoulder-blades.

'That's nice,' he said, and cradled my elbows in his hands. We swung slightly, from side to side.

'Who was it you planned to murder, John?'

'No one you knew.' He spoke right into my ear, calmly, as though he had expected the question. 'Someone in London. Years and years ago.'

'What for? For love? For money?'

'Uh. Money. Sort of. I saw the opportunity and took it. I'm not proud, Isabel, of who I was. I wouldn't do it now. Does that make you feel better?'

'I don't know.'

'That's a pity.'

We kissed. When our lips touched, I wanted to giggle. John put his fingers on the nape of my neck. I moved closer and stopped laughing. He smelled of dirt.

'John.' I brushed strands of hair from my eyes. 'I hope you have a safe journey back to Leeds. If you want to come and visit me here in the future, you'll be very welcome. Once I find somewhere to live and all that stuff. It was nice meeting you.'

'Let me walk you back to your hotel, at least.'

A man rode past us on a bicycle, swerving one way and then the other, sending drunken curses into the dark. I glanced into the estate agent's window again, saw our silhouettes, like two mountain peaks, over the pictures of houses.

'If it's no trouble.'

I held open the door to room nine. John slipped through. We did not turn on the light but I left a small gap between the curtains. A splinter of moonlight cut across the floor and bed-spread.

We kissed again and perched on the edge of the bed. As John's fingers slid under the waistband of my skirt, the bed on the other side of the flimsy wall let out a long and horrible creak. We took no notice at first but then it began to knock against the wall, a repetitious jolting that shook the floor. It was rhythmic, first slow and then faster, but there was no human sound, no groan or sigh, just a banging headboard and squeaking springs. John and I stopped kissing and slid together to the carpet. I put my head in my hands.

'Fucking hell,' said John.

'Jesus Christ.'

We waited for several minutes but it did not stop. With our backs against the bed, we rocked with it, somehow too over-whelmed or too caught up in the rhythm to move away to the other side of the room.

'It's making my head hurt.'

'Let's not do this,' I said. I was listening to the bedsprings, thinking of Mete, and I wanted to cry.

Footsteps passed on the landing. A key went into a door on the other side of the landing. A woman laughed.

'Yeah.' John kissed the top of my head. 'You're probably right. Let's not.' He pushed hair out of my face and tucked it behind my ear. 'I must get the next bus.'

'Yeah.'

I padded downstairs with him. In the porch I pecked his cheek and squeezed his hands.

'You should have a hot bath, Isabel, get an early night and sleep off the horrors of today, if you can.'

'No, I'm not going to sleep yet. I'm on my way out again now. The day isn't over for me. I've got one more friend to see.'

'Oh, for God's sake.' John hit his forehead with the palm of his hand, deliberately melodramatic. 'You're not still pursuing this non-murder investigation, are you?'

'I have to. I'm stuck with it, for now. 'Bye, John.'

I blew him a kiss and began to walk away down the street. John remained in the guesthouse porch. I could see myself through his eyes, growing smaller and more distant in the dark, almost disappearing, but he came after me. His hand grabbed my shoulder. 'Wait, Isabel.'

'I've got to go, John. I can't rest until I know the answer.'

'I understand, but I think you're wrong. What about Mete and Elif? What about them? Get some sleep now and in the morning go home to them. Forget everything else.'

'Look, if you're such an expert on my life, explain to me why Owen told his mother that I was dead.'

'You were dead?'

'She thought I was dead. Why would that be? Why would Owen say something like that?'

'Maybe he thought you were. You never got in touch with him.'

'No. It's something else. I think it was Owen's way of making me disappear for him, having convinced his mother that I'd led him astray and Julia's death was my fault. It's a sign of guilt. And there was blood on his clothes.'

'Are you sure?'

'That's what she said.'

'You know, I really don't think he bumped her off. We've looked at the logistics and it doesn't work out. We've done everything we can and it just seems as though you got it wrong.'

'I didn't.'

'I've got it.'

'What?'

'The reason they thought you were dead is that, as far as they were concerned, you were. You didn't live here any more. This is the only place there is. When you leave this village you cease to be alive. You're nobody unless you're here.'

'They think they're the whole world?'

'They are the whole world, to themselves.'

'Perhaps.'

'No wonder your aunt Maggie couldn't stand it and went to open a bookshop in London. What sane person wouldn't?'

'So Maggie's dead too, then?'

'In a sense.'

'In that case I don't follow your reasoning. Hang on, did I tell you about Aunt Maggie opening a bookshop?'

'Yeah. You said she runs a second-hand-book shop in Hounslow with a man named George.'

'Oh. Well, I suppose I must have. I've spend too much time with you today. But I meant Richmond. She lives in Hounslow but the shop is in Richmond. That's what I must have meant to say.'

'If we'd had sex, you know, it would have been good, but I'm glad we didn't.'

'Maybe. Sorry if I made you do things you didn't want to do today. I mean, the allotment and everything.'

'Don't worry about it. None of it matters to me. Gotta go, Isabel. Got to travel to the edge of the village, the city and beyond, to the big wide world and the horizon if I can get there, see if the earth is flat after all.'

'Yeah.' I punched his arm. 'Hope it is and you fall off.'

John laughed and winked. ''Bye, and good luck, Isabel.'

''Bye.'

There was a moment where we were not sure whether to hug and kiss again or shake hands so we did none of them. John lifted a hand in a sort of salute, and I smiled with my arms folded. John sauntered along the dark street, gradually blending into the night until I could not see his edges at all. He was right. We had almost had sex but we had stopped in time. So far I had done nothing too dangerous, nothing that would stop me going back to Mete.

I ran John's words through my mind. I might have mentioned Aunt Maggie to John, but I had not told him about the bookshop or George. And yet it did not surprise me that he knew. Fine raindrops began to fall.

I checked my phone. Another message.

She's still here, playing with Elif. Can sleep on sofa – x

This made no sense. Who did he mean? I stared at the text until I could find an answer. Mete could only have meant Bernadette but she would not be playing with Elif. I would call him later to find out, but at the moment I did not feel like speaking to him.

John had left and the only friend I had now was Kath. Kath would help me decide what to do, if she was still here. She had been a better friend than Owen. Next to Julia she was pale, somehow watered-down, but when Julia had disappeared, Kath and had I become inseparable.

Kath was a good, kind person when I knew her, and I was sure she could not have changed. She would be in her parents' house and probably had a husband and children, but she would not turn me away. The more I wanted to be with her, the more certain I became that she knew I was here and that she would want to see me too. John didn't understand. Kath was at home and she was waiting for me, I was sure. I had Owen's letter in my pocket. I'd show it to her and she would help me.

While this was going through my mind I found I had not walked to Kath's house but had taken the side-street that led, of all places, to the house I grew up in. I was standing in front of my old house and looking at the for-sale sign in the garden, wondering how much it would cost me to buy. The walls blurred as I stared. It was smaller than I remembered it. The bay window and door were the same gloomy shade of green they always were. I think it was my father's choice. There was nothing of my mother's presence now, but I could almost see her on the doorstep, a plastic rainhood pulled down over her ears as she watered the hanging basket from a small metal watering-can. 'The hanging bastard', as my father had called it. It wasn't there any more. My father was quite funny sometimes. I had forgotten that. My mother too, in her odd housecoats, putting on her best clothes when the vicar came for tea. I used to hide upstairs when he visited. He once told me that my mother was an extraordinary woman. I must have been young for I had never heard the word before, or perhaps it was the way he pronounced it. I had thought he meant 'extra ordinary', and I took offence. When my parents moved into the house it had a ghost, so my mother said, of an old man who had died there fifty-seven years before. A different vicar came round to perform an exorcism and the ghost left through the front door. When I was little, I sometimes held open the gate for him, in case he'd got trapped in the garden and was still haunting us.

Paving-stones now covered the scrap of lawn my father had been so proud of. I picked a stem of foliage from the narrow border left behind. I slipped away. I didn't remember getting here. I was very tired. I tried to remember the route to Kath's family home. I knew it was not far, but which way?

I texted Mete again.

Who is this friend?

I walked up and down the pavement until a reply came.

Leila of course.

This was impossible. As I had thought, it had to be Bernadette. He had heard me talk of Leila in the past and mixed up her name with Bernadette's. Mete sometimes confuses words and names. Even when we are speaking English together we have to talk about Tuesday and Thursday in Turkish – *salı* and *perşembe* – because he can neither hear nor properly pronounce the difference in English. It has led to terrible arguments where I have wasted hours waiting for him on one day or the other. I once had friends in Izmir named Lucy and Louise. He called them both Lu-icy and hoped for the best. Those words sound similar, though. Bernadette and Leila are hardly easy to confuse. But he was tired and, after all, had only met Bernadette once before.

I read Mete's texts again. I closed my eyes and opened them. I was in Istanbul, walking beside Mete. I closed and opened them again. I was nowhere. Then I was here, in the village. There was another cigarette in my hand. I was acting like the person I used to be, years ago. I flicked ash on the pavement as I clopped along the street in my pointy, muddy shoes.

I must know who is with Mete now. I pull on my shoes, button up the big coat, and tiptoe onto the landing and downstairs. It takes me a moment to unlock the back door and then it swings open. I shut it gently behind me and crouch on the back step. The rain has stopped. The sky is clear and the stars prickle my skin, as if spines are dropping from their rays. The cold stings my nose. We said we would only send texts: calls are too expensive. The phone rings and rings. He must be asleep. I wonder if this woman, my friend, is still there and whether she can hear the phone ringing and is wondering whether or not to wake him. Then I get his voicemail message. It is not even his own voice but some pre-recorded woman. I press 'end call'.

I remember that I also have Bernadette's phone number and scroll through my call register to find it. I dial the number.

'Hello?' She answers quickly, no trace of tiredness in her voice.

'Bernadette. It's Isabel. How are you?'

'Oh, not so bad. Got a headache I've had for days. Sorry I never returned to see you in Istanbul. I had to get back to

London in the end. I don't like this travelling thing. I was homesick so I went straight to Athens and flew home. I should just stay at home, I've discovered. Are you calling me from Istanbul? What's this going to cost us?'

'I'm not sure where the phone thinks it's calling from but I'm in Britain, on the edge of the moors where I grew up.'

'Oh.'

'I thought you were in Istanbul now, with Mete.'

'No.'

Bernadette is not lying. I know it. I doubt that she could lie if she wanted to.

'We're speaking to each other in the same country, then. That seems funny. Never mind. Sorry I bothered you. It's late, isn't it?'

'It's all right. I wasn't in the middle of anything. Call me any time.'

'Thanks. It was good to see you in Istanbul last week.'

'Yeah. You too.'

'Bye, Bernadette.'

'Goodbye.'

So no one is in my flat but Mete and Elif. I suppose I'm relieved to know this, but now I worry about Mete.

'What's she writing?' I once asked Bernadette about Maggie. 'I know it's called *The Missing Girls' Club*, but what's the story? Is it all right to ask her?'

Maggie used to go to her study and type for hours at a time.

I'd hear her, tap-tapping away. George had a new computer with a word-processing program but Maggie said she would always keep her typewriter. Sometimes I became so used to the sound of the typewriter that I only noticed it when it stopped. She would say whether or not the book was going well and would tell us how many chapters she had written, but she never discussed the plot. Leila's name was mentioned from time to time. 'Leila's had a good day today,' she'd say. 'Getting up to all sorts.'

'Why don't you go up and see? She leaves the door open. She doesn't lock her stuff away or anything.'

'Have you looked?'

Bernadette shrugged. 'I couldn't care less what's in her books. I'm not going to read them.'

'Why not?'

'I'm not interested. I don't read books.'

'I can't look, though. I probably shouldn't. What do you think?'

As I have mentioned, Maggie's books were usually more embarrassing to me than interesting, but the title of this one intrigued me. The only missing girl I knew of was Julia. I was convinced that the book must have something to do with her.

'Go and look.'

'No, no. It would be wrong.'

Maggie was leaving for the shop. I said goodbye to her in the hall and went upstairs to watch from the landing window. *She has definitely walked along the street and cannot be back within the next five minutes now, even if she has forgotten something. I* pushed open the bedroom door and went to look beside the typewriter.

I flicked through the pages of *The Missing Girls' Club* but couldn't find Leila. I read parts in detail and I skipped pages in between. A rich philanderer had been murdered. On investigation it transpired that before his death he had tried to contact five ex-girlfriends he had treated badly, begging for reconciliation. The women discovered each other, worked together to set a trap and, eventually, murdered him. The police couldn't work out which of the five was guilty and they all went missing before the police could interview them. In the last chapter I learned that the women had moved from London to different parts of the English countryside and created new identities for themselves. One was an art teacher on the North York moors. Another followed her childhood dream to work on a farm. There was no character called Leila.

I heard someone moving around on the landing and assumed it was Bernadette. She was in the bathroom with the taps running. Then the bathroom door opened. I kept still. The bedroom door opened. George and I screamed together. He was naked, but for the towel over his arm.

'Hello, Isabel. Sorry. So sorry.'

George backed out of the room. I replaced the pages of Maggie's novel and waited until I heard the bathroom door shut once again.

I sat on my bed with the covers over my head for the next half-hour.

'Sorry about earlier,' he said to me later, calm as anything.

I suppose he was embarrassed, too, but was trying to make me feel better. I pretended not to hear him. I could think of nothing to say. And now he would tell Maggie about this, that I had been snooping at her book.

I loved working in the shop but because of Maggie, or perhaps because of Owen, one day I had to leave. I had to go far away from the shop and from Maggie's house.

George's Second-hand and Antiquarian Books was made up of three small, interconnecting rooms on the ground floor, and a tiny basement. I spent most of my days in the basement where there was no window, just a light on the ceiling that never worked and a standard lamp in the corner. There was also a kettle down there, a broken armchair and a couple of cushions. I would climb down the ladder early in the morning and only surface when I needed to carry a box of books up or down. Maggie taught me the pricing system so I sat, usually at the bottom of the ladder down to the basement, with a pencil and wrote the prices carefully inside the covers.

Even with the lights on, the shop was always dark. Maggie and George took it in turns to work at the till. George was a smiling, grey-haired man who peered at the world over the top of his spectacles. He taught an evening class in drama and acted with the local dramatic society. In the shop he was almost silent. Maggie and George communicated in hushed voices and exaggerated gestures even when the shop was empty. I think they enjoyed the theatre of it.

I liked to sit among the books, reading extracts between pricing and stacking them. Sometimes I worked on all fours, sorting through new books, putting them in piles according to their categories. I liked looking inside them for names, inscriptions and dates. People used all sorts of things as bookmarks. I found photographs, postcards, bank statements, receipts and letters. There was once a letter from a clinic telling a woman that her smear test showed no abnormalities. I put the photographs around the wall and created an odd assortment of friends. There was a christening, a wedding, holiday and party snaps. One showed a group of girls, about my age, holding pints of beer and laughing, pink-faced, at the camera. I used to look at the photo and wonder who they were. There was also a photograph of an empty park with leaves rustling on the grass. When I gazed at the scene, I could feel the leaves around my shoes, the cold wind against my ears.

I had been working at the shop for a few weeks when I found a box of books with 'Leila' scrawled on the side in thick black ink. I wondered why she had her own box and if, perhaps, it contained books that Maggie thought Leila would read. They were mostly classic novels. There was a book called *Fear of Flying* which I thought to be about flying. I found *Delta of Venus* by Anaïs Nin and hid it under a pile of dictionaries. I imagined Leila reading these books in the white bedroom. When no one was around I read them, a few pages at a time. At Maggie's house I read and reread *Jane Eyre* but here I read Leila's books. The pictures in my mind of Owen and Mr McCreadie were drawn in hazier lines as I began to leave them behind. In one book I discovered a character named Leila and wondered if this was where Maggie had found the name for her novel.

I often went out with Bernadette. I never knew whether she enjoyed or wanted my company but she would slouch along with me to the park, or we would walk by the river for hours at a time. We didn't talk about ourselves but what we could see around us, boats, kissing couples, traffic jams. We went to the cinema or theatre, occasionally to the pub. I had enough money to pay for both of us, and Bernadette was happy to let me. I never understood Bernadette's situation but I liked the way she seemed to belong to no one, seemed to live outside any kind of system. Her face softened as I grew to know her. As the layers peeled off I began to catch glimpses of the person who might once have been a happily married opera singer.

Maggie would come looking for me, sometimes, if I had been gone for long, if it was getting dark. I always told her not to. I reminded her that I was nineteen and perfectly capable of fending for myself but Maggie would tell me that I had to make allowances. 'I know I'm an interfering old woman, but indulge me, won't you? Just for a little while. We don't want to lose you again.'

'It's all right, Maggie. I don't mind. I really don't mind.' And I would laugh. I also laughed whenever she bought me a quarter of toffees or gave me a packet of tissues to carry in my pocket. Yet if we went to the pub together, she was happy to treat me as a drinking partner, gossiping with me about men and sex, always probing to find out whether I had slept with Owen, whether there had been any other boys. I told her the answer to both questions was no, and she would sigh. I once heard her say to George, 'I'm sure Isabel was more than just friends with Sheila's son. I think they were sleeping together. I'm sure of it.'

A special customer in New York ordered a rare book from the shop. Professor Mehmet Parlak was a world authority on Middle Eastern history and we had a first edition of an illustrated history of the Russo-Turkish Wars. It was heavy and expensive, and Maggie decided that the book should be delivered by hand. Without telling me, she bought me a return ticket to New York.

'You could visit Leila,' she joked. 'That's where I sent her. Ha-ha-ha.'

'Maggie, I don't want to go. I'm not interested in travel. I won't know how to do things.'

Maggie told me that Professor Parlak was an important customer and it was worth paying for my flight to make sure the book arrived safely in his hands. I didn't want to leave the basement of Maggie and George's shop. I had found a safe place and I was happy. In an unknown city I would be lost, could get blown away. I became angry.

'Why don't you go instead? You know him. You know New York and how to get around.'

'I would if I could. Mehmet is an old flame of mine from a long time ago, before I met George. It was a fling, nothing more, but George knows about it and he'd hate me to go. He's not a jealous man by any means but we've had our ups and downs. It's always worse, of course, when the competition is in another country. I don't want to cause any upset but I do want Mehmet to get the book safely. You'll like him. When he learns that you're my niece he'll be delighted. He'll probably take you to dinner or something. If he offers, let him. He's charming and funny, and rich, too.' She nudged me. 'I think you're getting very het up about nothing.'

'But, Maggie, I don't think I've got time to go to New York.'

'What on earth were you planning to do instead that's so important?'

'I was going to sign up for a dance class and I need to go to the dentist. A bit chipped off my tooth last week so I need to get it seen to as soon as I can.'

'For goodness' sake. I'm asking you to go for a couple of days. There's time for you to go to the bloody dentist and a dance class as well. Isabel, this is an opportunity for you to see a bit of the world. You told me you wanted to travel.'

'Did I?'

'Well, of course you do. I wanted to travel at your age but I never had the opportunity. No, you need to have fun, expand your horizons. You'll love it when you get there.'

'Where will I stay?'

'I'll book you into a nice hotel. You could be doing it for

yourself but I'll sort you out this time. It's what you need. If you stay at the bookshop for ever you'll turn into a pile of dust. You'll be like that crumbling old book we found yesterday.'

I had pulled the book out from under the radiator. As soon as I tried to dust the cover to look at it, the title disappeared and fell away in powder and flakes.

'I won't know anybody. It'll be horrible. I don't want to go on my own.'

I was probably afraid that Maggie was sending me away because she didn't want me any more, that I would slip out of the picture-frame into the land of the missing and not find my way back again.

'Mehmet is a lovely man. He's very friendly.'

'I don't know him.'

Maggie was quiet for a while. I knew she had not given in but was dreaming up ways to persuade me. Eventually she spoke, but it took her two or three attempts to articulate her idea. 'I'll tell you what to do. Imagine you are Leila.'

'Your character from the book?'

'She goes off to New York to live because she's an adventurer. I told you. She doesn't worry herself stupid about a new experience. She can't wait. And that's why it works out for her.'

'But she isn't real.'

'It doesn't matter. Good grief, Isabel. Have an imagination. The point is that she can be a version of you, or you of her. Use her as your role model. Think to yourself, What would Leila do in this situation? and you'll be able to do anything in this world.'

I went to sleep dreaming of meeting Leila. I had many

dreams about her. Some were frightening. What if I met her and she didn't like me? Leila was impatient, an adventurer. I was a homebody and a drip, and I knew it. But often the dreams were rich and beautiful, and when I woke up I tried to sleep again to finish off the dream. I had a sense that Maggie had not told me everything about this trip but I didn't worry. I thought perhaps it had something to do with the professor, her old flame. I wondered if she was trying to match-make me with someone in New York. The professor? Surely he must be too old for me. Perhaps she wanted to rekindle her own romance with him and I was a go-between.

The next day another letter from Owen arrived. In this one he told me that he was ready to come and see me. We had to talk about Julia. He was angry and I was the only person he could speak to. That stupid Julia was getting inside his head and wouldn't leave him be. He was in London and wanted to meet me in the next few days.

Maggie stood behind me and read the letter over my shoulder. 'You should call him.'

'I don't want to see him. I don't want to think about any of that stuff any more. How does he even know I'm here?'

'I must have mentioned it to Sheila. Sorry, I didn't think. Why don't you just meet him?'

'I can't,' I said. 'I'm going to New York to deliver a book.'

I took Maggie's advice, and in New York I pretended to be Leila. I enjoyed the heat and the noise, the speed, the distance from home as I sat in cafés and walked in Central Park. I met the professor and he invited me for lunch. In the afternoon we strolled around the university campus and he took me to his study to see his collection of picture books on East and Central Asia. He told me that, if I wished to travel more, I should go to Turkey next. I must have expressed interest or even excitement at this – after all, Leila would have done – because Mehmet then gave me the addresses of his brothers and sisters in Istanbul and Izmir. One brother had a bar in a resort on the Aegean near Izmir and, if I wanted, I could work there for the summer. He would write to his brother and recommend me. I tucked the paper into my pocket and kissed him on both cheeks. He asked me how Maggie was. *My dear and beautiful Margaret Eva.* I told him that she was fine but, even as I said it, I knew that it was time for me to move away from Maggie and the bookshop. Leila seemed willing to act as a kind of guide to help me navigate my new life. Owen's letters were dropping through the letterbox almost daily – and it was Maggie's fault – but Leila and I were headed for Turkey.

– vi –

Near the station she picked up the rental car and drove to the town. She parked outside the guesthouse. She had chosen this place because it was cheap. She had imagined dirty carpets, old smells, grimy surfaces you didn't want to touch but, in fact, she had a clean, white-walled room with a springy bed and a clear view of the town. On the phone she had dealt with a rather sullen woman. In person, the woman was perfectly friendly.

It was late in the evening so she would do no more work until tomorrow. She would wake early and take a walk before visiting her old friends. The funeral was today but she had arrived too late for it, on purpose. She would wear the black outfit tomorrow as a sign of respect. People round here liked that sort of gesture.

Maggie had a desire to lay some flowers by the water, at the scene of the tragedy. It was mawkish and she had often shuddered at the sight of dried-up bouquets in lay-bys, tied to bus shelters or lamp-posts, but Isabel had been only nineteen and nineteen-year-olds are sentimental. It wouldn't make any difference but it was one thing that she could do.

★

It was raining so she drove. By the cottages near the reservoir, she saw Isabel. She was certain it was Isabel. She even tapped on the window and called her name. The girl ran off. Shiny raindrops splashed up from her heels like small coins.

Maggie came to a beech tree and laid the flowers by the trunk. As an afterthought, she scrawled a message on the card.

– 6 –

I am safely at Kath's house now, directly under the room where we once lit candles for Julia. I marvel at Kath's sticking power. She is incredible. After all the years, she is still here in this village, in this house. In the next room she sleeps soundly. Her gentle snores slip across the landing and under my door.

I am sitting in warm lamplight. I close the window and now my feet swish back and forth against the deep carpet. There is a cosy bed where I shall soon snuggle up and sleep. The question turns over and over in my mind. *What if I die while I'm here in this town? I shall never have escaped.* Is that what Julia thought, if she had time to think it? What if my life ends here, in this street, less than a mile from where I was born? Who will help me out before that happens? Maggie is the answer. *The Missing Girls' Club* was no help at all but there is *Goose Island*. I'll read it now.

In bed I send a final goodnight text to Mete. I don't ask about Leila. One of Maggie's books has a pilot on the cover, crawling out of a light aircraft on the moors. He is dark and handsome, an Action Man doll. It reminds me of Mete when he was in the Turkish Air Force, before his accident. It reminds me of the café in Izmir where I worked as a waitress. Mete and his pilot friends were drinking beer and laughing round a big table. Mete pointed out the shape of the mountain peaks beyond the main part of the city on the other side of the bay and told me that they were known locally as Marilyn Monroe because they resembled a voluptuous woman lying on her back. I look at the handsome soldier on Maggie's book cover and remember Mete's sweet smile as he sat there in his blue uniform and cap. I kiss the air in his direction.

Kath answered the door. She didn't recognize me. I almost didn't recognize her. Her face was fatter than it used to be and somehow sunken. Her hair was long. In the 1980s we'd both had short, angular cuts, occasionally permed, always dyed one colour on top of another. Kath had softened. She wore a pink, knitted jumper. It was thick and fluffy, made her look like a cuddly toy.

'Kath.' I wanted to smile but I couldn't.

Her eyes ran all over my face, confused. I tried to catch her gaze in mine.

'Kath, don't you remember me? It's Isabel.'

'Isabel. Isabel?' Her voice dropped to a whisper. 'Izzie?' The word snagged in her throat and she gave a sudden small cough. 'My God.' Her fingers gripped the edge of the door and for a second I thought she was going to shut it in my face.

'Well.' She laughed, a little too loudly. 'Let's have a hug. How are you? It must be – I don't even know how long. But how are you?'

'I'm all right.' I smiled.

Kath held out her arms. It was a slippery hug. Neither of us was certain enough to embrace fully.

'Come in. Has it been raining? Get inside and warm up.' Kath stepped back and I entered the dark hall. The walls were painted a deep shade of crimson. The air smelled musty, perfumed. Bowls of rose petals stood on the table and the radiator. 'I can't believe it. Let me take your coat.'

'Thanks.'

'Are you staying in the village? Are you visiting someone?'

'I'm just here for the night. I've got a room in a guesthouse up the road.'

Kath draped my coat over a chair in the hall. I followed her into the living room. It was the same dark colour as the hall. Around the walls and on the furniture were patchwork quilts, lace doilies, embroidered mats. Yellow balls of wool filled a large basket in front of the television. A pair of knitting needles stuck out in a V.

Kath turned on the gas fire. Blue flames jumped and sub-sided. 'Oh, but you won't have heard about Owen Carr. He had an accident and—'

'I know. I did hear. That's why I've come. I was at the funeral this afternoon.'

Then I noticed the pictures on the mantelpiece. A boy and a girl, both with fair hair and Kath's face. 'They're sweet.'

'Cara and Jake. Yeah, bless 'em. They're five and seven. This week they're with their dad. You married?'

I told her about Mete and Elif. She seemed pleased with this news and gave me a soft pat on the shoulder. 'And you still have family around here?'

'No. No one. Not any more, thankfully.'

'But someone told you about Owen. I'm glad. I thought about going to the funeral but I chickened out. It seemed hypocritical to grieve in public when I'd hardly spoken to Owen in years. And, actually, I'd forgotten it was today. I didn't pay attention to the date when I saw it in the paper.'

'But you live – lived – in the same village. You must have seen him around the place.'

'I know, but it's very easy not to see someone if you don't want to. We'd say hello in the pub if we saw each other after a few drinks, but not in the street, cold sober. I wish I'd had a proper conversation with him. All these years and we were too embarrassed, I think, to say. "How are you?" and have a chat about old times and what we were doing. It's ridiculous. What were we so embarrassed about?'

I shrugged and shook my head.

Kath rose heavily to her feet, moved around the room fiddling with light switches. Lamps came on, brightened and dimmed. She turned the gas fire up another notch. I listened for sounds outside but there was nothing. I leaned back on the sofa, half thinking I would just like to close my eyes and sleep, hoping she wouldn't put the television or music on. Kath sat down in the armchair, upright and just on the edge of the cushion as though she were the guest, not quite comfortable in her host's living room. It would have been perfect if we didn't have to speak now and could rest in silence but, of course, we had to talk. Kath buried her fingers in the crocheted blanket that covered the sofa.

'That's a pretty blanket,' I said, for something to say.

'I made it. It was easy, just crocheted squares. It was an early effort. I like to make things in the evenings, if I'm watching telly and the kids are in bed.'

I looked around the room and realized that all the cushion covers, the framed embroideries on the wall, must be her handiwork.

'I'm getting better, gradually. I can start to put some of these things up in the attic as I make new ones. Quite a store of treasures growing up there. I keep them for Cara, so that she can start learning from them in another year or so. Jake's hoping to join the church choir next year. Remember when we belonged, with Owen?'

'Yeah.'

But talk of Cara and Jake made me worry about Elif. I didn't like to imagine her growing up here, going to my old schools, being friends with the daughters of my friends. I didn't want to go through the same old cycles, season after season, until Elif reached the age of seventeen or eighteen. If I lived here, I would surely have to take her to the lake to feed the ducks, teach her how to identify the different species. It would be my childhood all over again for Elif. And what might happen to her when she turned fifteen? I couldn't bear it.

SUSANNA JONES

'Your parents moved away from here, didn't they?'

The last time I had heard Kath speak, she must have had the voice of a seventeen-year-old, yet she sounded just the same to me as she always had. A fat, solid voice from deep in her throat.

'What was the question? Oh, yes. Years ago. I don't know where they are. I don't know *if* they are.'

Kath smiled and exhaled a sympathetic sigh.

'Well, Maggie would tell me if they'd died, I guess. So I suppose they're still somewhere. They sold their house here some time in the nineties. I know that much but I don't know where they went. Possibly up to Scotland where my mum was born.'

'Where in Scotland?'

'Near Stirling somewhere. But they never told me they'd gone.'

'Would it have been easy for them to find you, though, if they'd wanted to? You've been living abroad for a while.'

'They could have asked Maggie. They could guess that she'd kept in touch with me. There's never been anything to stop them.'

'But they probably think you don't want to know them. I bet they feel a lot of guilt about all that stuff with Owen. Perhaps it's that way round and if you made a move they'd be delighted.'

'I don't think so. They didn't even hang on for the trial.'

'It seems sad and it was such a long time ago,' Kath said. 'My dad died ten years ago and my mother's not well. She's deteriorated over the last couple of years but it's a comfort to me that she's there. It would be a pity to lose your parents without coming to some sort of peace, at least finding out whether they have regrets. I bet they do.'

'I can't say it would make that much difference now. Kath, can we sit on the floor? I don't much like chairs.'

Kath laughed and slipped from her chair to the carpet. I did the same. I warmed my toes in front of the fire. Fake flames danced, blue and orange, to the gentle hiss of gas.

Kath went into the kitchen, returned a few minutes later with a tray of tea things. The teapot was wrapped in a pink knitted cosy. There was a plate of shortbread and two china mugs. We drank tea and talked. All the time I could see soil sifting through my fingers, more and more of it. It was thick and dark, smooth as it fell and fell. I tried to concentrate, none the less, and learned that Kath is now a primary-school teacher, not here in the village but a few miles away. Her children go to the local primary school, though, the one we went to. They probably sit cross-legged in the same hall and sing 'When a Knight Won his Spurs'. Her ex-husband, Simon, is a computer engineer from Whitby and they were married for eight years.

'He left, a long time ago, but lots of his things are still here, cluttering the attic and spare bedroom. I wish he'd take them so I could feel I was getting on with things, but he can't see what the problem is. We've got a big attic, unfortunately.'

I saw the attic room, bursting with Kath's knitting and embroidery, Simon's boxes of clothes. 'I remember that room,' I said. 'It used to be your bedroom.'

'Yes, that's right.' Kath's voice was bright. She was not thinking about our ceremony for Julia, the candles and perfume. She had probably forgotten.

There was a silence and we drank more tea. When the pot was empty, she went to put the kettle on again. 'I'm an addict,' she said. 'I can't have less than three cups.'

'You sit down. I'll do it.' I went to the kitchen.

Kath called out to me, 'Look, Izzie, why don't you stay here tonight? I've got a spare room and you don't want to be on your own in some lonely guesthouse.'

'Oh, no. I couldn't intrude.'

But I already knew I was not going back to the Lake View. I would rather have slept on the street than in that poky room.

Kath stood in the doorway. 'You wouldn't be intruding. I'm quite lonely, actually, when the kids aren't here. I'd love to have some company for the evening. We'll cook a nice dinner and catch up on the past. You look so well. You haven't aged at all. It's amazing.'

'Thanks, you too.' In fact, Kath looked much older. She was more attractive, though, than she ever had been when I had known her before. She looked happy. I was glad I had come. 'Let's do that.'

I think of my parents in a village in Scotland, for some reason in a brick bungalow. I see them playing bridge with friends of the same age. My father is laughing gently at a bad joke of my mother's. She likes to pun, to play with words, and remarks that

248

she is even better at Scrabble than she is at bridge. They pour drinks for their friends and offer snacks – nuts and chocolate – eager to please. A standard lamp casts a pool of white around the table. The bulb shines through a fringed, faded lampshade. I am filled with sadness. It ebbs and flows around my bones. Sometimes it rises up to my eyes and a little spills out. Then it passes.

I chopped tomatoes while Kath measured fistfuls of spaghetti into a pan of boiling water. 'Things have changed round here, you know,' she said. 'You don't have to go to the foreign-food section of the shop to buy spaghetti any more. We even have a Mexican restaurant.'

I said nothing but tipped the chunks of tomato into the frying-pan and stepped back as oil spat up at me.

Kath continued, 'I couldn't live anywhere else now. It's a small place and I don't know why I like being here, but I do. It's having the house, I suppose.'

'Your parents left it to you?'

'And that's why I love it. It's completely mine. I don't have to remember my memories, you see, because I'm among them. It's only when I go away that I'm aware of what's past and what's present. Except for tonight, though. I never expected this. When an old friend you heard was dead walks through the door, glowing with health and youth, well—'

I dropped the knife into the sink. 'Not again. Who told you I was dead?' I turned on the tap and rinsed pink tomato juice from my fingers. 'Go on,' I said. 'How did I die? It's a bloody lie anyway.'

'I can't remember where I heard it. It was a rumour that went around years ago. It wasn't very consistent. Once I heard that you died in prison and another time that it happened afterwards.'

'You're the third person who's said that to me today. I don't feel very good now. And, to be pedantic, it wasn't prison.'

I leaned against the sink, unable to think what to say next. Kath stopped too. She perched on the back of a chair, reached out and rubbed my arm.

'Sorry. I was never sure about anything I heard. Your parents left the village and that seemed to fit with the story, in a way. I didn't like to say anything before. I thought I'd just assume that you were real and not a ghost or *doppelgänger*. It's a bit eerie, though. The power of gossip that it can make someone alive or dead.'

'But where did it come from?'

'I don't remember, and I didn't necessarily believe it at the time but it stayed in the back of my mind. Somehow it ended up as the truth.'

'I suppose I spooked a few people at the funeral, then.'

'Never mind that. People round here need shaking up once in a while.' Kath opened a bottle of ruby-red wine, filled two glasses almost to the brim. 'Cheers. To old friends.' She held her glass up high.

'Old friends.' We clinked glasses. The wine was sweet and heavy. I savoured it. 'So what did I die of?'

'Oh. I can hardly remember what nonsense it was. It doesn't matter.'

'No, please. What was it?'

'It was terribly vague. I – um . . .'

I could see that Kath was trying to come up with something acceptable, not too gruesome, nothing that would upset me. 'What was it? I can take it. I'm not superstitious or over-sensitive. Just curious.'

'They said you committed suicide. The story was that you cut your wrists in prison – sorry, detention centre, whatever it was – and bled to death.'

'Oh.' The story must have come from Owen. Why would he have said that? What kind of revenge would it be?

'But the other version was that you came out of prison and had nowhere to go because your family didn't want you, and you took an overdose somewhere. In a field, I think. A field of flowers by a lake.'

'That's nice. No, that's sweet, isn't it? A field of poppies, maybe. I could have drifted off to sleep. Of the two I certainly prefer that one. Jesus Christ.'

'Sorry, Izzie. Have I upset you? I shouldn't have said anything.'

'No, no.' I tried to laugh it off. 'I almost believed it for a second there. It was like waking from a nightmare. What a relief that I'm alive. I suppose those things could have happened to me. They will have happened to someone, after all. If you look at it objectively, perhaps there's no difference. I wonder if I'll show up in the funeral photographs.' I giggled.

'Blimey, who took photographs? That's a strange thing to do. Anyway, you're here now.' Kath sat down at the kitchen table. She nudged the other chair from under the table with her foot.

'Yes, so it seems.'

'And I'm so glad. I'm so glad to see you again. I can tell that life has been good to you in the end, after everything. Owen was never going to do as well as you. I tell you what, shall we do something together tomorrow? If you haven't arranged to meet anyone else, we could go for a walk in the country, then find a pub for lunch. I'd like to spend a bit more time with you. When do you have to go back to Istanbul?'

'I'm supposed to leave in the morning but do you know what? I applied for a job here today.' I laughed again. 'You won't believe what came over me when I saw the new supermarket. I don't know what I was thinking.' I told her of my ten minutes in the supermarket and we laughed until our knees buckled, our sides hurt and we couldn't breathe.

'Do you really have to go back to Istanbul so soon?' Kath wiped her eyes. 'I can see lots of reasons why working at CostRight wouldn't be the best thing for you to do – that beige uniform for one thing – but there are other jobs.'

'I do, really.' I realized we were not quite laughing at the same situation as I had neglected to tell Kath about John, Annie and our attempt to dig up the remains of Julia Smith. Should I explain? Not yet, but perhaps in the morning. 'I suppose I could look into changing my ticket. I miss Mete and Elif so much, though. Oh, I don't know. Let me think about it.'

We moved back into the living room to eat. We sat on the floor at the coffee-table and opened a second bottle of wine. Kath talked about her children, asked questions about my life in Istanbul. She wanted to know how I had ended up there but I couldn't explain it well. It was late, I was tired, and I had forgotten the exact story.

'I'd love to see more of you, Isabel. You haven't changed, you know. You're just the same. In fact, I have photographs somewhere. Shall we have a look at them?'

Kath opened a small cupboard in the corner of the room. Letters and loose photographs fell onto the floor. She flicked them to one side with her fingertips and rummaged around. Eventually she pulled out three or four thick albums, red and blue. We sat next to each other on the floor to see what was inside. The pictures lay under sticky plastic. Many pages had lost their stickiness and the photographs went lopsided as we flicked through.

'Here's the school trip to London. That's the *Cutty Sark*.'

'Oh, yes.'

A group of girls, familiar faces and hairstyles, stood in front of the ship. It was a flat, grey day. The water looked cold and the girls were drab in jeans and raincoats but they were trying to make the best of it, pulling faces at the camera.

'Is that you there?' Kath pointed to a girl at the end of the row whose face was not in focus.

'I think it is, yes. I remember seeing the *Cutty Sark* but only vaguely. I don't remember this picture being taken. The evidence says I was there, though.'

'I don't think Owen will be in any of these. I don't seem to have been interested enough in the boys to have taken any pictures of them. But look, there's you and me on the bus.'

'Is that Julia behind us?'

The back row of the bus was filled with boys, a whole heap of them, but in the centre was a girl. Her head was turned away and, again, Kath's camera shake had blurred the picture. The boys were just a lump of dark heads and blue legs. The girl was no more than a dark pony-tail, over a featureless face, and a white shirt.

'It might be. I tend to forget about Julia. She comes back to me in the middle of the night sometimes, when I'm feeling worried or depressed, or when I read bad stories in the newspapers. I always think of her in the science lab that time.'

'Which time?'

'Don't you remember the day she tried to pierce her own ears? In chemistry with Mr Pilkington. It was hilarious. I fainted and there wasn't even any blood.' Kath shuddered. 'Anyway, let me clear away the plates.'

She bumped her hip on the back of a chair as she left the room. I offered to help but she waved me away. She giggled again.

I did remember that day. It had been a disaster.

Julia showed up in the science lab one afternoon with a needle, a small silver stud earring, and an orange ice lolly wrapped up in a small towel. The classroom contained eight large square tables, each with gas taps, a big square sink, strange pockmarks and burns in the wood. Kath, Julia and I sat at a table in the back corner.

'What are you doing with that?' I asked. 'You're not going to eat it now? It's going to melt.'

'I know. That's why I've got to do this quickly, when Mr Pilkington's over with the boys.'

The boys in our class were riotous in all lessons but a particular pain in chemistry. Lab coats, safety goggles and Bunsen burners created a thrill they rarely found in other classes. Mr Pilkington would move from table to table trying to prevent fire, singed hair, broken test tubes, would try to stay on their good side by humouring their silliness and taking an interest in their jokes. The girls' side of the classroom was usually left to take care of itself, apart from the occasional perfunctory visit to see how our experiments were coming along.

'Do what?'

Julia had heard that if you froze your ear-lobes with an ice cube, then stuck a needle in a flame for a few seconds, you could pierce your ears without pain or injury. There were no ice cubes to hand so she had been to the corner shop and bought the lolly. She wanted Kath or me to do the job. We winced and squealed at the very idea. Julia got angry. It was unfair, she snapped, because the rest of us had pierced ears but she couldn't afford it. She called us cowards and said that we were pathetic and not her friends. She didn't want to look like some virgin who had unpierced ears and still wore white knee socks. She was bare-legged that day, as always in the summer, but I understood what she meant. The ice lolly was beginning to drip from its paper packet so we had to hurry. I said I thought it would hurt and I couldn't pierce her ears, but I agreed to hold up a hand mirror so that she could do it herself. Julia gave me a sarcastic 'Oh, thank you so much.' She grimaced and pressed the lolly against her right ear-lobe. A trickle of orange juice ran down her ear and neck onto the white collar of her school shirt. Kath and I watched, fascinated by Julia's stoicism, the unmoving scowl on her face. The ice turned slushy and crumbled over her fingers as she pressed it hard against her skin. Kath screwed up her face in horror and held the Bunsen burner forward so that Julia could put the needle into the flame with her free hand. When Julia thought her ear was cold enough and the needle hot enough, she took a deep breath and pushed the needle into her skin. It went through and stuck. She gasped in pain and fell forward to the table. Kath saw the needle sticking out, groaned, and fainted. She clonked her head on the table, then crumpled to the floor. Julia wouldn't lift her head. Her dark hair spilled over the gas taps. She cradled her arms around her face and continued to gasp.

The rest of the class dropped their experiments to see what was happening. Stools crashed to the floor and a crowd formed. Mr Pilkington pushed through. Amid the fuss and chatter, his lab coat caught fire in the flame of our Bunsen burner. One of the boys put out the flame by banging it with a textbook until Mr Pilkington was shouting, 'Yes, yes, you've put it out now, that's quite enough thank you,' and the boy moved away in a huff. 'Sorry for saving your life.' I stood beside Julia and tried to prise her hands and face from the table while Kath lay on the floor, a heavy white lump.

The school nurse removed the needle and disinfected Julia's ear. Smelling-salts brought Kath round. Julia was embarrassed, afterwards, and threatened to punch the gob of anyone who mentioned the incident. I knew that she was furious with herself, not for trying it but for failing. A few weeks later she had her ears pierced by the local jeweller. She had the biggest gold hoops in the school. I think Owen paid for them.

Kath returned with coffee. When she had wriggled into position on the floor, we opened another album.

'Here's one of your aunt Maggie.'

Maggie, Kath, Julia and I were sitting on a large rock on the hills. Maggie had her arms around Kath and me. Julia was holding on to Kath. She was smiling but her knuckles were tight on Kath's sleeve. Our hair blew to the right in coarse lumps. We looked like mermaids under water.

'I don't remember this. Who took it?'

'Your mum did.'

'Did she? I suppose it was one of those Sunday-afternoon walks when we all got together.'

'I think it was. I remember your mum and Maggie arguing a lot. They didn't get on very well, did they?'

'Chalk and cheese. I think there was some love underneath it all – maybe still is – but Maggie was too wild and unconventional for my family. The funny thing is, I'm not sure she ever did anything particularly daring or outrageous. It was an image she cultivated. My parents were much more eccentric in their attempts to be the most normal people in the village. In fact, Maggie's life has been steady. Her books are a bit spicy but not shocking. Quite sweet, if anything. You should see the book-shop in Richmond. It's like going back in time fifty years or more.'

'She had a special kind of charm, though. I remember looking up to her and thinking she was wonderful. Her house always smelled amazing. Did she burn incense or something? Whatever it was, it seemed exotic back then. And Maggie was a good listener too. I remember pouring out my troubles to her when I thought I was overweight. She listened, then gave me a box of some kind of herbal tea to take home. She also told me something I didn't really understand, that I should look around, choose myself a thin girl and pretend I was her, do all the things that girl would do. It was probably good advice but I didn't follow it. I just wanted someone to moan to. Maggie was a sort of village elder for girls.'

'It's a pity she'd moved away by the time Julia disappeared. The whole thing was buried so quickly. If Maggie had been around she would have made people talk about it.'

'I buy all her books. I don't really read them but it seems disloyal not to.'

'Is her identity out of the bag, then?'

'It's an open secret. People want to believe it's someone who still lives around here so they pretend it isn't her. Different names come up, usually women who live in old cottages on their own with lots of cats, but I think everyone who knew Maggie knows that she is Eva Carter.'

We flipped through the pages of the album for another half-hour. By now I was seeing double and my mouth was struggling to pronounce words properly.

I yawned.

'I've worn you out, Izzie. You've had a long day. I expect you're ready to sleep now. Is your stuff at the guesthouse?'

'Yeah. I'll leave it there and get it in the morning.'

'Maybe we should phone to let them know you're not coming.'

Now that I was snugly at Kath's, Doreen Fatebene's big house distorted itself in my mind. It was cold and creaky with hundreds of dark rooms and long, narrow corridors. Empty beds rocked and clattered in the rooms, as though the place were caught in a storm at sea.

'I don't think they'll notice, not until breakfast. I could slope in then.'

'I'll give them a ring,' Kath said. 'I'm a bit tipsy but I think it's for the best.'

Kath's lips were stained black. Mine must have been too. I wiped them with the back of my hand and accidentally scratched my chin with my thumbnail. It hurt, and for some reason this surprised me.

I gave Kath the number for the Lake View. She dialled it and slurred into the phone that I wouldn't be coming back tonight, after all. Doreen Fatebene wanted to know why and what had happened. She said my bag was a security issue and she might have to call the police. Kath gave her address so that the police could bring the bag round, if necessary. She was laughing as she put down the phone.

As we cleared away our plates and glasses, Kath said, casually, 'So, had you kept in touch with Owen?'

'Me? No. Not at all. I'd almost forgotten about him.'

'I thought you might have kept up your friendship, you know, when that stuff was all over. I thought the two of you might have stayed – uh – friends.'

'No.'

'Did you try?'

'No.'

I told Kath of my suspicions. I did not mention my day's work, just that I had always wondered about Owen and what he might have done one afternoon in 1982.

Kath considered my words. 'Funny how when the idea's in your head it's hard to shake it out again. I always assumed some stranger in a car abducted her, someone who didn't live round here. That was what they led us to believe, isn't it? Awful for her parents. Her mother became an alcoholic after that.'

'She was already an alcoholic, wasn't she?'

'Was she?'

'I thought so. Or her father was. I'm not sure any more.'

Kath had got it wrong, I knew, but it didn't matter.

'I might be wrong about Owen,' I said.

'We'll never know.'

I considered this a disappointing response. We might find out, if only people would make the effort.

Kath changed the subject. 'I always envied you, Izzie. It's hard to believe, in the light of what happened, but I felt envious and relieved at the same time when you and Owen were arrested. You'd had this adventure without me. And yet, of course, I was glad I hadn't gone out that day and ended up in the same situation. I was very confused about it all.'

'If you had come with us, I'm sure we would never have done it. You were a good influence on people.'

'Maybe.'

'You were.'

'I should have written to you or visited you and Owen in prison. Especially you. I could have visited you easily.'

'It doesn't matter. I wasn't exactly round the corner.'

'I was scared. I think I was waiting for you to say that it would be all right, that I could go. I wasn't able to make that kind of decision for myself. I always wondered what became of you. I'm so glad it's turned out well. Your life has been more exciting than mine.'

Kath stroked the corner square of the crocheted blanket, poked her finger through one of the small holes. Her guilt was nice to know about but it changed nothing. I didn't want Kath to pity me. I don't think I would have wanted her life.

'I always knew it could so easily have been me.'

'No.' I shook my head. 'It would never have been you.'

'I almost came with you to the boat that day. I remember.' Kath's eyes misted and she rubbed her nose.

'But you didn't. You stayed at home to study. That was you.'

'And look how things turned out. But you're back now. The job application might have been a strange moment of madness but, still, won't you want to come home more often now that you've done it once?'

'I'll have to see. This was a special occasion.'

I would sort it all out before morning. If there had been no Elif or Mete, I would come back, of course, but it was not so simple. Would Mete want to come and would I want him to? Would it be good for Elif to live here or would the place poison her too? Or would I poison Elif by returning to Istanbul and not solving the problems here? All I had to do was work it out in my head. Then I would know the answer, I could tell the police, and I could leave. It was not worth telling Kath about the allotment. We had found nothing. It was a secret between John, Annie and me. We turned out all the lights except the one in the hall, and I followed Kath upstairs. She showed me to the spare bedroom. It was large, with a double bed and an old-fashioned dressing-table, a tall oak wardrobe. The room looked out onto the street. Beyond the terraces of small houses I could see the school playing-fields. There was a piece of clothing, a sweatshirt perhaps, between the goalposts. I leaned my back against the window to feel the sharp, cold glass on my arms and neck. I was smiling. Kath moved about in her room for twenty minutes or so and then her light went off.

I am in the garden again. There are no clear sounds, no birds or cars, but the night is noisy with the swaying of trees, water trickling from roof tiles, down pipes and drains. I am thinking of Maggie and trying to understand about Leila. I remember the pink mug on the shelf above the sink with LEILA in black capital letters. Who was drinking from that mug?

I call Bernadette.

'Yeah? What? Can't you sleep tonight?'

'Bernadette, when you flew out to Istanbul, was there someone with you on the plane? You said something about a friend but I didn't pay attention at the time.' I use my free hand to rub my legs, try to warm them. My jaw is stiffening with cold.

'There was Leila. Didn't she talk to you?'

'*Leila?*'

'We sat together on the flight but we didn't talk much. It was Leila's idea for me to do the trip. She had air miles and helped me out with my ticket. I thought I told you that.'

'No, you didn't.'

I am panicking now, trying to remember conversations I had with Maggie that make no sense at all. All of a sudden everyone seems to think Leila is real.

'Do you know what she wanted to do in Turkey?'

'She lives there. She was going back to her husband. You know, the three of us were all in Maggie's house at almost the same time, but you two never got to meet each other. We're like sisters, in a way.' Her voice is growing quieter, smaller, as if she is running away from me, into the distance, into rainy West London streets. 'I don't know if I can afford this call. Is it charging me as well as you?'

'I don't know. I don't know how it works. I'll hang up now. Take care, Bernadette.'

'Yeah, 'bye.' Her voice is tiny now, a speck of sound, and it disappears.

I must have slept. I am awake, not rested but confused, and I pick up Owen's letter and the copy of *Goose Island*, stuff them into my coat pockets. My sense of why I'm doing this is vague. I walk down the street as I walked up it yesterday.

Here I am, now, near the reservoir. I'm hiding behind the beech trees. Julia has just passed by. I hold my breath and watch her edge along the path. She seems nervous. She must know what's going to happen. Against the green water she looks too solid, too heavy. I can see her back and legs but not her feet. It is as though she is walking just a few centimetres above the ground. She steps soundlessly through the air, away from me and back towards the village. I won't follow her. I breathe the dank water. Mallards and coots sleep somewhere out of sight. I'm having an adventure. Elif's spirit is playing with my shoes, bumping around at my feet and I know she will be safe. Perhaps I will fetch her from Istanbul. I will bring her here to share my life. The lake blinks its heavy green eyelids. I have come far enough and I must stop here.

Another beep from my phone. The tiny screen lights up. A text message has come from Mete. **Günaydın**, it says. Good morning. I press Names and scroll down to Mete's number. Then I press Options and Erase. *Erase Mete?* it asks me. I don't know. *Erase Mete?* But I don't know. I don't think he is talking to me any more. The message is meant for someone else.

I am almost at the spot where Julia disappeared. And then I see something. A kind of light I never noticed before, a gap between the trees that was always just air. I see the car – clearly green, not blue – and I see Julia again. She is still walking. I realize I have always been able to know what happened to Julia. It is not a mystery at all. Owen is nowhere to be seen. It has nothing to do with him. Owen did not kill Julia. He did not harm her. The blood on his shirt must have been his own. I am so excited I want to run back to the house, wake Kath to tell her what I know, but I do not. It is not the right time yet. Julia was safe, but what about the rest of us? There is the bag of newspapers. There is the car. I walk to the tree and sink down to look at the reservoir. I drop the book and the letter into the water, swish them back and forth with my hand, and push them downward.

I am in bed. The sun is up. I have slept for another couple of hours. Kath is still sleeping so I tiptoe out once more. I set off to retrieve my bag from the Lake View guesthouse. The tricycle is still there in next door's garden. I whisper good morning to it and step up onto the garden path. As I approach the door, it opens and a figure pops out. I scream, a quick but shrill sound, like a silly woman who has just seen a mouse. It is my aunt Maggie.

'Isabel.' She almost jumps. She drops her suitcase and her face breaks into a wide smile. 'Fancy seeing you. What are you doing here?'

'I came to Owen's funeral.'

She hasn't aged one bit. There are no wrinkles, no crevices around her eyes and lips, no sagging pockets of flesh, but she has gone rusty. Her auburn hair is wiry and tired, her nails polished in brown. Patches of dark orange smear her forehead and chin.

'So it *was* you I saw from the car last night. I banged on the window but you didn't seem to recognize me. How thoughtful of you to come. All the way from Istanbul?'

'Yes. You're too late, though, Maggie. It was yesterday.'

I think of Owen and me and the kite. I smile to myself. Now I know that I was safe with Owen all along, it is all right for me to remember. This is a new feeling. I like it. My eyes are filling with tears. I grimace and blink them back. I don't want Maggie to think these tears are for her.

'Oh, I know that, Izzie. No, unfortunately I couldn't get here any sooner. There was a sort of clash with something else I had to do. So I've hired a car and come up now for a few days to give Sheila some support. You know how these things are. The funeral is only the beginning.'

'So how come you're staying here?' I nod towards the

guesthouse. I am finding it easy to sound cold, to make her nervous. Maggie is uncomfortable. She doesn't want me to ask these questions.

'Sheila's house is full until tomorrow. Apparently they have several elderly relatives staying. They're leaving today and I'm going to stay with her for a few days, maybe longer. It doesn't matter too much about the funeral, at least I hope it doesn't. I never knew Owen very well, not as well as you did.'

'How's George?' My voice is smooth, my posture perfect. Maggie is taller than I, but we both sense that I am looking down on her.

'He's fine. He often asks after you. We're married now. I suppose I told you that. We went conventional in the end, as you see. I always read your email messages out loud to him. He's a bit long-sighted for the computer now, I'm afraid. He leaves everything to me but then that's the way I like it. You really should come and stay some time. Oh, give me a hug.'

I allow Maggie to hug me. I touch her back, in what I hope is a vaguely patronizing gesture, and put my cheek almost to hers for a mimed kiss. Doreen Fatebene presses her face against the window and watches.

'Guess where Leila is,' I say.

'Leila? *Leila?* I haven't the faintest idea. What do you mean, exactly?'

'Leila. Where is she?'

'I never heard from her after she went to – uh – where was it? New York?'

But Maggie's eyes are darting all over the place. The parts of her skin that aren't orange turn candy-floss pink. She avoids eye-contact with me and lifts her lips into a stiff smile.

'Maggie, didn't we agree a long time ago that Leila doesn't exist?'

'Oh. Yes. Actually, I don't remember—'

'You seem confused. Does she exist or doesn't she?'

'She does.'

'Is that right?' I can see the workings inside Maggie's head, little clicks around a circuit that switch on the small, single lightbulb. Ping. She's got it.

'There once was a real girl called Leila, but she wasn't with me for long. I adapted her to help you. You needed a role model. I think – I think you were rather nervous when you came to stay and were very intimidated when I talked of Leila and Bernadette. You wouldn't go out and do anything so I changed Leila's character to inspire you. I'm sorry. It was a foolish thing to do. I'd forgotten all about it. But look how it made a difference to your life. Look how you went off and travelled because of me. But, really, I had forgotten about Leila.'

Maggie says this as though she believes I should have forgotten about Leila too.

'Is that right? So it wouldn't be the case that you introduced her by mistake and then had to deny her existence? Why would you do that?'

'You're right, I wouldn't. Can't we talk about this some-where—'

'You'd do it because I might realize who she was.'

'I've told you, Isabel. I'd forgotten about Leila. I don't know what you're so upset about.'

'You keep saying you'd forgotten her. That's a great shame because, apparently, our imaginary friend is still going strong. Leila's in Istanbul right now, as it happens, with Mete.'

'Ah. That's – uh. Really? Will she still be there when you get back? It'd be a shame if you missed her again. You two have so much in common. When you say Leila do you mean – the real one? The one you didn't meet?'

'I mean Leila. I have no idea what she's even doing there. I'm guessing that she heard about Owen's death and thought it was time to pay me a visit. But, no, Bernadette said she lives there.'

'Quite.'

'But I'd rather hang on here for another day and spend time with you, Maggie, than go there to find her. I haven't seen you for years. Leila is not important to me but you are.'

'Well, good. I'd like that. Sheila will be exhausted today. She'll be in pieces so I don't want to bother her yet. You and I could go off on our own for a chat. It's a very fresh day. I think it's going to be nice. We could have a walk on the hills, if you'd like to.'

Maggie looks up at the sky. Her thin face seems to broaden as a smile spreads across it.

'Yes, let's do that. You rescued me when I was younger and I'll always have to be grateful for that.'

'Oh, you shouldn't be. It was my hobby to pick up the waifs and strays. I liked to help out young women who were lost. I saw myself as a sort of guide, a force for the good of the next generation. I tried to put into practice what I wrote about in my books.'

'Always a happy ending for the girl, as you like to say. Bernadette, for example. I saw her the other week. She came to Istanbul, too.'

'Oh, Bernadette. She was a funny one. What's she doing now?'

Maggie has noticed Doreen at the window and is uncomfortable. She tries to pass me on the path but I will not let her.

'Odd jobs. She's getting her singing voice back.'

'Is she? Good for her. Good for Bernadette. Back on her feet. I always knew she would.'

'I discovered her real name for the first time when I saw her passport. It's Chloë. Isn't that strange? Bernadette doesn't look or seem like a Chloë in any way. She could never be a Chloë to me. I suppose you knew her name before she changed it.'

'I did. It doesn't really suit her, I agree, but neither does Bernadette.'

'Maggie, why the name Leila?'

'That's her name, Isabel.' She is becoming exasperated. She tries to hide it but I know that rising tone in her voice, those wide eyes. 'Nothing to do with me.'

'What was wrong with Julia?'

'I don't know what you're talking about. Who's Julia?'

'You knew Julia. Don't pretend you didn't. She was my

friend and you met her. I've seen a photograph of us all together.'

'Possibly. I wouldn't remember all your friends from the old days.'

'She's the one who disappeared. We thought she had been murdered. Even her parents thought that.'

'Oh, that Julia. Of course. But that happened after I left the village. I don't think I ever met the girl.'

'If you say so. Leila's with my husband now, and my child. What's she doing?'

'How would I—? I expect she wanted to visit you.'

'Will she come here?'

'I doubt that very much.'

'No, because Leila is Julia and everyone thinks she's dead.'

'No, because your Leila doesn't fucking well exist and the one I knew was not Julia. Oh, excuse my language but you're really pushing this. You've been disturbed by Owen's death. Can't you see? You should have kept in touch with him back when you were in London, as I wanted you to. Then you might have had the strength to cope now.'

Maggie steps past me. I let her move towards the gate. I turn away from her, arms folded, and she returns with a drippy, sweet expression all over her face. I want to wipe it up with a cloth and shove it down her throat.

'Isabel, I'm sorry. Why aren't we getting along with each other, like we used to? In the old days, we were close. Can't we go to a nice café and—'

'What about her parents? How terrible for them to think of their daughter murdered.'

'I'm not sure what you want from this conversation. Fine. You're not going to understand me. If someone shows up on my doorstep needing help – and Leila did – then that's all I care about. She didn't tell me her age but she looked sixteen or more. I don't know anything about Julia. You had so many friends at school. It's not as if I could have got to know them all.'

'You should have told the police.'

'I don't believe in the police. That young girl came to *me*. She was my responsibility. The police had nothing to do with it. And she wasn't Julia.'

'Whatever you say. I'm not going to hang around here. I just have to get my bag and that's it.'

I go up to room nine. I look out of the window. Maggie is padding down the street, too fast to keep my eyes on. She seems to disappear before she even reaches the corner. I expect she's on her way to Sheila's house. I lie on the bed, as I did yesterday. I don't believe a word she says. Now what do I do? I haven't had much sleep. I'm sure Doreen won't mind if I doze here for a little while.

My eyes open and I am on a sofa in a room that smells of rotten apple cores. Maggie is at the table, writing something. I wonder how she got here so quickly.

'Maggie, you might like to remind me who I am.'

'Well, you're Isabel, sweetheart.' She doesn't look at me.

I frown and rub my forehead.

'Isabel's dead,' I say. 'I remembered when I was at the reservoir. Isabel drowned herself there after her release. The memories I have from after that time aren't mine. I saw them when I looked into the water and they didn't belong to me.'

'If you're anyone, you're me. You're Maggie. You're both of us.'

And that is exactly how it feels. Her answer does not surprise me.

'But why?'

'Leila. Julia. You had a bad time because of her and I never had the courage to tell you the truth. Shall I tell you now?'

'Yes, please. I mean, yes, tell me.'

'You know her life at home was unhappy. She had to take care of herself, bring herself up and, in a way, bring her parents up too because they weren't responsible adults. She had some idea of running away from it all with the soldier. When his letters stopped coming, and she understood that it was a fantasy, she started to call me. It was every week at first, and then every night. She used to cry and cry, begging for my help. So I drove up from London and took her away.'

'You should have called the police.'

'I was going to, just as soon as she was safe with me, but she pleaded with me not to tell anyone. She made threats and I was frightened for her.'

'You shouldn't have taken any notice. Why didn't you call her parents? It was criminal to let people believe that she was dead.'

'She told me she would phone her parents herself. I sat there and watched as she dialled the number. She chatted to them for a while, or so I thought, and put the phone down. She told me that they didn't want her back and had said that she could stay with me. I didn't realize how devious she was, though. It was just the Speaking Clock, or something like it.'

'You believed her? You didn't insist on talking to them yourself? Oh, come on.'

'I thought I'd leave it until she was stronger. She was very distressed for a while and my only intention was to see that she became well. By the time I found out the truth – Sheila mentioned in a Christmas-card letter that Julia had never been found – Leila was sixteen and was used to her new life and new name, so I didn't think it was my business to go to the police. I wanted her to be happy, that's all. I wanted her to have some of the adventures I'd had when I was young. I sent her off to New York, then Turkey, where I had been. She met her lover there and, years later, had the baby girl. The one you know. Emel, her name is. It worked out well for her. But you came out of prison just after she left my house.'

'It wasn't prison, actually.'

'The point was, you still thought Julia was dead and that somehow it was all your fault. I should have told you the truth. I didn't know you were going to come back here and wait for her to be found.'

'I remember.'

I had arrived back in the village to discover strangers living in my home. The neighbours wouldn't tell me where my parents were. And so I went to the reservoir and did what I thought they wanted, with a bottle of bleach.

'I wanted you – Isabel – to have a happy ending. It's my fault that you died and I wanted to right the wrong. That's what I do for the women I write about, to show them that I'm on their side.'

'All right. I'm not sure that this justifies—'

'I gave Julia's – or Leila's – life to you. It's what you might have done, had Julia never gone missing and had you not died. I thought that Julia could just stay missing. I didn't think I had to kill her just because you'd come back to life. But she kept creeping in and taking the life right back again. You and Julia can't both win. It was my belief that you could, and now that has gone, so there's no point in writing it any more. There's no point in my old stories where everything works out.'

She drops her head into her hands and curses under her breath.

'You're too full of your own importance.' I force a laugh. 'John said that this place is known as Eva Carter country. I nearly choked, Maggie, when I heard it. What a laugh. As if anyone ever called it that. Only a handful of people have even heard of you.'

'That's harsh, Isabel. There's no need to be mean. This place is my terrain and I understand it well. That's why I had to help Julia get out. Her parents would have destroyed her, and no one would have noticed. *You* never noticed what they were doing to her, did you?'

'I guess you'll walk out of here now and we won't see each other again. I'll go down to the water and get on with it.'

'Shall I take the flowers away?'

'No. I want them. Leave them there. It's the least you can do.'

We hug. When Maggie has gone, I walk out to the garden. I look behind me and the house is no longer the Lake View guesthouse but my old house and there is a for-sale sign in the garden. I set off for the water because I have no choice. Julia has won.

— vii —

Tomorrow she would knock on Sheila's door and tell her the truth about Julia. Isabel had gone and now Owen. There was just Julia. The two girls had smiled from the photograph as if they knew the riddle they would become, as if they had made a pact and planned for this moment to last and to tease. But the question was simple. If two young girls set off on their paper rounds at the same time on the same day and one of them disappeared without a trace, then what could have happened to the other?

There was a message on Maggie's phone. If the message was from Julia, she didn't want it. She did not plan to contact Julia again. If Maggie was partly responsible for Isabel's suicide, Julia was too. She read the message.

Let me know when you'll be back.
I'll meet you at the station.
Love you – G

Maggie set out into the hills. She'd like to read George's words

*again without this town and its buildings and its people all gathered
around her. She'd like to read them with wet grass under her feet and
the sting of the wind on her ears. She followed the road out of the
village and picked up a stick to tap against the dry-stone wall as she
strolled. After half an hour or so, she glanced over her shoulder and saw
that the houses were losing their height and shape. They looked, she
thought, like elderly people whose strength had diminished along with
their bodies, and now they were small and harmless. Maggie decided
that she did not need to see Sheila tomorrow or ever. After her walk she
would drive to the station, take the train southwards, back to George.
It would be better to leave the village and the moors behind.*

*She clambered up the hill, stumbling over bumps and stones,
quickening her pace as she climbed higher. The wind whipped her hair
into her eyes. On the summit she bent forward to catch her breath. The
landscape revolved, a blur of stone wall, gate, sheep, stile, gorse bush.
She did not feel right. Perhaps it was the terrible memory of walking
here once with Isabel, Bess and Julia. Cold fingers of wind tightened
around her neck and wrists.*

And now I lead my aunt Maggie to the grassy spot from
which she can see the whole village. There it is, the long green
pool. My place. But she doesn't want to know and she turns
her head away. I have to make her see that it is still my story.
She is going to forget.

*The wind fell. Maggie smiled and shook herself free. She narrowed
her eyes to take in the view of the village and beyond. The dead girl
might win after all. She might win.*